DEADLY DOLL

Brooke Cox

Mantle Rock Publishing
www.MantleRockPublishing.com

Published by Mantle Rock Publishing
2879 Palma Road
Benton, KY 42025
www.mantlerockpublishing.com

Printed in the United States of America

ISBN 978-0-9961734-3-8

Cover by Diane Turpin, www.dianeturpindesigns.com

Thank You

I want to thank my husband Tim and my daughter Sara for always believing in me and encouraging me.

I want to thank Lynda, Susan, Paula, Pamela, my mom and my dad for putting up with me. And Karen for helping me to get started on my writing journey.

And I want to thank Kathy for giving me a chance.

Prologue

June, 1976.
Knoxville, TN

"You better hurry, the storm's almost here." While holding her pinky up, Grandma Emma, Brooksie's great-great grandmother on her mother's side, took a sip of sweet tea. She was always the Southern lady. Every Sunday she wore gloves and one of her many hats to church.

Brooksie stood at the edge of the carport and scanned the darkening sky. The wind picked up the edges of her hair. "Bye Grandma." She dashed off toward her home next door as thunder rumbled in the distance.

Running up the front porch steps, she saw her father's car sitting in the driveway behind their house. He didn't call her after he got home. Could she really blame him? She hadn't spoken much to him since he took the doll she found away from her last week. He refused to tell her why he did it, even though she was twelve years old and not a little girl anymore. What was the big deal about a little doll?

She jerked the front door handle, but it was still locked. "Daddy are you in there?" There was no response. "Daddy?" All of the lights were off inside the house and she couldn't hear the TV. Her daddy always had the TV on.

"I'm coming Daddy." She dug her key out of her jean pocket. A loud bang caused her to jump. The key fell from her hand. The last time she heard that noise, she hadn't shut the back door all the way closed and the wind had blown it open to slam against the house.

Did he run out real quick and just forget to shut it? There was one way to find out. She stepped out into the rain. Large drops splattered on her nose and scalp sending cold chills down her back.

"Daddy?" Thunder rumbled as if it was answering her call.

Her heart pounded with each step as she made her way to the back of the house. Rain was coming down so hard now that she had to put her hand over her eyes to see where she was going.

Rounding the back of the house, she saw the back door swinging in the wind. She stepped inside and shut it. The wind howled around the corner of the house, sounding like a low moan. She locked the door and heard the moan again, but this time it was different.

"Are you here Daddy?" She wiped the water from her eyes and walked forward a few steps. "Yikes." She stumbled over something and slammed into the wall. Slowly her eyes focused onto something big lying on the floor in front of her room.

"Daddy!" He was lying in a pool of blood and blue paint swirls. Blue paint dripped out of the small can still clutched in his left hand. When she turned him over, blood gushed out of a hole in his chest. In his eyes she saw pain and fear. He opened his mouth and made a gurgling sound, then his whole body went limp.

"Don't leave me Daddy," she begged. "I'm going to get help." Standing up, she noticed the destruction of her room.

Chapter 1

April 10, 1982

"There. It looks awesome next to my window." Brooksie stood back and admired her new poster of Rick Springfield.

"Yes, it does." Darlene nodded in agreement.

"Face it, he looks good anywhere. Why don't we get one for your room?"

"Why do you think I need one?" Darlene crossed her arms.

"Your Christopher Reeves Superman posters are so…" Brooksie shrugged, "seventies."

"Sorry, Cuz. Christopher Reeves is always in," Darlene sighed. "He's so handsome."

Darlene had called Brooksie "Cuz" because they were best friends and cousins. Brooksie's Papaw Clyde and Darlene's mom, Aunt Bobbie, were brother and sister. Grandma Emma had Aunt Bobbie late. In fact, Bobbie was only a couple of years older than Brooksie's mom, Mimi. It worked out well since Brooksie and Darlene were the same age.

"Forget handsome old guys." Brooksie waved her hand. "The baseball team's having a carwash during lunch at the Pizza Barn."

"Christopher Reeves is not old. And you don't have a car."

"No, but you do. We can eat pizza and enjoy the view." Brooksie walked off and beckoned Darlene to follow her.

"I see Uncle Clyde's truck, but I don't see Uncle Clyde in it." Darlene pointed to the window.

The driveway to Papaw Clyde's barn ran behind Brooksie's house. She'd watched him drive up and down it her whole life. "He's letting somebody else drive it, so what?"

"You don't understand I don't think anybody's driving it."

Brooksie peered out the window. "You're right and it's just turned this way. Run!" She grabbed Darlene by the arm and dragged her out the bedroom door.

The house shook and there was a thunderous boom. They stood in the doorway to the bathroom. Brooksie's and Darlene's hair flew up from the surge of air that gushed from her room. There was crashing sounds all around them. Within seconds, everything was quiet again.

The girls coughed and waved their hands to get rid of the dust hanging in the air.

"Thankfully I saw the truck coming." Darlene put her hand to her chest and coughed some more.

"My room." Brooksie pointed to the pile of glass, wood, and other things from her room lying out in the hall way.

"Brooksie. Darlene. Are you all right?" Papaw Clyde screamed with fear in his voice.

"We're okay. What about you?"

"Yeah, I had a little accident," he replied.

"I'd hate to see what a big accident is." Brooksie ran her hand through her hair. "I have to look." She took in a deep breath and walked over the debris.

"Me, too." Darlene followed along behind her.

"It looks like a bomb went off in here." Brooksie fought back the tears as she scanned the destruction.

"Wow." Darlene peered over Brooksie's shoulder into her room. "The truck came right through you window."

Sitting where Brooksie's window used to be was the front of Papaw Clyde's farm truck. Her bed that had sat under the window was broken in half and pushed against the other wall. Pictures and posters were thrown everywhere and all the things that were sitting on her book case and shelves lay scattered across the floor.

"Thankfully you girls are okay." Papaw Clyde leaned over the truck's hood and peeked into the room.

"What happened, Papaw? Did you hop out and forget to put the emergency brake on?"

"No, I was loading my tractor onto the trailer." Papaw Clyde gestured behind him.

A cool breeze lifted Brooksie's hair when she looked through the gaping hole. She could see the top of the tractor over the truck's cab.

"Oh yeah, I see the tractor now," Darlene piped up.

Papaw raised his hat up and wiped the top of his head with his sleeve. "I wanted to get the hay loaded before it rained and I didn't have anyone to press the truck's brakes while I loaded the tractor on the trailer." He paused and glanced toward Brooksie. "So I put on the truck's emergency brake while I drove the tractor onto the trailer behind it. For some reason, the truck started to roll."

Brooksie bit her lower lip instead of asking him if he had heard of something called gravity. What else did he expect to happen when the truck was sitting on a hill?

"Let me get this straight Uncle Clyde. You were sitting on the tractor, which was on the back of the trailer, while the truck rolled by itself?" Darlene asked.

"Yeah, at the time it seemed like a good idea." He wiped his forehead again.

"I'll call your momma and then I'll call Dennis. I dread telling your Mamaw Mary. She won't be too happy."

"She never is," Brooksie mumbled under her breath. Her grandma, Mamaw Mary, was always mad or aggravated at something.

After he walked off Darlene asked, "Who's Dennis?"

"He's our insurance agent and he's on the deacon board at church with Papaw."

"It's a good thing the agent knows you guys so well. I

don't think anybody else would believe how this happened. We could've helped Uncle Clyde load the tractor."

"He doesn't like to ask me to help with anything around here, and I don't want to talk about it." Brooksie took another look around her room. "I haven't seen my room in such a mess since…" Her heart fluttered. She quickly pushed the memory back down. What good could it do her now? She couldn't change what happened.

"Since when? I've never seen your room in a mess."

"It doesn't matter." Brooksie picked up the broken pieces of the solar system that used to hang in front of her window. Her dad helped her make it when she was in the sixth grade. She even got a science award for it. Disgusted, she tossed it over into the clutter of her other broken possessions.

"I know you're upset, Cuz, and I don't blame you, but God needed this to happen for a reason."

"Like what?" Brooksie threw her arms out. "My room needed to be aired out the hard way?"

Darlene didn't say anything. Instead she walked toward the pile of glass and bent metal that used to be the window.

"I'm sorry." Brooksie ran her hand through her hair. "It's not your fault."

"It's okay, Cuz. You've got a good reason to be upset."

"At least my T-Rex is okay." Brooksie picked up the wooden dinosaur that her dad had helped her put together. She made her way across the room and sat the T-Rex in her remaining window. Her new Rick Springfield poster lay at her feet, ripped into shreds. She wadded it up and tossed it behind her.

"Hey, here's an old cookie tin. They've made these cookies since the seventies. Mind if I open it?"

"I don't care." Brooksie picked up her new Go Go's album that was cracked in two.

"Cool. I didn't know you played with dolls."

"I had a few Barbies, but I kinda destroyed them." Brooksie tossed the record album. "That was more fun than playing with them. Did you find what was left of one?"

"This isn't a Barbie. I've never seen a doll like this before. With her long dark braids and beaded dress, I'd say she's Native American."

It couldn't be. Brooksie's memory came flooding back and her knees buckled.

"Cuz, what's wrong?"

Chapter 2

Brooksie plopped down on top of some old books. She wrapped her arms around her knees and rocked herself back and forth as she fought to keep the images from emerging all at once.

Darlene stepped over the debris to her. "Cuz, what's wrong? Are you in pain? Are you about to throw-up?"

"Where did you find it?" Brooksie squeaked.

"Find what?"

Brooksie's reached out to touch the doll, but pulled her hand back.

"This?" Darlene waved the doll around.

Brooksie nodded.

Darlene picked up the cookie tin. "I found it in this, under what's left of your window. It was wrapped up tight in tissue paper. Why is this doll so upsetting to you?"

Brooksie's voice quivered. "It's Mom's doll and I haven't thought of it since the day I found… " Her chest tightened as a couple of tears escaped. She hated to cry, especially in front of someone else.

Darlene dropped the tin and rubbed Brooksie's back with her free hand. "I'm sorry. If I had known the doll would upset you, I would have left it where I found it. Do you want me to get rid of it?"

Brooksie didn't pray as often as Darlene did, but she needed it now. *Please give me strength.* She took in large breaths until the pressure eased off her chest and the memories burrowed back into her mind.

"No." Brooksie picked up the cookie tin and glanced back to where her window used to be. "So that's what he did with it."

"Who did with what? Cuz, you're not making any sense."

"Daddy used to eat these cookies all the time. They were his favorite." Brooksie focused her attention on the tin. "He must've hidden the doll in it and sealed it inside the wall when he fixed the hole over my window."

"Why in the world would your daddy hide Mimi's doll in the wall?" Darlene scrunched her nose.

"You were right about it being Native American. Papaw Asmus lived in Alaska for years." Brooksie wiped her nose with the back of her hand. "While he was there, he had an Alaskan friend hand make the doll especially for Mom."

"Papaw Asmus is Aunt Mary's dad right?"

"Yeah. I found the doll at Papaw and Mamaw's house and brought it home. Daddy took it away from me and I never knew what he did with it until today." Chills ran down Brooksie's back, but she suppressed the shiver. "For some reason he went through a lot of trouble to hide the doll and I want to know why he did it."

"How do you plan on finding that out? This was years ago and your…" Darlene paused. "We have no clues."

"Yes, we do." Brooksie stood up and stiffened her back. "I need my diary and I think I remember where I hid it." She tip toed over to her closet and pulled down her old bug collection. "It's under here." She lifted up the piece of cardboard and what was left of the bugs pinned down onto the top of it.

"You were afraid that somebody else might read it?"

"Not exactly. I didn't want to see it again for a long time." Reaching in, she pulled out her diary with a glittery moon and stars all over it. The key was hanging by a worn thin ribbon. Brooksie tried to put the key in the tiny lock, but her hands shook too much.

"Let me do it." Darlene took the dairy. "There's some stuff on the front of it." She snarled her nose.

"They're just old bug legs and other parts." Brooksie puffed them off.

"Oh my." Darlene unlocked the diary and handed it back to her.

Brooksie sat back down and laid it on her lap. "I can't do all of this at once."

"I don't expect you to. Go at your own pace, Cuz."

Brooksie flipped through the yellowed pages. "April 10, 1976. It was a Saturday morning and I was staying down at Mamaw and Papaw's house until Mom and Daddy got off of work. As usual, I sneaked into the attic to play."

"Sneaked? You weren't allowed to play in the attic?"

"Are you kidding? Mamaw Mary has never liked for me to play in the house. She thought I should be doing chores instead. It's like she didn't remember being a kid." She was never overly affectionate like grandmothers were supposed to be and she'd often wondered if Mamaw Mary even liked her.

"I was playing spaceship. On this day, I saw a blue-tailed lizard run across the attic floor. I pretended it was an evil lizard alien who traveled back in time to sabotage the Civil War by eating all the Yankees. One of my daddy's ancestors fought in the Union army, so I couldn't let it do that. My mission was to capture the evil lizard alien and send it back to its own planet and time. I chased it under an old cabinet standing against the wall. I couldn't get the lizard alien to come out, so I scooted the cabinet over. And that's when I saw it."

"The lizard alien's spaceship?" Darlene winked.

"Ha. Ha. That's when I saw the hidden door that led to a secret room. There was a crack that ran from the floor to a few inches from the roof. And there was a crease in the wall about two feet away from the crack. I wanted to see what was on the other side and I tried several ways to pry it open, but nothing worked. Frustrated, I leaned against the wall and my shoulder nudged an old picture hanging next to the door. It creaked opened." Brooksie spread her hands out.

"No way. That's sounds like something out of *Scooby Doo*."

"I had one of Papaw's flashlights tucked in my jeans. I whipped it out and turned it on."

The front door slamming against the wall echoed down the hall way. "Brooksie."

"It's Mamaw Mary." Brooksie shoved her diary into Darlene's free hand. "Don't let anybody know about the doll or my diary. It's our secret."

Darlene crammed both under her shirt just as Mamaw Mary came around the corner.

"I swannie, look at this mess. It makes my nose want a sip of coffee." Mamaw Mary kicked Brooksie's stuff out of her way. "Now I have to stop doing my work and go through all this stuff."

"Mamaw, it's my stuff. If anybody is going to go through it, it's me. It's my house, my room, and my stuff. Stop kicking since some of it may not be broken."

Mamaw Mary had a mole on the side of her left eyebrow. It was big, plump, and pink, but when she got mad, it grew bigger and pinker. Right now it was pulsating pink like a volcano ready to erupt

"It all looks broken to me." She gave another kick, causing the cookie tin to scoot across Brooksie's books. "I haven't seen one of those in years." She walked over and picked it up.

Brooksie held her breath as Mamaw Mary opened the old tin.

Chapter 3

"What did Aunt Mary mean by her nose sipping coffee?" Darlene rubbed acne lotion on her chin.

"It's something she says when she gets mad, especially at me." Brooksie laid the lid down and sat on top of the toilet. "One time after she yelled it at me, I asked if her nose wanted a lump or two of sugar to go with its coffee. I was the one that ended up with a couple of lumps."

"You're not going to have to worry about hearing that again for a while."

"Yeah, I'm glad Mom's gonna let me stay with you until my room gets fixed. She knew it would be hard for me to live with Mamaw Mary."

"And she'll be stopping by after her work to visit. So you shouldn't be too homesick."

"Homesick?" Brooksie blew her bangs up. "Yeah right. I have never fit in on the farm and you know it."

"It's not that bad." Darlene wiped her hands on the towel and headed toward her bedroom.

"Oh yes it is." Brooksie followed along behind her. "They watch *Hee Haw* and *Lawrence Welk*; I watch *Land of the Lost* and *Star Trek*. They listen to country and I like rock. Instead of wanting to ride on a tractor, I pretend my bike is a spaceship."

"But they still love you." Darlene sat down on her bed.

"But they don't understand me." Brooksie threw herself

across the other bed, landing on her stomach.

"Let's face it, Cuz, I don't understand you either."

"Yeah, but you still accept me. In fact, you enjoy my uniqueness." Brooksie flipped her hair.

"Yes, I do." Darlene pulled her covers back. "I'm never bored when I'm with you."

"We can't go to bed yet," Brooksie protested.

"Why not?"

Brooksie reached into her bag and pulled out her diary. "Did you forget about this?"

"No, I thought you could read it tomorrow since it's so late and we have church in the morning."

"Just a couple of pages," Brooksie pled.

Darlene rolled over onto her side and propped up on her elbow. "What did you see once you went through the hidden door?"

Brooksie let a few memories escape as she read over the old pages. "I walked into a small dark room full of cobwebs. It was like being in an old horror story with some monster standing in the corner waiting to grab me."

"You enjoyed that."

"Yeah, I did," Brooksie smiled. "But I shined the flashlight around to see if there was really anything in there interesting enough to investigate. The only things I saw were a pale blue funky shaped box on the floor and a toy sword lying next to it."

"What kind of box was it?"

"Beats me." Brooksie sat her diary down. "I do remember seeing a strange word on it that started with an M. Is that a big deal?"

"Could be a clue."

Brooksie puffed her bangs up. "It was mi...mil...milker..."

"Milliner," Darlene announced. "That's an old word for a hat maker. It was a hat box."

"So the person who did this was a woman?"

"Not necessarily. The box could have come from a friend

or relative," Darlene suggested.

"That still doesn't really tell us anything." Brooksie went back to reading. "There were cobwebs hanging everywhere, so I went back in the attic and found an old fancy hand fan with Chinese women holding umbrellas painted all over it."

"They were parasols."

Brooksie shrugged. "Whatever. I used the fan to swipe away the cobwebs. I imagined myself being like that Howard guy who discovered King Tut's tomb."

"Howard Carter."

"There was tape wrapped around the box's lid, sealing it. I used the pocket knife Daddy had given me to cut the top off. I imagined a long lost treasure like what that Howard....Howard Carter guy found. I did a countdown from ten and then I jerked the lid off."

Darlene leaned forward. "And you saw the doll inside it."

"At first all I saw was a bunch of envelopes."

"Envelopes?" Darlene repeated. "Did you look in them? Was there anything written on them?"

Brooksie scanned over the page. "I didn't mention that and I don't remember. But I was so disappointed that I stood up and kicked the hat box over. The envelopes spilled out and a small black bag rolled out on top of them. The top of the bag was tied up with string. I love knots, so it didn't take me long to untie it. I was going to reach in the bag, but I was afraid there might be a dead spider or bug in it."

"Good thinking," Darlene agreed.

"I held the bag upside down and shook it."

"And..." Darlene gestured with her open hand.

"And something wrapped in a piece of cloth fell out. When I unrolled it, I knew immediately it was Mom's missing doll." Brooksie glanced up to Darlene. "It was the same one you found. Anyway, Mom had described it to me several times when I was a little girl."

"Did Mimi put it there and forget about it?"

"No. It came up missing when Mom was about five years

old. Somebody must have gotten it and hid it in the secret room."

"Wow." Darlene sat up and plunked her pillow in her lap. "It's like they wanted to make sure the doll stayed hidden for a long time."

"Yeah, just like my dad did." Brooksie turned her attention back to her diary. "I heard Mamaw Mary fussing at me as she climbed the stairs, so I slid the doll under my Bionic Woman shirt. Mamaw chased me out of the attic while waving a pair of her white panties as big as a wagon cover in her hand and yelling her nose wanted a sip of coffee."

"Why in the world would she be waving her white underwear? Was she surrendering?"

"Saturday was her laundry day and she wanted me to know I was bothering her. Anyhow, I went on home by myself. I couldn't wait to give Mom her doll after she got in from work. I was going to be the hero. In my mind, I pictured Mom pinning a medal on my Bionic Woman shirt."

"And that never happened."

Brooksie shook her head. "Daddy got home first. I showed him the doll and told him where I found it. At first he told me that wasn't Mom's doll. It couldn't be since it had supposedly been burned up."

"Burned up? But you said Mimi lost it." Darlene tilted her head.

"No, I said it came up missing. I've heard Mom say they looked for the doll for days and couldn't find it. The next Saturday, Grandma Emma and Mamaw Mary saw what was left of it in Papaw Clyde's trash fire."

"No way." Darlene hugged her pillow.

"This is way past Scooby." Brooksie ran her fingers over the diary page. "There was a knock at the front door and Daddy left to see who it was. When he came back, his face was drawn and red."

"Who was at the door?"

Brooksie shrugged. "I never knew. He said hello to someone and after a few seconds I heard him shut the door. At the time, I didn't think anything about it."

"What happened next?"

"He demanded that I give him the doll. I refused and clutched it to my chest." Brooksie's heart pounded and her palms moistened. "He said we weren't going to give it to Mom just yet and he needed to put it up for safekeeping. We'd give it to her at a better time. Then he told me not to tell anybody else about the doll."

"Did he tell you why?"

Brooksie shook her head. "He never had the chance. I shoved the doll in his hands and ran out the back door." She paused and stiffened her back. "He called out after me, but I didn't answer him. I ran to Papaw's smelly old barn. Normally I hated to go there, but all I wanted was to get away."

Brooksie slammed her diary shut, causing Darlene to jump. "That's enough for now."

"And that's when he hid it in the wall?"

"Had to be. I remember that Monday he began to work on fixing the hole that had been on the inside over my window. Mom had been nagging at him to do it for about six months. I guess that was his idea of safekeeping like the secret room was somebody else's."

"Didn't you say that the doll was handmade in Alaska?"

"Yeah, so what?"

"Maybe that makes it a rare and valuable collectable. Your Dad and whoever hid it the first time may have been afraid somebody would steal it?"

Brooksie's mind went back to seeing her room after she found her daddy. Blood gushed in her ears. "That would explain it. And if I'm right, then Daddy's death is my fault."

"How do you figure that?" Darlene demanded.

"I think you're right about somebody wanting to steal the doll and it being valuable." Brooksie shut her eyes and allowed herself to go back to seeing her room the day she found her daddy, but she blocked his image out. "My stuffed animals and pillows were cut open with their insides pulled out. My drawers had been turned upside down and everything was thrown across the floor. It was obvious they were looking for something. That's why the police thought a burglar had gotten in the house."

"I remember Momma saying something about your dad interrupting a burglar."

"I bet the burglar was looking for Mom's doll and ransacked my room to find it. If I had left that doll in the secret room where I found it, then my dad might still be alive today." Brooksie covered her mouth with her hand and stiffened her back to keep from shaking.

"You're jumping to conclusions." Darlene laid her hand on Brooksie's back. "For your theory about the doll to be right, somebody else would have to have known you found it. Did you show it to anybody else besides your dad or tell any of your friends at school?"

Brooksie shook her head. "I only wanted to tell Mom."

"So then how could anybody else have known you had the doll?"

"I don't know, but it's too much of a coincidence for me. Somebody had to have found out."

There was a knock at the door. "May I come in?" It was Alfie, Darlene's dad and he has been like a father to Brooksie for years. She was the only one he'd let call him "Alfie."

"We can hear you two talking. It's getting late and we have church in the morning."

"Sorry, Daddy."

"Brooksie, you look a little pale. Is there anything wrong?" He crinkled his gray bushy eyebrows.

"Thanks, Alfie, but I'm good." Brooksie squeaked. "We're just talking."

"Okay. If you need me, feel free to wake me up." Alfie shut the door and turned off the lights.

Chapter 4

Brooksie expected to have weird dreams all night, but she didn't. Instead she stared at the ceiling as she went through cycles of confusion and guilt. Would her daddy still be alive if she had left the doll where she found it? How could she have known somebody was after it? If the doll was so dangerous, why didn't her daddy warn her? Why didn't he call the police? What did he know and who told him?

One thing was for sure. She couldn't go through the rest of her life wondering if she had a part in her father's death. There was only one thing to do: investigate and find out everything she could about the doll. Too bad Scooby and the gang weren't real. She could use their help right now.

During church, she tried to focus on what the preacher was saying, but she couldn't. Lunch wasn't much better. After Alfie said grace, Brooksie listened to everybody else talk while she ate her broccoli casserole. Back at her grandparent's house, the only time they said grace before a meal was when the preacher was visiting. And then there was usually fried chicken, mashed potatoes, and apple pie on the table. She didn't perk up until Aunt Bobbie set out the strawberry cobbler.

"Yum." Brooksie wiped her mouth. "This cobbler tastes just like Grandma Emma's used to."

"Thank you. I used a recipe out of one of her old recipe books." Aunt Bobbie pointed to the recipe books sitting on top of the refrigerator.

Brooksie ate another helping of cobbler with a big scoop of vanilla ice cream. It brought back happy childhood memories when Grandma Emma and her daddy were both still alive. After they got through eating, Brooksie and Darlene helped clean up the kitchen and went to Darlene's room.

"Nap time." Darlene yawned and flopped across her bed.

"Naps are for babies. I need your help."

"Help on what?" Darlene half whined and demanded at the same time.

"On investigating Mom's doll, remember? Questions buzzed around in my head last night and I didn't get much sleep. I have to know if Daddy died because I brought Mom's doll home." Brooksie put her hand up before Darlene could say anything. "I know there was no way I could've known that, but it still happened."

"Cuz, you do realize it could all be a strange coincidence?"

Brooksie shrugged. "Yeah, I know, but I need answers and I know Mom needs them too. And if it's nothing more than a coincidence, then maybe we'll get an adventure out of it."

"Do we have to start right now?" Darlene tapped her watch with her fingernail. "How about in thirty minutes?"

Brooksie crossed her arms. "You can, but I'm going to get started." She picked up a chair and carried it to Darlene's closet. Being a little over 5 foot tall, Brooksie was used to climbing things. She lifted up a purse on the top shelf and pulled out the cookie tin. "Whoa." Brooksie slung her arms in the air as the chair tilted back.

"Gotcha." Darlene dashed over and placed one hand on the back of the chair and the other on Brooksie's back. "It's not a good idea for you to climb."

"Yeah, I know." Brooksie handed Darlene the cookie tin and stepped off the chair.

"Let me do this." Darlene sat the tin on her dresser and gingerly lifted out the Alaskan doll. "This doll was made with such craftsmanship. I would love to be able to make a doll that is as beautiful and elegant as this one. She truly is one of a kind."

"What are you two up to? You're getting a little loud." Aunt Bobbie opened the door and poked her head into the room.

Darlene hid the doll behind her and leaned against the dresser. She glanced at Brooksie with wide eyes.

"I'm working on a family project and Darlene's helping me," Brooksie spoke up.

Aunt Bobbie pursed her lips together. "Why didn't you two mention it earlier?"

Darlene looked down to the floor.

"We just started and a lot happened yesterday." Brooksie smiled.

"That's for sure. You know you all can ask me questions. I know a lot about the family history," Aunt Bobbie offered.

"This is about Mamaw Mary's side, but thank you anyway."

"I'll be praying for you." Aunt Bobbie closed the door.

"I don't like lying to my momma," Darlene grumbled.

"It wasn't a lie. This is a family project and you're helping me."

"You know Momma thinks it's a school project. We were not completely truthful and that is the same as a lie."

"You didn't say anything, I did." Brooksie pointed to herself.

"I participated by not speaking up."

"You're right and I'm sorry. I know Aunt Bobbie is cool, but I don't want anybody else to know just yet."

Darlene sighed sat down on her bed. Brooksie plopped down next to her.

"I'm ready to look at her now." Brooksie plunked her hand out.

Darlene gently placed it in her palm. "Be extra careful."

"I had forgotten how beautiful she was." Brooksie ran her fingers over her dark braided hair and the tiny delicate blue beads sewn onto the buckskin dress. The boots on her feet were the softest fur she had ever felt. She turned the doll upside down and lifted the back of the dress hem up.

"Cuz, what are you doing?"

"I wonder if she's got a signature on her rear like the Cabbage Patch dolls have on theirs. You know that Extra Rodgers guy."

"Xavier Roberts. Let me look at the doll before you do any damage to her." Darlene gently held the doll. She carried it over to her desk where she placed it under a suspended magnifying glass. After switching the lamp on, she turned the doll around, examining it.

Brooksie watched over her shoulder. "I don't see anything."

"Me either. Her buck skin dress ties in the back. I'm going to untie it to look over her body." Darlene slowly untied the back and carefully lifted the dress away from the doll. "Aha."

"Aha what? I don't see anything but a line of stitches."

"See right here?" Darlene pointed to a place below the doll's neck. "There are two different sets of stitches in this one seam. This doll has been opened up and sewn back. Whoever sewed it up the last time didn't have the expertise of its maker."

Brooksie knew Aunt Bobbie was a talented seamstress and Darlene was just as talented, so she knew what she was talking about. "Our first clue. We need to investigate every one we find. Do you mind to open the doll and sew it back up when we get done?"

"Why?"

"To see if somebody put something inside of it."

"Oh, Cuz, I don't know. What if we don't find anything else and I've messed up Mimi's doll? Maybe there was an accident and it just needed some repair."

"I have faith in you. I know you can do it and the doll won't be messed up. A lot is riding on this, including my sanity." Brooksie clasped her hands together and stuck out her bottom lip.

"I'll do it as long as you stop doing that." Darlene pulled

her sewing box out from under her bed and carried it back to the desk where she opened it. Brooksie was amazed at all the little tools and colorful thread she had in it. Darlene took out a small tool and carefully plucked out the stitches in the doll's back.

"That's it." Darlene pulled out the last stitch. She picked up her tweezers and slowly prodded around inside the doll. Brooksie held her breath. All she could see inside it was stuffing that looked like dingy pulled apart cotton balls.

"That's odd," Darlene mumbled.

"What's odd?"

"There are two different types of stuffing inside. See?" Darlene moved some of the cotton ball stuff around to give Brooksie a better look. "There's a bundle of coarser and darker fibers along the back seam. The rest of the stuffing is white and soft. I think some of the original stuffing had been taken out for some reason and different stuffing was put in the doll to maintain its shape."

"So that's it."

"That's what?" Darlene furrowed her eyebrows.

"You were wrong. It's not the doll itself that's so valuable, but what was inside it."

Chapter 5

"What are you talking about? What did I say that was wrong?" Darlene tilted her head.

"You thought the doll could be a valuable collectable, but that's not it. Think about it, how many times have you heard about a burglar breaking in and killing to get their hands on a doll collection? None. It's obvious that something was smuggled from Alaska to here inside Mom's doll. And it was something somebody killed my daddy to get."

"You're getting ahead of yourself, Cuz," Darlene put her index finger up. "Like I said, the doll could've been in some kind of accident on its way here and had to be fixed."

"That doesn't explain why my dad and somebody else went through a lot of trouble to make sure it stayed hidden." Brooksie leapt up and paced the room. "Papaw Asmus sent the doll, so he had to be the one to put something in it. Since it was handmade, they put whatever it was inside the doll before her back was sewn up."

She quickened her pace. "After it got here, somebody took whatever was inside it out and sewed the doll back. They didn't think anybody would find out, but somebody did and that's why the doll was hidden the way she was. And to make sure nobody suspected anything, they went a step further by putting a replacement doll in Papaw's trash fire so people would think the doll was destroyed."

"Let's say you're right, that he smuggled something

27

valuable inside the doll, what could it have been?" Darlene stretched her hands out over the doll. "It's a little bigger than both my hands together, so whatever was in it had to be small."

"Just because something is small doesn't mean it's not important." Brooksie tapped her chin with her index finger. "Hmm?"

"I probably shouldn't ask, but what are you thinking now?"

"Papaw Asmus lived in Alaska sometime in early 1930 to mid-1950."

"Yeah," Darlene drew out. "So what?"

"Not only was he up there during WWII, but also when the cold war started. And," Brooksie held up her index finger, "Alaska is close to the USSR. He may have gotten involved in some cold war espionage and did some spying. That would be so cool." She rubbed her hands together.

"You can't be serious," Darlene said more than asked.

"Why not?" Brooksie jammed her hands on her hips.

"What did your Papaw do while he lived in Alaska?"

"He worked for an oil company. I think he helped build roads. Why?"

"I'm not trying to sound mean, but I think your Papaw Asmus being mixed up in cold war espionage is a farfetched idea, even for you. He's from the backwoods of East Tennessee. Where would he have learned to be a spy?"

"What if he was out in the wilderness and came across a spy who was dying or hurt and needed to get something back down here?" In her mind she saw Papaw in a thick fur parker with a sled and dog team behind him. Lying in the deep snow in front of him was a man holding out a small canister in his bloodied hands. "Micro-film is small. Papaw Asmus could've put a top secret microfilm or a coded message inside the doll. Who would suspect it?"

"Cuz are you listening to yourself? That sounds like something out of some old campy spy novel."

"Even if it wasn't exactly like that, Papaw could've gotten

involved into something. Maybe it was a pretty spy and she talked him into it."

"I've heard enough." Darlene rubbed her temples. "I'm going to sew the doll back up. And then I'm going to take a long nap." She threaded the needle and pulled the edge of the seam out. "What's this?"

"You found something else?" Brooksie leaned over her shoulder.

Darlene gently pulled back the flap of the doll's body. "Someone has written 817 on the inside. Please don't say it's a secret code."

"What else could it be?"

"It could be how much it cost or a serial number the maker used to keep track of the dolls he or she made," Darlene suggested.

"Or it could be a clue incase the doll was ever found again. It may lead to what was hidden inside it."

"So now we're going to try to find out what 817 means," Darlene groaned. "There goes my nap."

We'll need to get to school early tomorrow morning so we can do research on it in the library."

"We don't have to wait until tomorrow. Did you forget about Daddy's books downstairs in his study? He used them to teach Political Science and some history classes at Maryville College."

"What are we waiting for?" Brooksie threw the door open and ran down the hallway toward the basement steps.

Chapter 6

"**M**y goodness. Be careful." Aunt Bobbie stepped back into the kitchen as Brooksie whizzed by.

"I will. I promise." She missed the bottom two steps and hit the landing with a loud plop.

"I'll keep an eye out, Momma." Darlene followed along behind.

Brooksie grabbed hold of the ladder attached to the bookshelves behind Alfie's desk and pulled herself up on the first rung.

"Wait. Let me do that." Darlene marched over and gripped the ladder with both hands.

"Rats!" Brooksie hopped off and stepped out of the way.

Climbing up, Darlene sang, "Now, let's see which books we want."

"Hmm?" Brooksie tapped her chin. "On the far end are a couple of books I think would be good."

Darlene moved the ladder over making a screeching sound. "Which ones, Cuz?"

The phone rang.

"There's one about the cold war. And a shelf up is a book about Alaska in World War II."

"Good choices. We'll start with these." Darlene handed Brooksie the books and climbed down.

"Darlene, pick up the phone. It's Aaron," her mother yelled.

"Okay, thanks, Momma." Darlene grabbed the phone on Alfie's desk and went over to the window with her back to Brooksie. "Hi, Aaron."

Aaron and Darlene had been dating for the past three years. He graduated high school last year and was studying architecture at the University of Tennessee.

Brooksie leafed through the books and tried to block out all the sickening cooing coming from Darlene. Maybe that was one of the reasons she didn't keep boyfriends too long. She wasn't as sweet as Darlene, and she didn't like talking lovey dovey.

Nothing jumped out at her in any of the books. As long as she was careful, she could get a couple more and climb back down before Darlene was through talking.

Brooksie inched up the ladder. Leaning back, she scanned the multitude of books until she spotted *War Codes.* Why didn't she think of that? She leaned over and stretched her arm out as far as she could, but it still wasn't close enough to touch it.

There was no way she could move the ladder over without making that screeching noise again. She placed one foot on the edge of the book case and the other on the end of the rung. She grasped the ladder with her left hand and reached for the book with her right. Her finger tips barely touched the book's binding. If she could get her fingers down a little further, she could scoot it out enough to grab it. Adjusting her weight to her other foot, she leaned forward. Her foot slipped off of the rung, throwing her sideways and downward. On the way down, she grabbed at the shelf causing it and the books to tumble down with her.

"Hmph." Brooksie crashed into the floor, barely missing Alfie's desk. She covered her face with her hands as books flew down and landed around her and on her.

"I gotta go, Aaron." Darlene slammed the phone down. "What did you do? Are you okay?"

"Yeah." Brooksie sat up and gazed at the mess lying around her. "Oh, no. Will Alfie be upset?"

"Not if we get these up before he gets back from his deacons meeting."

"Everything all right down there?" Aunt Bobbie shouted.

"It's fine, Momma." Darlene shook her finger at Brooksie. "Why were you on the ladder? You know how klutzy you are?"

"I saw a book I wanted to look at." Brooksie massaged her leg where a big brown book had popped her. "That's gonna leave a nasty bruise."

"I could've gotten it when I got off the phone. Aaron's on his way over. Maybe he can help us figure out what 817 means."

"No way." Brooksie stood and brushed dust off her legs. "I don't want anybody else to know about this yet."

"You know we can trust Aaron," Darlene huffed while replacing the bookcase shelf.

"Yeah, I know, but I want to figure this out on my own."

Darlene cleared her throat.

"Okay, on our own. I want to prove to my family that I can do something worthwhile and it's okay to be me."

"You don't have to prove yourself to them." Darlene bent down and snatched up two books. "The most important thing is for you not to feel guilty over what happened to your dad."

"I know." Brooksie glanced over to the pile of books. "Here's the one I wanted." She picked it up and tossed it down on the desk.

"We'll look at it after we get this mess picked up."

Brooksie picked up a couple of books and shoved them back on the shelf.

"Don't do that. Daddy keeps them in a certain order. Just give them to me."

"Here." She held them out.

"Thanks, Cuz. Uh-o, there's space for one more."

"I'll look under the desk." Brooksie crawled under it and saw a book lying open. "No way."

Chapter 7

"I know why I fell off the ladder and the books came down on me," Brooksie announced.

"You fell off because you're clumsy and you take too many chances," Darlene replied.

"It's like you said in my room yesterday. God meant for all of this to happen. He wants us to solve...solve the doll mystery." She threw her arms out.

"Doll mystery?" Darlene tilted her head.

"I like the sound of that. Forget Scooby. It could be an episode from *The Hardy Boys*. Too bad Shawn Cassidy isn't here to help us." Brooksie saw the opening scene with her and Darlene walking in the dark with flashlights while creepy music played around them. Then they heard somebody calling for help.

"Cuz. Snap out of it." Darlene snapped her fingers.

"Oh, yeah. I found this book under Alfie's desk." She crammed it under Darlene's nose. "What do you see on this page?"

"I could see it better if you got it out my face." Darlene pushed it back.

"Sorry." Brooksie laid the book open on Alfie's desk and ran her left index finger down the page. "This is the Jewish alphabet and the numerical representations for each letter."

"So you think 817 means something in Hebrew. Do you know what a longshot it is to have an Alaskan doll with a Hebrew code inside it?" Darlene crossed her arms.

"I don't care. It's a start and we can work on it until Aaron gets here."

"This had better be worth my nap time." Darlene sat down at the desk and pulled out a piece of paper. Brooksie knelt down next to her.

"Let's see what 817 represents. According to this book, 800 is Final Pe, 10 is Yod, and 7 is Zayin. And no, I don't know what those words mean," Darlene warned.

"Let's listen to how they sound all together. You know, like some of those new license plates where you have to say it a certain way for it to mean something," Brooksie suggested.

"Oh, yeah, they had license plates on the back of their chariots and animals thousands of years ago."

"Very funny. You know what I mean."

"Sorry, Cuz, I couldn't resist. Let's give it a try." Darlene took in a big breath. "Final p-e-a you lying."

"Do they have peas in Alaska?"

"I guess they ship them in. You do better," Darlene dared.

"Okay. How about Fin Alpo saying? It could be about a sled dog that only eats Alpo."

"Final peon slaying. It could be about one cousin killing the other one because she won't let her get any rest." Darlene crossed her arms on top of the book and laid her head down.

Brooksie ignored her. "Were there any Jewish Eskimos? I mean, why would anybody use an old language like Hebrew anyway? What's so special about it?"

"It's backwards." Darlene rose back up. "The Hebrews wrote and read from right to left instead of left to right."

"I get it. We need to read it from the right to the left so it will be right."

"Only you. But you're right about reading it from the right." Darlene knitted her eyebrows. "Now you've got me doing it too."

"Let's say the words backwards together." Brooksie stood and pressed her hands on the desk. "Ready?"

"Ready."

"Zaying Yod Final Pe," they said together.

"Let's say it faster. I can tell there's something there." Brooksie drummed her fingers.

"Zaying Yod Final Pe...Zaying Yard Final Pe....Laying Yard Final Pe." They looked at each other. "Laying Yard final Pe."

"Somebody's not planting peas anymore?" Darlene knitted her eyebrows.

"Not pea the vegetable, but as in going to the bathroom."

Darlene's eyes widened. "Are you telling me this clue refers to somebody's bathroom?"

"Since the yard is referenced, I think it's about an outhouse."

"Outhouse?" Darlene echoed. "Who has an outhouse? They've been out of use for decades, thank goodness."

"Papaw Asmus still has one and he's the one who sent the doll back."

Darlene scrunched her nose up. "You got anymore outhouses in mind? Though I can't imagine any of them being too pleasant."

"I think the word final means the outhouse isn't being used anymore." Brooksie drummed her fingers. "I found the doll in Mamaw and Papaw's house and it disappeared from their house. That's where we'll start."

"Start what, or do I want to know?" Darlene grumbled.

"Digging in the yard. You know where Mamaw Mary's tomato garden is?"

"Yeah, it's on the other side of the hill behind their house. Oh, my goodness, that's disgusting." Darlene covered her mouth. "I've eaten tomatoes out of there."

"Now you're the one jumping to conclusions. That's not where the outhouse was, but it was somewhere close by. I've heard Mamaw and Papaw talk, but I'm not exactly sure where it sat."

"I was ready to give up tomatoes." Darlene rubbed her

stomach.

"How anybody can stand to eat those things is beyond me." Brooksie shivered.

Darlene snapped her fingers. "I know exactly where the outhouse used to sit. It's not too hard to figure out. There's a thick patch of weeds and thistles not far from the tomato patch. They're always green and plush. You've never noticed?"

Brooksie shrugged. "I never thought much about it before. I was too busy digging for worms and slugs in Grandma Emma's flower garden to notice that little patch."

"Why would you dig stuff like that up?" Darlene snarled her nose.

"Because Mamaw Mary would scream when I'd carry them into the house." Brooksie grinned and winked.

"I have a question."

"I put the slugs back in the garden," Brooksie answered.

"No..." Darlene shook her head.

"I didn't feel bad about making her scream at all. I rather enjoyed it."

"No. My question is about your Papaw Asmus. Did he speak Hebrew? Whoever had access to the doll had an understanding of it and that's not a lot of people."

"Not that I know of." Brooksie tapped her chin. "Hmm? Come to think if it, I've never heard him mention any Eskimo names."

"That's my point. How do we know we're not on a wild goose chase? This whole thing is kinda weird."

"No, it's exciting and fun. Who knows what we'll dig up?" Brooksie rubbed her hands together.

"I have an idea," Darlene replied. "And I'm bringing my rubber gloves."

Chapter 8

"See anything yet?" Darlene peered over Brooksie's shoulders in the dim evening light.

Brooksie focused the binoculars. "The kitchen light is still on. Papaw Clyde should be finished fixing the popcorn right about now."

"Does Uncle Clyde fix popcorn every night?"

"Yeah and at the exact same time, 8:45. They'll eat popcorn for about fifteen minutes in bed and then they'll turn the TV off. As for Mom, she'll be watching TV in her old bedroom, which is upstairs and on the front side of the house. The spot where we're going to dig is behind the corner of the house, between Mamaw and Papaw's bedroom and kitchen windows. As long as we're quiet and careful, there shouldn't be any problems."

"You know I wouldn't do this for anybody else," Darlene told her.

"You mean you wouldn't dig where an outhouse used to be for Aaron?"

"Aaron would never ask me to do that. To me it's almost like telling a lie or stealing. It doesn't feel right."

"You worry too much," Brooksie taunted. "We'll clean the mess up after we're done. It's no big deal. Besides, who's gonna pay attention to a pile of weeds? Just relax and enjoy the adventure."

"I won't be able to relax and you know that. But I did remember my gloves." Darlene held them out.

"As soon as the light goes out, we'll sneak through the field and up to Papaw's barn where we'll get the shovels. By the time we're ready to dig, they'll be turning the TV off. Then we're home free."

Darlene rubbed her temples. "Home free?"

"Think of it this way; we'll have a fun story to tell our grandkids one day." Brooksie raised the binoculars back up to her eyes.

"I don't want mine to know how I became a delinquent."

"Papaw just turned the kitchen light out. Let's go."

"I want to pray first. I've never been on a secret mission before."

"Okay." Brooksie lowered her head. "Make it quick."

"Dear Lord, please be with us and keep your hand on us as we try to uncover answers we believe you intend for us to find."

"Amen." Brooksie jumped out of the car and turned on her small flashlight. "Stay next to me."

"Where else would I go?" Darlene turned on hers as well.

Darlene had parked her car on a little gravel road on the other side of Cow Walk Creek, which ran through Papaw's farm. They walked across the small foot bridge over the creek.

"Now, I have to unhook the electric fence. Keep your flashlight on my hands so I won't get shocked." Brooksie unhooked it and stood to the side with the fence ends in her hands.

"Is it safe?"

"Yeah, now come on. We don't have all night," Brooksie grumbled.

"Okay." Darlene darted through the opening.

Brooksie hooked it back. "C'mon," she motioned with her flashlight. Soon she had to stop and wait on Darlene to catch up with her. "Why are you walking on your tip toes?"

"I don't want to walk on any snake and get bitten."

"Snakes are cold blooded. They only lay out in the open field when they need the sun's heat to warm up. I don't think moonlight quite does it." Squish. "Rats!"

"What's that horrible smell?" Darlene put her hand over her nose and mouth.

"To put it nicely, I stepped in a pile of cow pooh. I hate being out on the farm. Do you know anybody else who has to worry about stepping in a big pile of cow pooh?" Brooksie repeatedly rubbed her shoe in the tall grass.

"Headlights." Brooksie grabbed Darlene and pulled her down to the ground beside her as a car drove down the road.

"This feels stupid. Do you really think they can see us from the road?" Darlene complained.

"Some people like to look for deer and coyotes in the fields," Brooksie answered causally.

"What? You never said anything about wild animals." Darlene peered around them.

"Sorry, guess I'm just used to it. The way it smells here right now, I don't think we have to worry about any of them coming around."

Once they reached the barn. Brooksie opened the tall doors. "Gross. I hate that smell."

"It smells like a barn's supposed to," Darlene stated.

"And that's disgusting. When we get the shovels, keep an eye out for Sedrick."

"Is that a bull?" Darlene asked.

"Don't worry about it. Stay out here and I'll bring the shovels out." Brooksie went in, got the shovels, and handed one to Darlene. "Turn your flashlight off for now and follow me."

She led the way to a big maple tree not far from her grandparent's house. Within minutes, the light went out. "Mamaw and Papaw have turned the TV off. The patch is just a few feet away."

"Where are we going to start digging?"

"The weeds are thicker in the middle, so we'll start there." Brooksie crammed the shovel in the ground and pushed it in further with her foot. Darlene tried, but her foot slipped off, causing her to stumble sideways. Brooksie stifled a laugh.

"I've never used a shovel before, just trowels in Momma's flower bed," Darlene wheezed.

"It's okay. I'll dig and you use the flashlight to go through the dirt, but you'll have to be careful to hold it so its light isn't seen from the house." Brooksie chucked a couple of dirt piles in front of Darlene.

"What am I looking for exactly?"

"I'm not sure. Anything unusual." Brooksie tossed out more dirt.

"How far down are you going to dig and how many holes?"

"I'm playing this by ear." Brooksie leaned on her shovel. "I've got an idea how to make this fun. Wanna hear?"

"Do I have a choice?"

"We'll use our imaginations and pretend we're captive slaves of an evil and powerful witch." Brooksie tossed another clump of dirt. "She's forcing us to dig a moat around her castle. But we know she just wants us to find a magic stone so she can..."

"I see something." Darlene called out.

"Sssh, be quiet. Don't wake up Mamaw's beagle, Fido." Brooksie squatted next to Darlene. Her heart was pounding. "What is it?"

"I don't know." She picked up something white and twisted it around. "Whatever it is, it's pretty sturdy."

"Rats!" Brooksie had to stop herself from running her dirty hand through her hair. "These are dog bones. I think this is where Papaw buried Fuzzy Wazzy when I was little."

"Eeeew." Darlene threw the bone and slung her hands in the air.

"Sssh. You're being too loud again." Brooksie scolded.

"Sorry. I couldn't help it. Doesn't finding dog bones bother you?"

"Not really. If you grow up on a farm or out in the country, you get used to seeing dead animals. I think this means I need to dig somewhere else." Brooksie paced around the weed patch. *Okay God, where do I dig?*

"I just stepped on something hard." Darlene pointed her flashlight. "There's some small concrete blocks."

"Cool. You found the block foundation for the outhouse." Brooksie crammed her shovel in the dirt.

"First we need to rebury Fuzzy Wazzy and fill the hole back in."

"I will in a minute. I'm in the mood to dig." Brooksie chucked out a pile of dirt.

"Are we still digging for an evil witch?" Darlene sorted through it with a small twig.

"You got a better idea?"

"Why can't we be angels working to save some children who are captured by a mad scientist?"

"That'll work too." Brooksie pushed her shovel into the ground.

"Cuz, did you hear that? Your shovel hit something."

"I want to check it out for myself." Brooksie rummaged her hand through the dirt.

"Why don't you use my gloves?"

"I don't mind." Brooksie held up a fat juicy worm. "I used to thread Daddy's fishing hooks with these and insects when I was little."

"Gross, that's disgusting."

Brooksie tossed the worm and shoved her hand into the hole. "I just touched something soft and silky."

"What is it?"

"Uh." She yanked her hand out. "It's a small burlap sack and it's been buried for a while. Look at all the bugs and dirt on it. The small twisted roots sticking out of it are cool. They're like distorted fingers reaching out from inside their prison."

"Only you could think of something like that. Please tell me you're not going to stick your hand in it."

"I'm not that crazy." Brooksie turned it upside down and shook it.

A small box fell out onto the ground. She remembered her

mother's doll falling out of its bag.

"I don't believe it," Darlene gasped.

"We actually found something." Brooksie jumped up and shouted, "Whoo hoo."

Fido's howl pierced the night.

Chapter 9

Brooksie shoved the little box in her jean pocket and grabbed a shovel. "We have to get out of here. Grab the other shovel."

"We need to fill these holes back in first," Darlene protested.

"We don't have time now. Get the shovel." Brooksie barked.

Darlene picked it up. "This isn't right."

"I know, but we need to get back to the barn." Brooksie raced toward it with Darlene behind her. The carport light flipped on, throwing light around them.

"Get down, now." Brooksie yanked Darlene down and pulled her behind some bushes. "Be careful these are…"

"Ow."

"These are blackberry bushes and they have briars," Brooksie finished.

"Thanks for the warning." Darlene tugged to free her shirt sleeve. "Won't Fido sniff us out?"

"I doubt it. He's real old and only heard us because I yelled. He hasn't sniffed anything out in a long time."

"Then why did you fuss at me for being too loud?"

"I'm sorry." Brooksie puffed her bangs up. "I didn't want to chance it until we were finished."

"We didn't clean our mess up and now they're going to see it," Darlene grumbled.

Papaw Clyde walked out with his baseball bat. Mom followed behind him with a flashlight. Lagging after them was Mamaw Mary in her night gown and hair bonnet with a fuzzy ball on top.

"I bet Mamaw Mary didn't have time to put her false teeth back in," Brooksie whispered.

Fido barked and trotted over to the weed patch. Mimi went to it and shined her flashlight around. Papaw Clyde and Mamaw Mary joined her.

"I wish Fido would stop howling. I'm having a hard time hearing what they're saying. Can you make out anything?"

Darlene turned her head sideways. "I think Aunt Mary said something about the World's Fair and Uncle Clyde mentioned groundhogs."

Mom turned her flashlight on the yard. Brooksie and Darlene ducked down further and held their breath. Mamaw Mary went back inside while Papaw Clyde and Mom walked around the parameter of the house. After one round, they went back inside, but left the carport light on.

"That's it?" Darlene asked.

"As long as the cars are okay, papaw won't really worry about it."

They went back to the barn where Brooksie put the shovels up and rinsed her hands off at an outside spigot. They jogged across the field back toward Darlene's waiting car. The sound of Brooksie's thumping heart echoed in her ears. Finally, there was some real excitement around this place.

She tripped a couple of times, but Darlene helped to keep her on her feet. Somehow they didn't step into any more cow piles. Darlene quickly unlocked her car and they slid into the front seat. Darlene flung her gloves into the back floorboard. Brooksie took her shoes off and slung them there too.

"Use your parking lights. Mamaw and Papaw can see your headlights from their bedroom window."

"Okay, but I'll have to drive slowly." Once they reached the main road, Darlene turned her lights on and checked the clock on her dashboard. "Oh, no. It's after eleven. We're gonna be in trouble."

Brooksie dug in her jean pocket and pulled out the box. "It was worth it. This box is small enough to fit inside Mom's doll. I bet it was inside it."

"Honestly, I didn't think we'd find anything but bugs, which we did."

"And dog bones," Brooksie added, still holding the box out.

"Aren't you going to open it? I'd thought you would have already ripped into it by now."

"I'm savoring the moment," Brooksie replied. "I've waited my whole life to have something adventurous and fun like this happen to me."

"It looks like a ring box. Wouldn't it be funny if there was a ring in it like you get out of gumball machines?" Darlene turned on an overhead light. "Go ahead and open it."

Brooksie gripped the box. "Drumroll please."

Darlene vibrated her tongue against the roof of her mouth.

Goose bumps ran up the back of Brooksie's neck. "Viola." She flipped the lid open.

"Well? What is it?" Darlene gasped.

Brooksie plucked it out. "A folded up piece of paper. I hope it's a confession note from the person who hid the doll."

"I don't know, Cuz. It's awfully small to have a lot written on it."

"We'll see." Brooksie sucked in a deep breath to keep her hands from shaking as she unfolded the piece of paper. "'*Look behind Goliath's green face. To lead to another clue's resting place.*'"

"Another clue," Darlene hummed. "This is pretty cool. Why aren't you bouncing off the inside of my car?"

"I wanted an answer tonight. I wanted to call Mom and tell her I found her doll and what really happened the day Daddy was killed." Brooksie twirled the piece of paper around in her fingers.

"Cuz, you've always been impatient. Besides, you're the one who wanted to have an adventure. You know," Darlene tapped the steering wheel with her fingers, "this could be like a scavenger hunt."

"I haven't thought of that." Brooksie sat up straighter. "It could still lead to some microfilm or something else top secret and that's why they made it a game where it wouldn't be so easy to find." She said the whole sentence in one breath.

"I hope it leads to some kind of buried treasure. That would be totally awesome."

Brooksie saw Papaw Asmus standing over a treasure chest overflowing with gold and jewels. "Don't get your hopes up too high. Like you said earlier, the doll is small. There wouldn't be room for a lot of treasure."

"I can still dream about it." Darlene pulled into the driveway and hit her door opener button. The garage door opened up to reveal Alfie standing with his arms crossed and a stern expression on his face.

"Rats!"

Chapter 10

The room had no light. Brooksie knew it wasn't Darlene's bedroom, but she'd been there before. There was a shuffling noise. Was something coming at her? Where would she go to get away? A glowing light appeared. In it was her mom's Alaskan doll dancing on top of the hat box she was hidden in. The doll curtseyed. Not sure what else to do, Brooksie curtseyed, too.

The doll smiled and jumped off the box, flipping it over on its side. The lid popped off and envelopes swooshed out. They sprawled out across the floor around her muddied shoes. Suddenly a piercing sound echoed off the wall. The doll screamed and covered her ears.

"Aah." Brooksie jerked her head up and scanned the blurry room. People were talking and moving around her. She focused her eyes and saw a chalkboard. Rats! She had fallen asleep in class and the awful sound in her dream was the dismissal bell.

Please don't let me have snored. She gathered her books and ran out to the parking lot. They got into bed late last night after Alfie gave them a small lecture. Aunt Bobbie had been upset, but she hadn't seen any heavenly visitors, so she knew Brooksie and Darlene were all right.

Aunt Bobbie believed in Spiritual Warfare where angels take on the form of departed loved ones when they warn of impending doom. Brooksie wasn't sure if she believed angels did that or not, but she wasn't about to say anything to Aunt Bobbie. That thought gave her comfort and that was all that mattered.

Leaning against the car, Brooksie massaged her stiff neck.

"Hey, Cuz." Darlene tossed her book bag onto the back seat. "I yawned in every class."

Brooksie threw hers in too. "I fell asleep in Mrs. Holbert's class."

"She can't see past the second row and didn't notice unless you snored."

"Can we go to the Piggly Wiggly? I want to keep a journal of everything we learn. That way we can piece things together." Brooksie spread her hands out wide. "So we can see the bigger picture."

"That's a good idea." Darlene pulled out into the traffic. "I was so tired this morning that I forgot to tell you about my dream."

"Let me guess. It was about Christopher Reeves in his Superman outfit."

"Yeah, he was." Darlene gave a long sigh. "I dreamed we found a treasure map written in Hebrew. Superman helped us find a chest full of jewels and gold doubloons that were buried by your Papaw Asmus who had been a pirate."

Brooksie started to tell about her dream of Mom's doll, but decided not to. It sounded weird compared to Darlene's.

As they walked to the book section of the store, Brooksie tried to check out the bag boys without them noticing what she was doing it.

"I like this one." Brooksie ran her hand over the cover.

"I think that one's for boys. It has dinosaurs all over the front of it." Darlene picked up another one. "This one has blue and red polka dots."

Brooksie snarled her nose and grabbed another one. "Cool. This one has the space shuttle sitting on the launch pad at night. Isn't it pretty with all the spot lights on it?"

"You don't think polka dots are pretty?"

"I don't like them either." A voice sounded from behind

them.

Brooksie and Darlene spun around. Standing behind them was a cute bag boy with a toothy grin.

"I'm Eddie. Did you all find everything you need?"

Brooksie recognized him. Whenever she tried to talk to him, he gave her short answers and walked away. What changed? Why did he want to talk to her now?

"There's something else Brooksie hasn't found." Darlene nudged her.

"I can help you find whatever you are looking for." Eddie gazed at Brooksie with big light blue eyes. Honey blonde wisps of curls lay on his forehead. Unlike Darlene, she went for the boyishly handsome and Eddie was definitely that. Too bad he wasn't taller. She liked boys with a little more height. She said the first thing that popped into the head. "I need some pads."

Darlene's mouth dropped open and her eyes bulged. Eddie's face and neck were blood red. Brooksie needed to fix it and fix it quick. "Pads for applying make-up." She tapped her face with her left hand.

"O...k...ay," He stuttered. "I think the make-up aisle is this way."

Brooksie didn't dare glimpse back to Darlene as they followed Eddie. Now everything felt awkward and it was her fault.

"Here's the make-up stuff." Eddie swung his arm out. It reminded Brooksie of the models on daytime game shows when they were showing off potential prizes. "Now let's see where they are."

Brooksie immediately saw the make-up pads, but didn't say anything. Eddie needed to find them to feel like he'd actually helped her. They stood in silence while he scanned the small section. Did she need to give him a hint such as a strobe light? Boyishly cute or not, she was about ready to walk away.

"There they are." Triumphantly, he pointed to them. "How many pads do you need?"

"One pack is fine, thank you."

Smiling, he took a pack off the rack and handed it to her. "You're welcome Brucie."

"Brucie? Why did you call me that?" It was no secret that Brooksie didn't like her name, but hearing it butchered like that was like hearing fingers nails being scraped down a chalkboard.

Eddie's smile faded. "I'm sorry." He frantically looked over to Darlene. "I thought that was what she called you."

"She has a unique name. A lot of people get it wrong at first." Darlene draped her arm around Brooksie's shoulders and gently shook her. "She knows you didn't mispronounce it on purpose. Don't you Brooksie?"

"Yeah." She knew Darlene said her name so Eddie could hear how to say it. But his bungling of her name wasn't any worse than her asking for pads.

"To make up for it, I'll walk you all out." Eddie stayed with them as they went through check-out and he carried Brooksie's one small bag out to the car.

"Thanks." She snatched it from him and opened up the car door. It was embarrassing to have him carry her one bag. She hoped none of Mamaw Mary's hair buddies from the salon were around to see it. They'd tell Mamaw and she'd have a hay day with it.

"You all got a lot of dirt and mud on the back floor board." Eddie peered into the back side window. "And there's a nasty pair of gloves, too. What've you girls been into?"

"We were digging for buried treasure and forgot to vacuum the car out." Darlene grinned.

Eddie's eyebrows shot up. "Did you all find anything?"

Brooksie puffed her bangs up. "We worked in an old flower bed yesterday where we dug up lots of worms, bugs, and old dog bones. I don't think any of those could be called a treasure."

"This Mustang is a treasure." Eddie rubbed his hand down the side of Darlene's car and into the fender well.

"Thank you. It's a 1975 Maverick and my parents had it painted this custom sky blue." Darlene tapped the hood.

"It's very nice." He turned his attention back to Brooksie. "Would you be interested in going out sometime?"

"What did you have in mind?"

"I thought we'd go out to eat."

"Eddie." The store manager yelled. "Get back in here, now."

"I gotta go. Come back by and we'll make plans about going out." He dashed out across the parking lot, almost in front of a car.

"We have to get this car vacuumed before we go back home. Good thing Daddy didn't notice it last night."

"Why did you tell Eddie we were digging for treasure?" Brooksie slammed the door shut.

"Are you kidding? That wasn't as bad as you asking for pads. Besides, what difference does a little joke make any-way?"

Chapter 11

"Aunt Bobbie, I love your goulash." Mom took a big bite of the meat sauce and macaroni noodles. "Do you have a recipe?"

"It's something I throw together." Aunt Bobbie waved her hand.

"I'm surprised Brooksie likes it so much when she won't touch a tomato." Mom rubbed Brooksie's arm.

"I like the spices in Aunt Bobbie's meat sauce and it doesn't have a strong tomato taste." Even though her mother was joking, Brooksie was tired of hearing comments about her not eating tomatoes. You'd think not eating them was against the law. Maybe they should put her face on a poster under the words, "Beware. Tomato hater."

"Over the years, I've known lots of people who didn't like tomatoes, but would eat foods like ketchup and pizzas." Alfie winked at Brooksie. She smiled back. Alfie wouldn't put a poster like that of her up in his yard.

"How about going with us after church Sunday to visit Papaw Asmus?" Mom wiped the edges of her sauce stained lips.

Brooksie should've expected that since she didn't go last week. Talk about boring. Nothing exciting happened in a nursing home. "I need to study. I have a big test Monday in Algebra II." That was true, but she felt ready for the test. She loved working out equations, but she'd never told anybody that, not even Darlene. "Beware. Nerd Tomato Hater."

"Mimi, are you getting enough rest? You look somewhat tired." Aunt Bobbie pointed her fork full of food at her.

"I'm having a hard time sleeping. I'm ready to get back into my own home and my own bed." Mom scooped up a heap of macaroni noodles onto her fork. "But I have enjoyed seeing some of the old family stuff in there."

"Brooksie," Aunt Bobbie wiped her mouth. "I meant to ask you how your project on the family history is coming along."

"It's going okay." God had just given her the perfect opportunity to ask her mom about her Alaskan doll. "But I do have a question for Mom."

"Shoot." Mom lifted her fork up to her mouth.

"I'd like to know more about your doll Papaw Asmus sent back from Alaska and its disappearance," Brooksie said in one breath.

Mom's fork clinked as it slammed into the floor and bounced, sending goulash in every direction. Brooksie immediately got down on the floor and began to clean up her mom's mess.

"Aunt Bobbie, I'm so sorry." The end of Mom's nose turned bright pink.

Alfie slipped out of his chair and picked up macaroni noodles. "This is not the first time anything's been dropped on this floor and it won't be the last. So don't think anything about it."

"I wasn't expecting that." Mom covered her cheek with her hand. "I thought you were going to ask something like who fought in the Civil War and on which side."

Brooksie tossed goulash mess in the trash. "I want a different angle." She washed her hands and sat back down at her plate.

Alfie handed Mom another fork. "Thank you Uncle Alfred. Is this project for extra credit?"

Brooksie looked to Darlene who crossed her arms and tilted her head. She imagined her asking, "Cuz, are you going to answer with a lie?"

"No. It's not, but it's something I want to do."

Darlene grinned and took a small bite.

"Well, my doll came up missing on a Sunday night."

"Wait a minute, Mom." Brooksie held a finger up and ran to Darlene's room. When she came back, she didn't slow down quick enough and slammed into the table. The dishes rattled and the drinks sloshed in the glasses.

"Whoa there." Alfie chuckled and grabbed onto the table. "What's your hurry?"

Heat radiated up Brooksie's neck. "I'm sorry. I wanted to write notes about what Mom's gonna say." She held up her new journal.

"The space shuttle, imagine that." Mom knitted her eyebrows together. "Are you ready?"

"She is now." Alfie handed Brooksie a pen out of his shirt pocket.

"Thank you." She took it and opened her journal. "Okay, you said your doll came up missing on a Sunday night."

"Yes, after we got back from church that night, I went to get my doll and she wasn't there."

"You didn't take your doll to church?"

"Oh no, Daddy didn't allow that. Before we left that night, I remember laying her in her usual place, snuggled between my two pillows on the bed. We searched the house and all over the farm." Mom sighed. "I was heartbroken."

"I remember that." Pieces of garlic bread sprayed out as Aunt Bobbie took a big bite. "You cried for days and Mom cried with you."

"Did somebody stay at home that night? Maybe they did something with it," Brooksie suggested.

"Nobody stayed at home," Mom answered. "We all piled in Daddy's station wagon and went to church."

"You didn't stay at home unless you were very sick," Aunt Bobbie added.

"If nobody else was in the house, then how did your doll end up in Papaw Clyde's trash fire the next Saturday?"

"Grandma Emma wondered if Daddy's dog Fuzzy Wazzy

got it off the bed and carried it away." Mom pushed noodles around.

"Did Fuzzy Wazzy get in the house a lot?" Brooksie asked.

"The only time Daddy let her in was when it was storming, and it was clear that evening. He walked around the house and yard for hours with a flashlight," Mom answered.

"Then how did Fuzzy Wazzy get in the house?"

"Who knows? I'm tired of talking about it." Mom laid her fork down. "The doll is gone and there's nothing anybody can do to bring her back."

∂∾⟨∾

Darlene sat down at her desk and opened the journal. "I'm proud of you, Cuz. First, you told the truth to Mimi. And second, I can actually read what you wrote in here. And you wrote it right side up instead of upside down."

"That's what lefties do. We either turn our wrists or we turn the paper. I did what I needed to do," Brooksie shrugged.

"You should try it more often. But now we need to go over what Mimi said."

Brooksie leaned against the desk. "You thinking what I'm thinking?"

"That's a dangerous question." Darlene propped her head onto her hand. "Exactly what're you thinking?"

"Somebody within the family was involved with Mom's doll's disappearance. They either hid it or helped somebody else hide it."

"But your mom said everybody went to church that night."

"I know, but think about it." Brooksie drummed her fingers. "Everybody who lived in that house knew Mom's routine of putting her doll on her bed before they left for church. They could've passed that information on to somebody else as well as where the house key was hidden. They went in after everybody left and hid it."

"That actually makes sense." Darlene nodded.

"And furthermore," Brooksie paced the room. "It would

55

have to be somebody close enough to put the replacement doll in Papaw Clyde's trash fire for everybody to see."

"How about Aunt Mary? I can see her doing something like that."

Brooksie shook her head. "That's not her style. She would've just thrown it away somewhere. But I still think Papaw Asmus had something to do with it since he's the one who sent the doll."

"Just because he sent the doll doesn't make him the one who hid it." Darlene opened a drawer and pulled out the paper with the clue. "Whoever wrote this was involved in the doll's disappearance. Too bad it's typed and not hand written."

"Yeah." Brooksie took it. "They wanted to make sure nobody knew who they were."

Chapter 12

Being raised on a farm, Brooksie was used to getting up at the crack of dawn, and Saturday morning was no exception. She tip toed to the bathroom. Quietly she put the toilet lid down and sat on it with her feet propped up on the side of the tub. She turned to the back page of the journal. She could write her thoughts in it without anyone else seeing it. All their stuff was written up front.

Dear diary...no, it's not a true diary. *Dear journal*...no, that didn't sound right either.

"Hmm?" Brooksie tapped the pen to her chin.

April 17, 1982. So far, this whole experience has been like a dream. I've enjoyed being off the farm and not being fussed at or made fun of. But at the same time, I can't help but blame myself for daddy's death. Darlene says it's not my fault. Maybe she's right. I don't know and I won't know until we figure out the mystery behind Mom's doll. But that's not the only guilt I have.

When I read my diary to Darlene, I couldn't tell her that I was so mad at Daddy for taking Mom's doll away that I didn't talk to him or spend time with him much the week before he died. I should have trusted him more. I should have apologized to him. I should have left the doll where I found it.

Brooksie wiped a tear and closed the journal.

"I hope you're right about the green Goliath being a metaphor for one of Papaw's tractors." Brooksie gazed at her house as Darlene drove up the hill toward the barn. It was strange to see the wooden boards nailed on the wall where her window used to be.

"The first clue was on the farm and Uncle's Clyde's tractors are big and green." Darlene parked next to the barn. "It's so beautiful out here with the rolling hills and the creek twisting through the lush green fields. You don't miss this scenery at all?"

"What I don't miss is that wonderful aroma of cow pooh." Brooksie slammed her door shut and motioned for Darlene to follow her. They walked to a rusty metal shed. "We need to hurry. Papaw will be back soon from the stockyard and Mamaw from getting her hair done."

"What time does your mom get off work?"

"One thirty." The shed door opened with a loud creak. "I'll take this tractor and you take the other one."

"Okay." Darlene climbed onto the tractor seat. "So being back here doesn't make you homesick?"

Brooksie jumped up on the other tractor only to lose her footing and plopped back hard to the ground. At least she landed on her feet. "Let's just say I'm enjoying the change of pace." She grabbed hold of the steering wheel and pulled herself back up. "And I get to see Mom most days. So I'm okay."

Darlene climbed back down and shined her flashlight under the tractor. "Uncle Clyde took me for a ride on one of these when I was real little. Do you remember?"

"Papaw drove you around the outside of the barn and you cried the whole time." Brooksie jumped down. "Nothing up there."

"Yeah, I did." Darlene gave a sheepish grin.

"You even cried after you got off." Brooksie flashed her light behind the seat.

"I was embarrassed that I cried, which made me cry harder." Darlene giggled. "I think I made Uncle Clyde uncomfortable. I know you never cried on a tractor."

"No, I did something worse."

"Worse?" Darlene put her hands on her hips. "Did you cause Uncle Clyde to drive into a cow or something?"

"I used my imagination and pretended the tractor was my pet dragon and we were flying over a medieval forest."

"I can see that." Darlene nodded. "The tractor's green and it puffs smoke."

"Too bad Papaw didn't think that way." Brooksie ran her hand through her hair. "One day I told him I was ready to go flying instead of riding. He asked me what I was talking about. I told him and he got mad."

"Are you sure Uncle Clyde was mad. Maybe he was upset or confused because he didn't understand."

"Either way, I was embarrassed and hurt and Papaw never asked me to ride on a tractor with him again."

"Did you ever stop to think that maybe he felt uncomfortable himself and was waiting for you to say something?"

"No, I didn't." Brooksie toyed with the flashlight.

"I think you're misreading Uncle Clyde in as much as he doesn't understand how you think."

"So it's my fault for being weird? I thought you were on my side?"

"That's not what I mean and you know it." Darlene stomped her foot.

"I'm sorry." Brooksie sighed. "I've always wondered why God put me in a place where I obviously didn't belong. And then he took my daddy who was the only person here who was anything like me."

"In Isaiah it says that God's ways and thoughts are higher than ours. If you are here, then God needs you to be here."

"I guess." Brooksie shrugged it off. "Did you find anything?"

"I don't think so. It's not like we know exactly what we are looking for." Darlene wiped her forehead with her sleeve.

"Papaw has an old tractor in another shed. It doesn't run

anymore, but he can't bring himself to part with it. Let's check it out." They moseyed down to the old wooden shed. The door gave a shrill creak when Brooksie opened it.

"Ouch." Darlene shoved her fingers into her ears. "Uncle Clyde needs to oil the doors around here."

"I think he likes that sound. The shed doors have creaked for as long as I can remember."

The girls searched around the shed and the old tractor.

"There's nothing here. I guess you were wrong about this clue." Brooksie checked her watch. "It's almost twelve. Let's wash our hands and go."

Darlene chatted about Aaron on the drive back to her house. Brooksie didn't really listen. It felt like her heart had dropped to her stomach. What was the answer to the last clue and would they ever figure it out? What if Darlene was right about Papaw Clyde? Did they simply just not understand each other? What was Mamaw Mary's excuse? And why did God make it that way?

Chapter 13

"Cuz, have you heard anything I said since we left?"
"Oh yeah, sure," Brooksie lied as they walked up the basement steps. "Well, not really."
"Yeah, I can tell you're disappointed."

"Hello, girls." Aunt Bobbie popped out of the kitchen with a half-eaten honey bun in her hand and frosting stuck to the corners of her mouth. "I'm glad you're back. Alfred won't be home for a few more hours. I need to get some teaching materials at the Christian bookstore and I don't want to go by myself. I'll buy you two lunch at May's Burger if you'll go with me."

"Sounds good to me." Darlene licked her lips.

"Let me freshen up real quick." Aunt Bobbie wiped her mouth off. "Meet me at the car."

"Do I hafta go?" Normally, Brooksie would've jumped at the chance to have a May's Burger, but she wasn't in the mood.

"Yes, you do." Darlene placed her arm though Brooksie's as they headed back down the stairs and toward the garage. "This is perfect. There may be something about Goliath at the bookstore."

❧

"Wow." Brooksie twirled around. "This place is totally awesome."

"You've never been to the Christian bookstore before?" Darlene asked.

"Are you kidding? We don't get past Kmart or Sears."

"But Uncle Clyde sets up communion at your church."

"The church treasurer buys the stuff and delivers it to him." The more Brooksie thought about it, the more embarrassed she felt. Darlene's family lived their religion. Her side was religious, but they didn't live it. They went to church on Sundays and lived good lives during the week and that was it. Was that enough?

"You're here now. Let's look around and see what we can find." Darlene swung her arm out like Eddie had at the make-up section.

Brooksie closed her eyes and took in a deep breath.

"What are you doing?"

"I'm smelling books. Each bookstore and library has its own unique odor. You've never noticed that?'

"Not really." Darlene closed her eyes and sniffed so hard she snorted. "Oh, no." She covered her nose and mouth.

"It's okay. Only a couple of people turned around." Brooksie snickered. "Let's check this place out."

They started out in the paintings. Brooksie was amazed at all the breathtaking pictures of Jesus and other biblical settings. Her favorite painting had stars and planets with the verse from Isaiah 40:26 (NIV) written on it. "Lift up your eyes and look to the heavens: Who created all these? He who brings out the starry host one by one and calls forth each of them by name. Because of his great power and mighty strength, not one of them is missing."

She didn't remember ever hearing or reading that verse, but she loved it. If she had any money, she would buy that painting and hang it in her room once it was fixed. But with her $10 every two weeks allowance, it would take her a while to save for it and by then it would probably be sold.

It would be great if she had the extra money to totally redo her room. There would be planets and stars painted on the ceiling. She'd have a real library like Alfie had and her own telescope. And she'd get her own personal computer and printer.

"What planet are you on now?" Darlene snapped her fingers.

"Still on this one. Did you find anything?"

"There's a section over there," Darlene pointed, "with costumes and props. Looks like they have all kinds of masks hanging on the wall."

"What are we waiting for?" Brooksie hurried over with Darlene behind her.

"I've always wanted a pair of angel wings." Darlene ran her hand down a pair that was made of white feathers with gold trim.

"If anybody deserves them you do." Brooksie yanked them off the hanger and tried to slip them onto Darlene.

"No, I don't want to do that in here." She pushed the wings away.

"Then I'll wear them." Brooksie slipped them on and twisted around to get the wings to flap. "How do they look?"

"You need a halo to complete the ensemble." Darlene gently slipped a golden one onto her head.

"And what about this?" Brooksie lifted up a plastic sword. It wasn't as shiny as the one in the secret room, but it was still pretty cool.

"Do you ladies need any help?" A lanky clerk sauntered up to them and eyed them over the top of his wire rimmed glasses.

Brooksie didn't like the way he emphasized the word ladies. "As a matter of fact we do. Do you sell green Goliath masks?"

"That's not funny." He snarled his pointy nose.

"Good, because I'm not joking. Do they make green Goliath masks or not?" Forgetting about the sword, Brooksie slung her hand out.

"Pay attention to what you're doing," the clerk shrieked.

With a loud whack, the sword struck a display of small New Testament Bibles. They flew off the shelves. One hit the clerk in his face, knocking his glasses off.

"Look what you've done," he snapped.

"I'm so sorry." Brooksie picked up his glasses and handed them back to him.

"Put that sword down before you hurt somebody or do more damage," the clerk barked.

"That's quite enough, Jeff." A little white haired lady suddenly appeared. "I'm sure it was an accident and everything is all right, including your glasses. Go cover the register please." Even though she used a sweet voice, Brooksie heard the authority in her undertone.

The clerk stomped off mumbling.

Darlene gave the little lady a hug. "It's so good to see you Mrs. Rice. This is Brooksie, my best friend and cousin."

"So nice to meet you, dear," she sang.

"You too. I'm really sorry about this mess I made. I'll pick them up."

"Let me have this first." Mrs. Rice took the sword from her and sat it on the counter. "If I heard right, you're looking for a green Goliath mask?"

Brooksie bent down and stuffed the small Bibles in the crook of her arm.

"Yes ma'am. Do you have any that we can look at?" Darlene asked.

"I'm afraid not dear. They used to make masks like that back in the forties or fifties. Unless somebody has one of those, I doubt if you all will ever find one."

"Rats!" Brooksie stood back up with her arm full of small Bibles.

"I'm sorry. If you'll excuse me, I need to check on Jeff. It's good to see you all." She trotted toward the register where he was arguing with a customer.

Darlene plucked the Bibles out of Brooksie's arms and placed them back on the shelf. "Wonder why this is so familiar?"

Brooksie felt as if a plug had been pulled on her hopes and they were draining away. "Now what? Where in the world can we find a green Goliath mask that was made back in the forties or fifties?"

Aunt Bobbie stumbled up to them with a basket full of books. "In the storage building in the graveyard behind your church."

"W...w...what?" Brooksie stuttered.

"That's where Mr. Bullard, the old choir director, used to keep props and old hymnals. He was quite the musical talent."

"So the mask was a prop?" Darlene placed the last Bible back on the shelf.

"When Mimi was little, there was a David and Goliath play at church. Momma volunteered to sew the costumes, so they brought this huge ugly green Goliath mask to the house. It used to sit at the top of the stairs. Mimi was so afraid of it that she wouldn't go upstairs by herself until it was gone."

"Mom never told me about that."

"I'd say she doesn't want to remember. It gave her the worst dreams. Anyway, come on girls, I need to check out. Brooksie, you may want to put the angel stuff back before they charge you for it." Aunt Bobbie walked toward the register.

Brooksie jerked the halo off. "Guess where we're going?"

"That's fine as long we're not digging there."

Chapter 14

"Here you go." Brooksie handed Mamaw Mary a brownie late Sunday afternoon.

"And here's your tea." Darlene sat the glass in front of her on the coffee table.

"We're so glad you all stopped by on your way home," Aunt Bobbie hummed. "I don't think Brooksie's seen Clyde or Mary since she's been staying with us."

Brooksie and Darlene grabbed their brownies and sat down on the couch next to Brooksie's mom.

"I'm ready for life to get back to normal." Mom rubbed Brooksie's leg.

Instead of agreeing with her mother, Brooksie shoved a huge bite of brownie in her mouth. She knew it was rude and not ladylike, but she didn't care. Even though she missed her grandparents, she was happy living with Darlene. It was nice being accepted.

"I hope Mr. Asmus is doing well," Alfie said.

"He's fine, thank you." Mom nibbled on her brownie.

Darlene leaned over and whispered, "I've got an idea."

"Humph." Brooksie tried to talk, but her mouth was too full.

"I don't think I've ever met Mr. Asmus," Darlene said casually.

"I did when he first came back from Alaska. His stories of the Eskimos and ice storms fascinated me." Aunt Bobbie placed her hand over her chest.

"So when was that exactly?" Darlene asked.

Brooksie managed to force the big bite down her throat.

"He came back in '51. His sister, Aunt Brooksie had gotten sick and he tried to get back before she died. Unfortunately he didn't make it." Mom nibbled again.

"I remember Aunt Brooksie moving in with us after she got sick." Aunt Bobbie took a bite of brownie. A big piece fell in her lap.

"Was she older or younger than Mr. Asmus?" Darlene asked.

"They were twins. Aunt Brooksie was a good Christian woman and raised Mary by herself after Papaw Asmus left for Alaska." Mom held up her glass and pointed it toward Brooksie. "That's why I named you after her."

"Lucky me," Brooksie said before she thought.

"You should be proud of that name," Mamaw Mary barked.

Heat rushed into Brooksie's cheeks. She was fair game for being fussed at no matter where they were.

"Brooksie mentioned Mr. Asmus worked for an oil company. Did he do anything else while he was in Alaska?" Darlene asked.

Mom, Mamaw Mary, and Papaw Clyde exchanged glances. There was something they didn't want to tell. Was she right about Papaw Asmus getting into espionage? The only noise was Alfie shifting around in his seat.

"He invested in a natural resource while he was there," Mom finally answered. "But he doesn't like to talk about it. After he first came back, he had a small fortune and people were hounding him for money."

"Does he still have it?" Darlene asked.

"I'm not sure how much money he has left. He bought his truck and the farm where he lived until he moved into the nursing home. I think he even took a few trips, but he stopped doing that in the early sixties," Papaw Clyde answered.

"You know, Mr. Asmus was always nice to me. When he sent Mimi the doll, he also sent me a beautiful pink crocheted hat and mitten set. It was made by his Eskimo friend Nookie." Aunt Bobbie turned to Papaw Clyde. "Does that sound right?"

"I think so. Nookie owned a trading post and his wife made things to sell in it." Papaw slurped his tea.

"Nookie was a man?" Aunt Bobbie crinkled her face.

"Do you still have them Aunt Bobbie?" Brooksie hoped they may hold a clue too.

"No, Fuzzy Wazzy ate them."

"So, Mr. Asmus went up to Alaska for work?" Darlene asked.

"I guess. He went up after Momma's mother died." Mom looked over to Mamaw Mary. "Momma had just turned two."

Except for her bright pink mole, Mamaw's face went pale.

Darlene opened her mouth. Brooksie crammed her foot into hers and gave a slight shake of her head.

"Clyde how are the plans for building the new church coming along." Alfie asked. "I know you are excited about it,"

For the next hour, the conversation was pleasant and lively. Mom was joking around as usual and had everybody laughing. After they left, Brooksie and Darlene went to her room.

"I'm sorry I kicked you in the foot," Brooksie apologized. "But I figured you were going to ask how Mamaw Mary's mother died."

"I was. Why did you stop me?"

"We're not allowed to talk about it." Brooksie flopped down on her stomach on the bed and propped her chin on her hands.

"You don't know how she died?"

"I have no idea."

"Does Mimi or Aunt Mary know?" Darlene sat down at her desk.

"Beats me. Mom told me years ago to never bring it up. Besides, I don't see how her death could have anything to do with what was in the doll." Brooksie raised her feet up behind her and swung them in the air.

"You're probably right." Darlene wrote in the journal. "Since Mr. Asmus worked for an oil company, I'd say that's what he invested in. And he did have some money at one time."

"The way Papaw Clyde talked, he spent a lot of it when he got back. What if," Brooksie sat up, "he put some crude oil in a small bottle and sent it back home?"

"To fit in the doll, it couldn't have been much. And with oil prices from that time, it really wouldn't have been worth much. Not enough to go through the trouble of smuggling it back in a doll."

Brooksie wanted to bring up spying again, but she didn't want to argue with Darlene about it. "The next thing we need to do is to get Crabby Crawly to let us in the storage building so we can look for the Goliath mask."

"Can't you get the key for it from Uncle Clyde?"

"He'll want to know what we're up to. I'm not ready to tell anybody else about the doll mystery yet."

"Who's this Cabby Crawly and why do you call him that? Or do I want to know?" Darlene hugged the journal up close to her.

"Crabby Crawly does the outside maintenance for Green Hill Elementary School and the church. He lives a couple of houses down from them in an old filthy single wide trailer. He never says anything nice and he looks down his nose at everybody else. No trespassing signs are all over his yard. The county made him chain his dog after it bit a salesman and the mailman."

"Is it safe to go to his place?"

"Papaw's a deacon and friends with the school's principal, so Crabby Crawly won't sic his dog after us."

Darlene shook her head. "Why is he like that? Did something bad happen to him?"

"Back in elementary school, there were rumors that he had been a prisoner of war in Germany in WWII. He was tortured and that made him mean and crazy." Brooksie crossed her eyes and twirled her left index finger at her temple.

"And we're going to his home tomorrow. I can hardly wait."

Chapter 15

"Oh my." Darlene's eyes bulged as they came to Crabby Crawley's house Monday after school. "What a horrible place."

Chickens and goats ran amok in the fenced in back yard. The grass in the front yard was tall and thick. The No Trespassing signs stood on tall rusted metal poles. Next to the rotten front porch was a huge growling dog in a small pen. He had slobber dripping off his jowls and his ears had places missing that looked like bite marks.

"And you all let this man do your church and school maintenance?"

"He actually does a good job." Brooksie shrugged. "Why don't you drive on over to the church and I'll walk over with Crabby Crawly. You don't want him in your nice car."

"I don't think you should be left alone with that man. I'll get a blanket out of the trunk and stretch it out on the back seat for him to sit on. And I'll keep the motor running in case we need a quick getaway."

"Okay." Brooksie grasped the door handle.

"Wait a minute." Darlene held up her index finger. "Don't sling my car door into his old beat up bug."

"Looks like he got a new one. This one's blue, I think. It's so rusty and has so many scratches that it's hard to tell exactly what color it is."

"New one? That car is a good twenty years old."

"No, I mean it's new for him. He keeps old Volkswagen bugs. Pray for me." Brooksie edged her way between the cars and crept toward Crabby Crawly's trailer.

She tip-toed by the dog's pin and tried to ignore the dog's threatening growls. The porch didn't look safe to walk on. Some boards were missing and others had gaping holes in them. *Please don't let me fall through.* Brooksie held her breath as she stepped on to the rickety old porch. It creaked and moaned from her weight. And there were stains on it that she didn't want to think about. She tried to step on the boards that looked halfway decent as she made her way to the door. Not wanting to knock on it with her hand, she took her foot and tapped against it.

"I am not buying anything you have to offer." He yelled as he jerked the door open. "I'll get my dog...Oh, it's you. What do you want?"

Brooksie stepped back and fanned as cigarette smoke billowed out the door. "I need to look at something that's in the old church storage building." That was the closest she had ever been to him and she was amazed at how blue his eyes were.

"And you want me to get it for you?"

"Actually I want to look in the building myself."

"Only certain people are allowed in there and you're not one of them." He started to close the door.

"Please. This is very important to me. I really need to find something that's in it." Brooksie didn't like to beg, but she needed this.

"What do you have for my trouble?" He demanded.

She didn't think about having to pay him. All she had was her ten dollar allowance her mother had given her Friday. Not having a choice, she dug it out of her jeans pocket and held it out.

He snatched it out of her hands. "It is not enough, but I guess it will have to do." He slammed the door shut behind him, walked across the porch, and gave a loud exclamation as his foot went through a board.

Brooksie cringed at his words.

"Come on girl," he barked after he got his foot back up on the porch. "I'm busy. Let's get this over with."

Grumbling under his breath, Crabby Crawly stomped to Darlene's car. He jerked the door behind Darlene open. "A blanket. I do not sit on blankets. You do not know who else has been on them." He reached down and threw the blanket off the seat and onto the floorboard. "Well? This car got a gas pedal?"

Darlene closed her eyes and gripped the steering wheel. Brooksie knew she was praying. After a minute, Darlene backed onto the road.

Crabby Crawly coughed and then he cleared his throat. It sounded as if he had coughed up his lungs. He rolled his back window down and spat.

Darlene rested her left elbow on the door and her hand over her mouth. Brooksie turned her head and blocked disgusting images from her mind.

They pulled into the church parking lot. The graveyard was on top of the hill behind the church, so they had to walk around the church to the back. As they walked through the graveyard, Crabby Crawly stepped on a few grave stones instead of going around them. He obviously had no more respect for the dead any more than he did for the living.

In complete silence they strolled up to the old storage building. It was made of wood and it looked like one of the old cabins in Cades Cove. Brooksie had never been in it and she often imaged it was haunted by pioneers.

"Here we are, what do you want girl?" Crabby Crawly unlocked the door.

"You know my name is Brooksie," she said, emphasizing the "k" sound. "We're looking for a green Goliath mask."

"A green Goliath mask?" He repeated slowly.

"That's right." Brooksie crossed her arms and stiffened her back.

"Wait out here." He coughed, leaned over and spat on the ground before he went inside.

Darlene scrunched her face up. "This had better be worth it."

Within minutes there were loud thumps of things being thrown around. He fussed in a loud voice.

"What's he saying?" Brooksie turned her head sideways.

Darlene cupped her hand behind her ear. "I can't tell. It almost sounds like he's speaking another language."

"Look out." Darlene yanked Brooksie back as a wooden chair flew over them.

"Heads up." He called from inside.

Small pillows flew out. A plastic manger soared out and bounced on the ground. "Things coming your way."

They stepped further back and watched as more things were chucked out of the building.

"What a creep." Brooksie blew her bangs off her forehead. "I bet he wanted us to stay outside so he could throw stuff at us."

"I know I'm not supposed to feel this way, but I don't like this man."

Crabby Crawly came to the door. "Found it."

"Whoa." Darlene backed up.

Brooksie understood why her mom was afraid of the Goliath mask as a child. Its face was a cross between an angry grasshopper and one of Papaw Clyde's bulls.

"I am not going to stand here all day and hold this thing." Crabby Crawly tossed it at them.

Brooksie lunged forward and caught it before it hit the ground.

"Good catch girl." Crabby Crawly scraped his back against a wooden post.

"Let's just get this over with." Darlene reached out for the mask.

"Not in front of him. Hey, old man." Brooksie waved the mask. "We're going to take this over to the other side of the graveyard for a second."

"It's Mr. Crawly to you," He hissed.

"As long as you call me girl, I'm gonna call you old man." Brooksie lead Darlene over to a tall obelisk shaped tombstone. "What's going through that mind of yours, Cuz?"

"I don't trust him and I don't want him overhearing anything about the next clue." Brooksie made sure the obelisk tombstone was between them and Crabby Crawly. She twisted the mask around.

"I see some scribble on the edge." Darlene reached in her Aigner purse and pulled out a small magnifying glass. "It's the next clue. Did you get the journal out of the car?"

"No." Brooksie tapped her head with her open hand. "I'll go back and get it."

"Wait." Darlene grabbed her arm. "I want to get away from that nasty man as fast as we can. I'll remember it and write down when we get back in the car." She held the magnifying glass over the scribble. "'*Cooking and baking are women's work and always will be. For the next clue, look behind the last letter zee.*'"

Darlene shoved her magnifying glass back in her purse. "Why can't any of these clues be easy?"

"Where's the fun in that? Let's take this creepy thing back and get away from here."

They dodged all the stuff lying on the ground. Brooksie laid the mask down on top of the upside down manger. "Here. Normally I would say thank you, but you made me pay for your help and you're rude."

"Cuz."

"Not so fast. You two are going to drive me back home after you pick this mess up." He gestured to the stuff he had tossed out. "You are the ones who bothered me to look for that stupid mask in the first place."

"We're not doing anything else for you." Brooksie crammed her fists on her hips and bobbed her head. "We didn't make this mess, you did. Instead of moving things around, you pitched them out the door because you were mad we bothered you."

Growling, he stepped out of the doorway toward them. Darlene stepped back, but Brooksie held her ground.

A wry grin formed on his thin cracked lips. "I should have known better than to help you anyway. Mary's talked about you over the years." He took another step. "How weird and strange you are from the rest of your family. You can't be normal like they are."

Darlene tugged at her arm, but Brooksie was frozen in place.

Crabby Crawly gave a hearty laugh. "You are a restless dreamer. That's why you will never amount to anything."

"We got what we came after." Darlene placed her hands on Brooksie's shoulders and pushed her back down the hill.

His laughter followed them though the graveyard. Darlene latched the gate behind them. "I would rather be around Brooksie any day than somebody like you. She's smart, interesting, and fun while you're mean and stinky." She stuck her tongue out at him.

Once they were in the car, Darlene locked the doors. "I don't see him coming after us."

"Why would he? He hurt me and that's what he wanted," Brooksie squeaked.

"I did stick my tongue out at him." Darlene reached in the back seat and grabbed the journal. "I'm going to write the clue down before we forget it."

"Thanks for getting me away from him. I was too stunned to do anything. It was hard to hear Mamaw Mary's words coming out of his mouth."

"What?" Darlene stopped writing. "Aunt Mary really said those things to you?"

"Several times. I don't know what's worse, the fact that she thinks I'll never amount to anything or the fact that she's telling people that."

"I'm so sorry, Cuz. Surely Uncle Clyde..."

Brooksie raised her hand. "Papaw Clyde believes anything she tells him with no questions asked. I've never told anybody else because I didn't want to cause trouble. But she's gone too far." She ran her hand through her hair. "There's one thing left to do. I have to go to Mamaw and Papaw's."

"Let's go on back to my house until you've calmed down. Right now you're too emotional and not thinking straight." Darlene backed out of the parking lot. "Have you prayed about how to handle this?"

Brooksie knew Darlene was right, but she was too angry for that right now. Did God listen to your prayers when you were angry? "I need to do this now."

"All right, Cuz." Darlene pulled out onto the road. "I'll take you there, but I think this is a big mistake."

Chapter 16

"What's that horrible noise?" Brooksie burrowed her fingers into her ear. "It sounds like metal scraping against metal."

"I probably have a flat tire and I'm driving on the wheel rim." Darlene crept along until she veered into the Green Hill School parking lot. She leapt out and ran to the back of her car. "I was right. It's the rear tire on the driver's side."

Brooksie joined her. "Wow. I didn't know tires could go down that fast."

"What in the world did I run over? I didn't see anything in the church parking lot. Did you?"

"Nope." Brooksie bent down and whistled. "That's a slash. I bet you ran over a shard of glass. Why didn't we hear it pop?"

"Who cares?" Darlene wrung her hands together. "Daddy's not going to be happy about this."

"Rats! I can't believe my luck." Brooksie threw hers hands up in the air.

"Luck? It's my tire."

"I'm sorry. I'm just frustrated." Brooksie kicked at the flat tire.

"I know you are, but first we need to get some help." Darlene pointed toward the school. "There are still a few cars there. We can walk to the office and ask if they'll let us use the phone to call Uncle Clyde for help."

"No way." Brooksie waved her hands in front of Darlene's

face. "When I confront Mamaw Mary, I don't want to give Papaw an edge over me by having him change your tire."

"Then we'll have to change it ourselves." Darlene rubbed her temples.

"Ourselves?" Brooksie repeated.

"Yeah, unless you want to get Stinky Crawly to help us. And he wouldn't do it without charging more money."

"It's Crabby Crawly."

"To me he's Stinky since I'll have to spray the back seat to get the cigarette smell out of it." Darlene popped her trunk open. "We'll do it ourselves."

"I don't know how to change a tire." Brooksie kicked a couple of small rocks.

"Don't worry. Daddy showed me how when I got the car."

"I can't afford my own car and I don't have a Daddy anymore." Brooksie sounded harsher than she meant to. "Sorry. None of this is your fault and I shouldn't take it out on you."

An orange truck drove toward them beeping his horn. The driver had his hand out the window, waving.

Darlene cupped her right hand over her eyes. "It's Eddie. I bet he'll be a gentleman and change our tire." She waved back.

He parked in front of them and hopped out of his truck. "Looks like you girls got a flat tire. Good thing I happened by." He tipped his cowboy hat toward them. "I'd be glad to change it for you."

Brooksie had never been into cowboys, but he did look cute in his old pair of Levis and tight green plaid cowboy shirt. She smelled his cologne before he walked up to them.

"That's very gentlemanly of you." Darlene nudged Brooksie

"Yeah, thank you," Brooksie added. "But, we're in a little bit of a hurry."

"Cuz."

"Guess I better get right on it then." He winked at Brooksie. "I'll get the tools out of my trunk."

She whispered to Darlene, "He winked at me. I'm not sure

if I like that."

"Unless you want to help me change this tire, stop taking your frustrations over Aunt Mary out on him. A cute guy is interested in you. Just enjoy it."

"I'll get the spare." Eddie sat his tools down on the ground and yanked the tire out of the trunk "This shouldn't take long."

Darlene whispered, "He's quite the hunky little guy."

While he was working, Brooksie couldn't help but notice his muscles straining against his shirt, pulling the front slightly apart. Darlene was definitely right about him. Every once in a while Eddie looked at her and smiled. Brooksie smiled back. It was a little mesmerizing to have a guy give you that much attention.

"Looks like you may have run over some glass in the church parking lot." Eddie took the flat off and tossed it off to the side.

"How do you know we were in the church parking lot?" Brooksie crossed her arms. Darlene nudged her with a little more force.

"I drove by a little earlier and saw Darlene's car. It's hard to miss." He shoved the spare on and tightened the lug nuts.

"Sorry. I didn't mean that the way it sounded. Thanks for the help," Brooksie apologized.

"Anytime." After a few more twists, Eddie stood up and wiped his hands on his jeans. "To be honest, I was hoping I would run into you again. We didn't get a chance to set up a date the other day. How about we do that now Brucie?"

"Brooksie," she corrected him.

"What?" He furrowed his eyebrows.

"We talked about this at the store the other day, remember? My name is Brooksie and not Brucie." Darlene nudged her so hard this time that she had to take a sideways step to keep her balance.

"I'm sorry Brooksie." Eddie drew out the "o" while accenting the "k." "How about going out Friday? There's a restaurant up in Union County called The Crowing Rooster.

They have great fried chicken."

Brooksie tried not to cringe. Not only did Eddie butcher her name, but he wanted to take her somewhere in Union County. She hated going up there to visit Papaw Asmus. There wasn't much to do there.

"Something wrong with The Crowing Rooster?" Eddie clinched his jaw.

Brooksie didn't like the strained tone in his voice. "I've never been there, but I like the Pizza Barn. It's not far from Darlene's house." She wouldn't be intimidated to go somewhere she didn't want to go. If he wanted to go out with her, he'd have to agree to the Pizza Barn. She crossed her arms and stiffened her back.

He flashed his toothy grin. "Pizza Barn it is then. We can go to The Crowing Rooster on our second date."

"I want to make it a double date with Darlene and her boyfriend, Aaron."

Darlene's eyes grew large. "Oh, yeah. That sounds like so much fun."

"I don't have enough room in my truck cab for everybody to ride," Eddie protested.

"No problem. I'm staying at Darlene's house for a while. I can ride with her and Aaron and meet you there. Is six okay?" Brooksie tried to say as sweet as she could without sounding sappy.

"Six is fine," Eddie answered. "I look forward to it."

"Me, too. See you then." Brooksie opened the passenger side door and slid in. "I have to take care of something right now."

"Bye and thank you again. We really appreciate your help." Driving off, Darlene complained, "I don't like leaving Eddie standing there like that on the side of the road. It's kinda rude, especially as he was gracious enough to change the tire."

"I want to get this over with before I explode." Brooksie balled her hands into fists.

Chapter 17

"Why don't you wait and talk to your mom first? She's always been cool about things," Darlene asked.

Brooksie shut the car door. "Mom doesn't always get what I tell her. And she doesn't always stand up to Mamaw Mary."

"Cuz, I think it's best if I stay out here and pray."

"Okay." Brooksie walked into her grandparent's house. Mamaw Mary was standing in the kitchen doorway with her hands on her hips. Her mole was pulsating pink.

"What is wrong with you?" Mamaw Mary bellowed.

"Me?" Brooksie pointed to herself. "Why are you upset with me?"

"Frank Crawly called and told me how you made him dig out the old Goliath mask and then wouldn't help clean up the mess you all made."

"Made him? Crabby Crawly made me pay him what little money I had. And there was a mess because he was mad and threw everything out of the storage building. I'm sure he broke some things."

"Don't you dare call him that name." Mamaw Mary clinched her teeth.

"Everybody calls him that name because that's what he is."

"At least he's not like you." Mamaw Mary jabbed her finger into Brooksie's chest. "You're never satisfied unless you have your head in the clouds dreaming of some crazy far away adventure. It's foolish and embarrassing. You need to act right and stay around here."

"Crabby Crawly told me what you've been saying about me. Don't bother denying it. He used the same words you yell at me when your nose wants some coffee."

"Don't play little miss innocent with me. Frank told me how you made fun of the way I talk. And you made fun of how I never finished school," Mamaw Mary yelled back.

"I didn't say anything at all about you to him." Brooksie stepped back "Darlene was standing there. She can back me up. If you want, we can go out to the carport and ask her."

"What is all the yelling about?" Papaw clomped in and stood next to Mamaw Mary. "I heard you two all the way to the barn."

Mamaw Mary buried her head in her hands and wailed. "Brooksie came in and accused me of saying things about her."

Papaw Clyde embraced Mamaw Mary and gave Brooksie a stern glare.

"Papaw, that's not…" Brooksie tried to explain.

"What's wrong with you? You were not raised to do that." His tone of voice made her want to sink into floor.

"But Papaw, that's not true. I wouldn't do anything like that." As usual, she was defending herself when she hadn't done anything wrong.

"Are you calling your Mamaw a liar?" His voice became fierce. "When I saw Darlene's car pull in, I got excited. I thought you came by to spend some time with us. But no, you're here to cause trouble."

Hot tears burst out and rolled down her cheeks. "That's not why I came here. If you'd just let me tell my side for once. Darlene was there and she heard and saw everything that happened."

"I don't need to ask Darlene anything. If you're happier living with them, then you need to leave and go on back home with her." Papaw Clyde waved his hand as if he was shooing away an animal.

Tears blurred Brooksie's vision as she raced for the door.

⤳⤙

Brooksie dropped to the floor next to Darlene's bed and wrapped her arms around her knees. She rocked herself back and forth. Whisperings found their way to her ears. Footsteps grew louder until they stopped at the bedroom door.

"Aunt Bobbie, can we talk about this later? I don't feel like it right now." She wiped a tear from her cheek and burrowed her head in her knees.

"We don't have to talk unless you want to. Do you mind if I come in and sit down next to you anyway?" Alfie asked quietly.

She jerked her head up at the sound of Alfie's soothing voice. "I don't mind." She had always admired Alfie's quiet wisdom. She had never seen him loose it at anybody like Papaw and Mamaw did at her earlier.

"Thank you." His knees complained with loud pops when he sat down next to her.

"You know Alfie; my life is like a cartoon."

"How so?"

"I've watched old cartoons where the stork was carrying a new baby to a family." Brooksie paused to blow her nose. "I think the stork that was carrying me crash landed at the wrong hospital. I belong with a family somewhere else." Feeling an escaping trickle, she hurriedly wiped her nose. "I'm sorry I keep blowing and wiping my nose so much."

Alfie chuckled and handed her his handkerchief. "A little runny nose never hurt anybody. May I suggest the serenity prayer?"

"Thank you." Brooksie wiped her eyes. "The what prayer?"

"You've never heard of the Serenity Prayer?" Alfie sounded surprised.

"I learned the Lord's Prayer in Sunday school when I was

little. I couldn't understand why it had snot in it."

"Were you crying then, too?" Alfie crinkled his eyebrows.

"No, not at all." Brooksie laid her head against the bed. "If you say the part where you pray 'lead us not into temptation' real fast, it runs together and sounds like lead us 'snot' into temptation."

"It does." Alfie slapped his knee. "I never realized that before. Do you want to hear the Serenity Prayer?"

"Sure." She snatched a decorative pillow off of Darlene's bed and fiddled with a tassel.

"God give me grace to accept with serenity the things that cannot be changed, courage to change the things which should be changed, and the wisdom to know the difference."

"Wow. That's pretty good."

"Good words to live by." Alfie patted her hand. "Darlene told me about the confrontation between you and your grand-parents."

"Yeah, I figured she had." She twisted the tassel around her finger.

"I know Mary and Clyde love you very much. I also know they're never going to change who they are and you need to accept that."

"But that's not fair," Brooksie exclaimed.

"Oh?" Alfie crossed his arms.

"It's not fair that I have to accept them for who they are, but they have never tried to accept me for who I am, especially Mamaw Mary. I learned a long time ago that if you have the audacity to be different from everybody else, then your feel-ings don't count." Brooksie clasped her hand over her mouth. She had never admitted that before to anybody.

"Think of it this way," Alfie rested his arm around her shoulders. "God anointed you to be different and unique and He doesn't make mistakes. You need to live to please God and not worry about what anybody else thinks of you. They'll have to answer to God for their own behavior."

"I know you're right Alfie, but it still hurts."

"Yes it does. It would be good if we could walk in other peoples' shoes for a day. You may be surprised how hard that other person's walk is."

"You're telling me to be the bigger person. Somebody should tell Crabby Crawly that."

"Darlene said he's the outside maintenance man at your church and at the elementary school."

"Yeah." Brooksie glanced down at the tassel that had fallen off and into her hand. "He's a rude and nasty man."

"Darlene also told me how he continued to hound you when he saw how upset you became over Mary's comments. Do you realize that he was playing you and Mary against each other for his own distorted pleasure?"

"Rats! I fell right into it." Brooksie tossed the pillow, less a tassel, back on the bed. "It's ironic that such a selfish man works for a church."

"Good point. So what are you going to do now?"

Brooksie wished she still had the pillow in her hand. Alfie had challenged her and she needed to come up with the right answer. "I need to…"

"Need to…" Alfie waved his hand as if he was drawing the answer out of her.

"Need to…call Mamaw and Papaw and talk to them?" Maybe his hand waving did work.

"And…" He coaxed some more.

"And talk to them about what happened?" Brooksie hoped that was enough.

"Yes, and apologize for your part of the confrontation."

"Neither Mamaw nor Papaw gave me a chance to explain or defend myself." Brooksie hopped up on her knees. "Papaw told me I needed to leave and go with Darlene. He even shooed me away." She mimicked Papaw's hand motion.

Alfie raised his hands. "I agree that they should have given you that chance, but did he say anything before that?"

Brooksie repeated everything Papaw Clyde said.

"I think your Papaw Clyde misses you and was disappointed and hurt you were there to fight with Mary and not spend time with them."

"But they were here last Sunday." She sounded whinier than she meant to.

"And so was everybody else. He wanted you to come to them and to know you cared."

"I didn't think of that." Brooksie puffed her bangs up.

"You need to spend some quality time with them. I promise you'll be amazed at how much better you will feel."

Brooksie snarled her nose. "It's not going to be easy Alfie, especially with Mamaw Mary."

"I know what stuff you're made of. One day you'll be able to talk with your grandparents about how you feel. You may be surprised at how they see some things." Alfie stood and extended his hand.

Brooksie took it. "I've had more than enough surprises for one day."

"I don't know about you, but I'm getting hungry. I could use a peanut butter and jelly sandwich."

"That sounds good." Brooksie didn't feel hungry until he mentioned food. And she would need her strength when she talked to Mamaw and Papaw again.

❧❦

Mom came by after work as usual. They talked outside about what happened. Papaw Clyde had called her at work and fussed at her. Unlike Papaw, Mom let Brooksie tell her side. She recanted everything, including Alfie telling her about the serenity prayer.

"Alfred is a godly and wise man. That's one reason why I'm okay with you staying here so long. As for that Crawly guy, something about him isn't right. He chooses to live in squalor and yet he acts haughty. And I don't like the look in his eyes."

"You mean that hateful 'I want to hurt you look?'" Brooksie could see and smell him in her mind.

"It's as if I can feel meanness emanating from him. And I

told him that to his face."

"You told Mr. Crawly he was mean? When? I've never seen you talk to him."

"I didn't tell you? It was after your father died. He told me the plans he had made for us to go out."

"No, you didn't tell me that." Disgust and anger welled up in Brooksie. Her mother was a very attractive woman with blond hair and big blue eyes. Since Brooksie's daddy died, a few men had asked her mother out, but she always told them she wasn't ready. But Crabby Crawly was a different story. She forced the bile back down her throat.

"Enough about him. I think you should spend some time home this weekend."

Brooksie knew there was no way out of it. She hoped she wouldn't need to pray Alfie's prayer this weekend.

Chapter 18

B rooksie bobbed her head to the tune. She loved listening to the blaring horns during band practice. Unlike Darlene, she couldn't play music on anything and march at the same time. After practice, she met Darlene in the band room.

"I've been thinking about the last clue." Darlene gently positioned her clarinet in the locker. "Something about it is familiar, but I don't know why."

"Really? It isn't to me." Brooksie leaned against the next locker. "I have a feeling a woman wrote the clues."

"Do you have one in mind?"

"Not really, but what if she's already dead?"

"What?" Darlene closed her locker.

"The doll's been hidden for years. This woman could've died or moved away since then." Brooksie slung her book bag over her shoulder.

"I think it's obvious who it is." Darlene dug her car keys out of her Aigner purse. Brooksie would love to have an Aigner purse. For that matter, she didn't have anything that was designer. If her dad was still alive, things would have been so different.

"Cuz?"

Brooksie shook her head. "What were we talking about?"

"I think the most obvious woman is Aunt Mary. Face it; she's had access to everything and she knows the family history."

"No way." Brooksie raised her voice. "Whoever wrote the clues had to be clever and creative. I've never seen her be either one."

"You're not being fair. 'Makes my nose want a sip of coffee' is clever and cute."

"Easy for you to say. You're not the one she yelled it to." Brooksie ran her hand through her hair. "You know, the last letter Z probably refers to a name that starts with a Z, but other than the zoo, I can't think of anything."

"I know one." Darlene snapped her fingers. "A couple of weeks ago I heard Mimi talk about Uncle Clyde being mad at a Zelda for stepping on his foot. She must be a big lady. Did it happen at church?"

Brooksie laughed. "No, they were at the barn. Zelda is one of Papaw Clyde's cows. He's lucky she didn't step all the way down or she would have broken his foot. Zelda was named after one of Mamaw Mary's hair salon buddies. The last calf born was named Gertie."

"Now that's true friendship. Are you going to name a calf after me one day?" Darlene grinned.

"I don't plan on having a cow of my own, unless it's on a bun and has pickles on it." Brooksie slid into the car.

"Speaking of food, I need to ask Aaron about Friday night."

"Sorry about that. I hadn't planned on asking for a double date, but I didn't like Eddie's reaction when I didn't want to go the Clucking Chicken."

"You know, Cuz, you have a lot going on in that creative head of yours. Give him a chance. You might be surprised. Besides, I've heard they have an awesome chicken casserole at The Crowing Rooster." Darlene emphasized the restaurant's name.

"You're trying to get me a boyfriend aren't you?" Brooksie crossed her arms.

"No…well…kinda sorta. I can tell you feel awkward

sometimes when you're around Aaron and me. I want you to have somebody who appreciates you for who you are."

"I'd like that too. How many boys want a girl with a vivid imagination, a girl who has no problem getting dirty, or would rather watch a show with spaceships or dinosaurs instead of a sappy love story? In fact, I don't like sap period." Brooksie stuck her tongue out as if she was gagging.

"You sell yourself short. I have no doubt that God has somebody out there especially for you."

"I guess." Brooksie leaned back in her seat.

Darlene's car topped the small hill next to her house. "Oh no."

"What's wrong?" Brooksie bolted up. "Did Mrs. Stout's' car roll back in the road again?"

"No, there's a police car in my driveway. Uncle Clyde called the police about the holes in his backyard and the police figured out it was us." Her voice quivered.

"Unless you told somebody else about it, there's no way they know it was us."

Darlene parked next to police car. "Do you think they'll put us in handcuffs?"

"Of course not. Do you really think Papaw Clyde would press charges?"

"No, he wouldn't."

Darlene extended her trembling hand to open the front door.

"I got it." Brooksie gently pushed her hand back. With a big shove, she flung the front door open. Standing at the top of the stairs were Alfie and a police officer who didn't look much older than her or Darlene.

"You finally got back. I need to ask you girls a couple of questions." The officer's voice was curt.

Chapter 19

Was the policeman that abrupt and rude to everybody? "We haven't been properly introduced. I'm Brooksie and this is Darlene." Brooksie pointed to herself and then to Darlene, whose cheeks were pale instead of their normal rosy color. "Now what's your name?"

Alfie's lips turned up in a small grin.

"I'm Officer Lanigan," he snapped. "Where were you two late yesterday evening?"

"Here at home." Darlene's voice was barely above a whisper.

"You didn't go back out at any time?" Officer Lanigan raised his left eyebrow.

"Listen," Brooksie jammed her fists on her hips and bobbed her head. "We're not the type of girls who sneak out at night and get into trouble if that's what you're trying to hint. Didn't you ask Alfie if we were here?"

"Alfie?" The officer raised his eyebrow again.

"That would be me," Alfie stated. "Yes, he did and I told him you two were here at home since late afternoon."

Brooksie could tell by the edge in Alfie's voice that he wasn't happy with the police officer either.

"I needed to hear it from them," the officer quipped.

"Why? What's happened?" Brooksie clasped the handrail and took a step up.

Officer Lanigan flipped open his note pad. "According to

Mr. Crawly, the maintenance man for Happy Valley Church, Brosky…"

"It's Brooksie." She corrected him.

"Brooksie and Darlene picked him up at his home and drove him to the graveyard. Once there, they had him hunt through things in the storage building looking for an old green Goliath mask." He closed his pad and pursed his thin lips together.

"So? Was that a crime? Are old Goliath masks outlawed?" Brooksie put her other hand on her hip.

"No, that's not the issue. When Mr. Crawly went to the cemetery this morning, there was a large hole dug next to the fence behind the storage building. In that hole was an uncovered skeleton of a Civil War soldier."

Darlene wheezed, "Oh, my."

"What? I grew up in that church and I've never heard anything about a Civil War soldier being buried there." Brooksie paused. "Well, there are some, but they have tombstones."

"From what I've gathered," Alfie interjected, "he was wearing a Union uniform and it seems as if he was buried in a hurry. He didn't even have a coffin. And there was no money or metal of any kind on him. Not even his sword."

"This is fascinating and all, but what has that got to do with us looking for an old mask?" Brooksie asked.

"That's what I hope to ascertain. I don't know what weird thing you two are up to," Officer Lanigan aimed his pen at Brooksie, "but I find the timing of everything to be a little suspicious."

Brooksie was glad he was standing at the top of the stairs. If he were right in front of her, she would've been tempted to smack that pen out of his hand.

"Like I told you earlier, Officer, it is nothing more than a coincidence. And coincidences by themselves do not make people guilty." Alfie puffed his chest out.

"In that case, there should be no problem with me checking out Darlene's car," Officer Lanigan sneered.

Pink sprawled across Darlene's cheeks. At least she had some color again.

"The officer doesn't have a search warrant, so it's up to you," Alfie told her.

"Let me assure you that I can get one if I need to," he barked.

"That won't be necessary. I don't have a problem with it." Darlene glanced at the door handle and back to Brooksie.

Brooksie opened the door and stood next to it. "After you all."

They walked out to Darlene's car. She unlocked it and stood next to Alfie, who laid his arm around her. Her lips were moving. Brooksie knew she was praying.

The officer pulled on a white plastic glove with a loud snap. He ran his hand over the dashboard. Next, he took out the floor mats. Brooksie was relieved they had vacuumed all the dirt out. He would have had a hay day with that.

"This is a very clean car. Was it recently cleaned?" His accusation was very evident.

"Of course it was. I taught my daughter to take care of her things. Do you have a problem with that, Officer?"

Brooksie grinned. Alfie was always a step ahead.

The officer snarled and proceeded to examine the driver's side. Not finding anything, he went over to the passenger side. He opened the glove compartment and immediately yanked things out and threw them onto the seat. It reminded Brooksie of the careless way Crabby Crawly tossed things out of the storage building.

"And who were you going to spy on with these?" Officer Lanigan leaned on the top of the car with a small pair of binoculars dangling out if front of him.

"I put them in there myself for Darlene to have in case of emergencies. I believe in always being prepared." Alfie used a harsh tone Brooksie didn't hear too often.

Snarling again, the policeman crammed everything back in the glove compartment and pushed the door back up, but it wouldn't close. He reached back in, shoved things around, and slammed the door with force.

Alfie crossed his arms and tapped his foot against the pavement.

The officer dug into the back of the passenger seat. "What's this?"

With a lopsided smirk, Officer Lanigan strutted over to Darlene and stuck his open palm under her nose. "Do you want to explain what this small twisted piece of metal in my hand is?"

"That's the earring I lost. It's made out of titanium like the space shuttle." Brooksie picked it up and crammed it in her earlobe. "Thanks for finding it. I've been looking for it everywhere."

"I lost a nice pair of cufflinks in the garage the other day. When you're done here, you may be able to help me find them as well." Alfie gestured toward the garage.

"I'm going to search the trunk next. Please open it," Officer Lanigan demanded.

Darlene did as he asked and moved out of his way. He bent down and tossed her stuff around.

"Aha. A gun. No..." He turned something around in his hand.

"It's my phasor." Brooksie snatched it up. "Mom made me a blue Star Trek Uniform Dress for the school Halloween Dance last year. I found this phasor in a specialty store at the mall. It took four weeks allowance to get it. It was either this or a tricorder and I thought the phasor looked cooler hanging on my side." She held the toy phasor on her hip with her left hand and twirled around. "See how cool it looks?"

Officer Lanigan slammed the trunk lid closed with so much force that his hair flew up. "I'm done here." He dug a card out of his pocket and handed it to Alfie. "If you hear of anything else about this case, call me. Good day." He stomped off to his car and spun the tires as he pulled out of the driveway.

"He didn't need to drive off like that," Alfie complained.

"I know many policemen and women who are polite and respectful. He was neither. I will be placing a phone call tomorrow.

"Maybe he doesn't like *Star Trek*." Brooksie spun the phasor on her index finger.

"I'm going to see what damage he's done." Alfie opened Darlene's trunk.

"Daddy, we're going back inside. I'm hungry after all that excitement." Darlene motioned for Brooksie to follow her.

"Wait a minute girls." Alfie pulled the slashed tire out and sat it on the ground. "When did your tire go flat and why didn't you tell me about it?"

Chapter 20

"I'm so sorry, Daddy. We've had so much going on lately that I forgot to tell you." Darlene rushed back to her car.

"Alfie, it's my fault. That happened the day I got upset at Mamaw and Papaw. We were driving to their house when the tire went flat." Brooksie explained.

"Eddie happened to be driving by and changed it for us. He asked Brooksie out." Darlene finished the story.

"Is that after you two looked at the Goliath mask?"

"Yes." Brooksie and Darlene answered together.

"Did you go anywhere else before the graveyard?"

"Stinky Crawly's," Darlene answered.

"Was Mr. Crawly with you two the whole time?"

"Unfortunately," Darlene answered.

"Alfie, do you think somebody intentionally flattened her tire?" Brooksie asked.

"I'm surprised that something could do that much damage and you two not see anything lying in the parking lot or on the road." Alfie put his hand into the slash. "It's almost as if a hole was gouged in the tire to make sure it went down quickly. But if Mr. Crawly was with you the whole time, then he couldn't have done it."

"Are you sure I didn't run over something Daddy? Brooksie thought it could have been a shard of glass."

"And I noticed we didn't hear a loud pop. Wouldn't it have done that?" Brooksie added.

"Not necessarily. You could have run over it anywhere and it worked its way in. Let's go on in before your momma comes out to see what's going on." Alfie shut the trunk and laid the tire next to the garage door.

"Sorry, Daddy," Darlene hummed.

"Things happen. I'll have to get another tire for your car." Alfie wiped his hands. "I think I may drive out tomorrow to the cemetery and look around the Civil War soldier's burial site."

"Alfie, why wasn't he found before now?" Brooksie inquired.

"Because he was buried so close to the woods." Alfie flung his hands around as he talked. "Whoever buried him didn't want him to be found for a while. If he was buried about fifty feet closer to the storage building, I think they would've found him when they put up the fence a few years ago."

"It's sad they had to bury him so quickly that they couldn't get a coffin for him." Darlene closed the front door behind them.

"Like all wars, it was tragic," Alfie answered.

Aunt Bobbie bounded out of the kitchen with a dish towel still in her hands. "So tell me about everything that happened."

"The officer found my phasor and a lost earring." Brooksie tucked her hair behind her ear. "See?"

"Well, wasn't that nice of him," Aunt Bobbie cooed.

"I wouldn't say that," Alfie quipped.

"It was silly of that officer to think you girls had anything to do with that soldier being dug up." Aunt Bobbie sauntered back into the kitchen.

"Hmm? You know," Brooksie tapped her chin, "that soldier being buried like that is very strange."

"Why do you think that?" Alfie tilted his head.

"You know how Mom loves studying the Civil War. A few years ago we went on a tour of the local battle sites and every one was close to the Tennessee River. There were none in our part of the county."

"That's correct. When the Union was moving through the

area, there were skirmishes here and there. Even though Knoxville was a Union town, there were a few Confederate sympathizers out in the county. If some of those people discovered you were hiding a Union soldier, then that could cost you and your family your lives."

An image of the sword flashed across Brooksie's mind. Could it have been real and belonged to a soldier hidden in that room? Could it be the soldier in the graveyard? "Hey Alfie." She blurted out.

"Yes?" He spun around.

She couldn't ask about the sword without telling him about the secret room. "Do you think we'll ever find out who he is?"

Alfie narrowed his eyes. "I think we will one day."

⌘

"Officer Lanigan had a point." Brooksie tapped her chin.

"What are you talking about?" Darlene stifled a yawn. "Except for Fuzzy Wazzy, we didn't dig up anybody."

"He thought the timing of everything was too suspicious, and I do also." Brooksie plopped down on Darlene's bed. "I think it was Crabby Crawly who dug up that soldier just to get us in trouble because he's mad at us. Look at what he did to me and Mamaw Mary."

Darlene sat down next to her. "Digging is a lot of work for him to do to cause trouble when all he has to do is talk. That tongue of his is a mean weapon."

"I still think the digging has something to do with us being at the cemetery. And the digger wasn't expecting to find a skeleton."

"The digger? What else do you expect to dig up in a graveyard?" Darlene picked up a pillow and turned it around. "There's a tassel missing. How did that happen?"

"Oh yeah, sorry about that. I laid it around here somewhere." Brooksie took the pillow and tossed it back on the bed. "Somehow somebody has found out about the doll and the clues and they're following us so they can get to the treasure or whatever it is first."

"I don't see how anybody else could know about them."

"What about what Alfie said? He thinks somebody may have sabotaged your tire."

"He didn't say that for sure. You're getting carried away again. Cuz." Darlene stifled another yawn. "I'm going to bed. I'm not like you. I can't take a nap in class."

Brooksie remembered the doll screaming and holding her hands over her ears. "I totally missed it. The answer to the last clue was in my nap dream."

"Nap Dream?"

"Whatever," she shrugged. "Saturday morning we need to go back into the secret room."

Chapter 21

The pencil flipped from finger to finger Friday afternoon. Brooksie shoved it back in the console. To her, first dates were exciting mini adventures, but after the newness wore off, she was bored. Would she ever find anybody who could keep her interest? And would they like the same things she did? Would Eddie be that one? He was certainly different from other boys she had gone out with.

Aaron parked in a space close to the Pizza Barn door.

"At least I'll have some fun tonight." Brooksie slung open the car door, barely missing the one parked next to them.

"What's that supposed to mean?" Aaron straightened his shirt.

"She has to spend the weekend with her family."

"Is that bad?" Aaron asked.

"It could be worse. I remember one time Mamaw Mary had some of her hair salon buddies over for supper. She asked me to help her and it was awful. They treated me like I was their personal maid and wanted me to wait on them hand and foot, especially Gertie."

"Is that the Gertie Uncle Clyde named his calf after?"

"Yep. I bet the calf is nicer and has more manners than she did. I hope I never have to see her wrinkly old sour face again."

"Ahem," a voice said from behind them.

"Oh, hello, Eddie." Darlene looked beyond Brooksie and smiled.

She spun around. Eddie's jaw was clinched and his eyes

narrowed. The last time she saw his jaw like that was when he was frustrated over the Clucking Chicken. Was that still the problem? There was one way to find out. "Hello, Eddie. Anything wrong?"

He relaxed his jaw and gave a toothy grin. "Just been waiting to see you again." He swung his hand from behind him to hand her a long-stemmed rose. "You're as pretty as a rose Brucie,"

"Again, it's Brooksie and thank you." She grasped the rose. "Ouch." She crammed her bleeding finger in her mouth.

"What did you do that for? You know it has thorns," Eddie scolded.

"I thought…"

Darlene interrupted her. "That was very sweet of you. Let's go on in. I'm hungry."

"C'mon." Eddie motioned for them to follow him. He reached the door first. Brooksie lagged behind, waiting for him to hold it open for them to pass through. Instead he shoved it out further.

"Watch it." Aaron caught it before it could crash into Brooksie. "Ladies." He held it open and motioned for her and Darlene to walk in.

Eddie sat down at a large round table in a dark back corner. Aaron sat down first. Darlene sat next to him and Brooksie sat between Darlene and Eddie.

"What took you all so long? You were right behind me." Eddie moaned.

Brooksie looked at Darlene, who shook her head 'no.'

"Where's a waiter?" Eddie roared.

"We've just sat down," Brooksie complained. "You have to give them time to get here."

"They're not so slow at The Crowing Rooster," Eddie spat.

"Sorry. I was filling a drink for another table." The waitress apologized as she laid napkins down in front of them. "Hey guys, how are you all doing today?"

"No need to apologize. We're good, Lynda. How are you?" Aaron asked.

"Pretty good. Can't complain too much. Now, what does everybody want to drink?" She wrote down their drink orders and twirled around. "I'll be right back with them."

"Where are you going? We're ready to order our pizza," Eddie snapped.

Before Lynda could get her pen and pad back out of her pocket, Eddie rambled off the order. "We'll have an extra-large pepperoni with olives and extra cheese."

"Wait a minute," Aaron objected. "We didn't discuss this."

"What's to discuss?" Eddie used a haughty tone.

"I don't eat olives," Aaron told him.

"And I don't like olives or cheese," Brooksie added.

Eddie threw his hands up in the air in an exaggerated manner.

"Lynda, can you do a half and half? Do one side with olives and lots of cheese and the other with pepperoni and regular cheese. I like olives, so I'd be okay with the other half." Darlene squeezed Arron's hand.

"Yes, we can." Lynda scurried off.

"I'm looking forward to next month. What about you Brucie?"

"What I'm looking forward to is ..."

Darlene broke in, "The opening ceremonies. Too bad we can't make it. I know Momma and Daddy would love to able to see President and Nancy Reagan."

"What are you talking about?" Eddie asked. "Why would they come to the annual Hog Festival?"

"Hog Festival? Darlene was talking about the opening of the World's Fair." Brooksie drew out the two words.

"World's Fair?" Eddie waved his right hand in a dismissive manner, almost smacking Brooksie in the head. "I'm talking about something really important. People from surrounding counties come in for the annual Hog Festival. Last year we broke the record and had close to a thousand people there. And we have the Hog Queen Pageant. I think it's something you should consider entering Brucie."

"You seriously expect me to enter it?"

"Why not?" Eddie shrugged.

"So you think Brucie here," Aaron pointed toward her, "would be a good Hog Queen candidate?"

Brooksie scowled and crossed her arms.

"Only the girls who are real pretty and can holler like a pig win." Eddie winked at Brooksie.

"What a compliment," Aaron chimed in.

"That's an honor." Eddie nodded his head.

Lynda walked up and placed their drinks on the table. Brooksie took a large gulp of her chocolate milk and wiped her mouth off. "I have no intention of ever hollering like a pig."

Again Lynda dashed away from the table.

Brooksie continued, "I'm not a country girl. I'd rather be on the bridge of the USS Enterprise instead of a tractor or in some stinky barn." She raised her glass to take another drink.

Eddie knitted his eyebrows together and scrunched up his nose. "I don't know much about the navy, but you don't seem the type to join the military."

"Pheww." Brooksie spit her chocolate milk out, spraying Eddie's left arm.

"What's wrong with you?" He slung his arm around.

"I'm so sorry." Brooksie wiped the shiny spots and streaks of chocolate milk off with her napkin. "You surprised me."

"What was there to be surprised at?" Eddie jerked his arm back and rubbed it against his jeans.

"Who doesn't know the USS Enterprise is the spaceship on *Star Trek?*"

Eddie's mouth dropped open. "You actually like *Star Trek?*"

He was not the guy Darlene was talking about when she said there would be one who would appreciate Brooksie for who she was. And to her, that included spaceships and dinosaurs. Now was her chance to get rid of him.

"Oh yeah. I love *Star Trek*. Darlene has a VCR." Brooksie shoved her foot into Darlene's. "I could bring *Star Trek the Motion Picture* movie over to her house so we all can watch it."

"That'll be a blast. Can't wait." Darlene nudged Aaron with her elbow.

"That sounds awesome. In fact," Aaron made eye contact with Eddie, "I have some of the old episodes back at the house that I taped off of the TV. I can bring them too and we can watch them all day."

Brooksie leaned over Darlene. "Hey Aaron, do you still have your *Land of the Lost* tapes?"

"I'll bring them too."

"I… I…ah," Eddie stuttered. "I have to work that day."

"Really? How do you know that since we didn't mention a date?" Brooksie propped her elbow on the table and rested her chin in her hand.

Eddie didn't answer.

"It's obvious we don't like the same things. I don't like hogs, cows, or tractors." Brooksie pointed to herself. "But it would be cool to have a tractor that had warp drive."

"That's the stupidest thing I've ever heard of." Eddie gave a derisive snort.

"Stupid huh?" Brooksie bobbed her head. "I bet you don't even know what a warp drive is."

"You really are a freak." His eyes bulged and he bit his bottom lip.

Heat radiated from Brooksie's face. "Where do you get off saying that? You don't know me at all."

Eddie clinched his jaw and narrowed his eyes as he had earlier.

"This date is over. You're leaving or we're leaving," Brooksie demanded.

"Brucie, you promised to go with me to The Crowing Rooster, and we're going to go." Eddie slammed his fists into the table.

"I never agreed to anything but the Pizza Barn. And I don't have to do a thing. And for the umpteenth time, my name is Brooksie. B-r-o-o-k-s-i-e. Brooksie."

Eddie jumped up, knocking his chair over. A hush fell across the Pizza Barn. "If you were a boy…" He let his threat trail off.

The manager, Mr. Gamin, appeared with two burly cooks by his side. "Excuse me, sir. You're going to have to leave these premises. We don't tolerate behavior like that here."

Eddie balled his hands into fists and glared at Brooksie. She held his gaze. He turned and ran to the glass doors, hitting them with both hands as he stomped out.

"I'm so sorry, Mr. Gamin." Brooksie sat Eddie's chair back up. "I wouldn't have suggested we come here if I had known he was going to act like that."

"I'm glad you found out what he was like here, rather than somewhere else." He wiped his hands on his apron. "Come on boys, we have more pizzas to cook."

"Here's yours." Lynda sat the pizza down on the table and passed out the paper plates. "Enjoy."

"Guys, I'm so sorry about what happened," Brooksie apologized while picking off olives and laying them in Darlene's plate.

"It's my fault, too, Cuz. I pushed you to go out with him. If anybody's a freak, it's him. He was so nice and sweet when he helped change my tire. It's like he has a split personality or something."

"I think he was putting on a show to get Brooksie to go out with him, but he was too arrogant and short tempered to keep it up. Or he could've just wanted a challenge." Aaron put a slice of pizza on his plate.

അ⌒⌒

With the journal in her lap, Brooksie laid her feet over the side of the bathtub and opened the journal in the back.

April 24, 1982. The date with Eddie last night was a fias-

co. *I should have known he wouldn't like the same things I do, but that doesn't explain his anger or attitude. What was bothering him? Did I do something to cause it? Was Aaron right about me being too much of a challenge? Is there nobody out there for me? One thing is for sure. I don't want to end up like Crabby Crawly, alone and mean.*

Chapter 22

"Almost got it," Brooksie exclaimed Saturday morning, standing on her tip toes and running her hand down the back of the wooden carport column. "Viola." She plucked the key off the nail and unlocked the front door to her grandparent's house.

Darlene followed her up the stairs. "Do you remember how to get back in the secret room?"

"It's been six years. I'll have to retrace my steps when I was chasing the alien lizard." Brooksie popped the old splintered attic door open. "Ready?"

"Wow." Darlene ambled around the attic. "I forgot about all the cool old stuff in here. Hey, check out this old manual type-writer."

"That used to be the control panel to my spaceship." Brooksie's fingers stroked the dusty keys. "The V button controlled the viewing screen. And the W was weapons control."

"Didn't you say you were playing spaceship the day you discovered the secret room?"

"Yeah," Brooksie laughed. "I was chasing a lizard. Wouldn't it be cool if there was one in here now?"

"No. It wouldn't." Darlene flung herself next to Brooksie and frantically looked around.

"A little lizard's no big deal." She shrugged. "I'm more worried about big hairy spiders."

"Oh, my." Darlene shivered and rubbed her arms.

"Help me move the cabinet out of the way." Brooksie took hold of one side.

"What if a big hairy spider crawls out from under it?" Darlene stayed in place.

"We'll scream, run, and look for something big to throw on it. Now get the other side."

"Okay." Darlene relented.

They scooted it over with ease.

"Do you see the crack?" Brooksie ran her hand down the wall.

"Oh, yeah, I do now." Darlene twisted her mouth. "You know, it's like God wanted you to find the secret room and the doll."

Brooksie's chest burnt. "And for my daddy to be murdered?" She immediately put her hands up. "I'm sorry. Forget I said it."

"It's okay, Cuz. So how do we get it to open since there's no handle?"

"This picture." Brooksie tilted the same picture she had years ago. The door creaked opened. "Scooby Doo hasn't got a thing on us."

"That's too cool," Darlene exclaimed. "Who's the lady in the picture?"

"Beats me. Did you bring your flashlight?"

"Yeah." Darlene pulled it out of her purse and handed it to Brooksie.

"Stay behind me." Brooksie's scalp tingled when she walked into the secret room.

"What a beautiful Chinese fan." Darlene picked it up. "How odd. It has cobwebs dangling from it even though it's been lying on the floor."

"I read that to you from my diary. That's the fan I used to tear the cobwebs down."

Darlene spun it around. "I see the parasols now."

Brooksie's flashlight reflected off something metal. "There's the sword."

"One of your toy weapons to use against the alien lizard?" Darlene asked.

"No, the sword was already here. I remembered it when Alfie told about the Civil War soldier that was dug up and it got me to thinking."

"You think it belongs to him?"

"Maybe." Brooksie shrugged. "What if our ancestors hid him in the attic from the Confederate sympathizers and he died in here. They had to sneak him out at night in order to bury him and left his sword behind. Or am I jumping to conclusions again?"

"I think you're on the right track this time. Daddy said the soldier didn't have anything with him. You know, if he was a Christian, they may have wanted to bury him next to a church. Is the house old enough for that to have happened?"

"I have no idea. We'll look into that later. Right now I want to get the letters." Brooksie shined the flashlight on them.

Darlene reached down.

"Wait." Brooksie pushed her back. "I need to do something first." She gently scooted the letters around with her foot and leapt back. A couple of hairy spiders crawled out from under them.

"Ooh," Darlene squealed and stepped behind Brooksie.

"I don't like those things either." Brooksie picked the envelopes up. "Let's go back out where it's lighter." She adjusted the picture and the door slid into place. The she flipped through the letters. "They're correspondences between Aunt Brooksie and Papaw Asmus."

"That's awesome. Let's go ahead and look at the last one like it says in the clue."

"Okay." Brooksie handed all but the last letter to Darlene. She ripped the top off and jerked it out.

October 1953

William,

I'm not doing too well. Clyde's family has graciously allowed me to move in with them. I'm not sure how much time I have left. I had hoped we could all be together again before it's my time. Mimi has asked about you ever since you sent her the doll. I have to answer her questions since Mary will not. There were a couple of times I thought about hiding Mimi's doll from Mary. I've never said anything before now, but Mary was upset that you sent Mimi that doll.

Even if we miss seeing each other, you need to work on your relationship with Mary before it is too late.

Your loving sister
Brooksie Asmus

"Mamaw Mary and Papaw Asmus have always had a strange relationship, but I didn't know she didn't like him sending Mom the doll."

"Obviously, Aunt Mary was jealous of it. Now we know your Aunt Brooksie hid the doll and you bringing the doll home had nothing to do with your dad's death." Darlene gave her a quick hug. "I know you don't like to be hugged, but aren't you relieved?"

Brooksie sighed. "No, because it wasn't her."

"What do you mean? It's right there in the letter. Aunt Brooksie was living here and had easy access to the doll. She hid it from Aunt Mary and then she managed to sneak the fake doll into the trash fire. So nothing valuable was hidden in it which means," Darlene held up her index finger, "there was no reason to kill for it. It's all just a coincidence."

"What about the clues we're following?"

"I don't know." Darlene shrugged. "Maybe it's some kind of game or there could be another letter somewhere or something they're leading to."

"Don't you remember what Mom said that Sunday they all stopped by to visit? Aunt Brooksie died before Papaw Asmus made it back here. And the doll disappeared after he got back. So it wasn't Aunt Brooksie unless her ghost had something to do with it."

"Oh." Darlene scratched her head. "I hate to say it again, but the suspect would have to be Aunt Mary. If she resented

Mimi having the doll, she may have hidden it so she wouldn't have to see it every day. She could've hid it after Brooksie died, the other Brooksie that is."

She shook her head. "All of this is too sophisticated for Mamaw Mary."

"We do know one thing." Darlene held up the letters. "They don't have the answer to the last clue."

"But they were put in the same box with Mom's doll, so whoever hid it, wanted to make sure they were read. There's something they're trying to tell us."

"I'll put them in my purse and we'll look at them after you get back to the house tomorrow."

Darlene stepped out of the attic first and went to the window overlooking the driveway. "Cuz, you need to see this."

Brooksie ran to the window. "Rats!"

Chapter 23

"It's time to face the music." Darlene lifted her chin. "The police are here."

"Don't sweat it. As long as it's not Officer Lanigan, I don't see a problem."

Brooksie and Darlene stepped into the carport.

"Girls."

"Mom? Did you get off work early?"

"Daddy called for me to come home." Mom gave Brooksie a tight hug, almost taking her breath away. "I miss you being here so much." Then she hugged Darlene. "It's good to see you here, too."

"So, do you know what's going on?" Brooksie tried to sound nonchalant.

"You know how your mamaw is." Mom rolled her eyes. "She has it in her head some criminal who has come in for the World's Fair dug holes in the back yard. Hey, I almost forgot." She went back to her car and brought an envelope back. "This came for you yesterday."

"Why would anybody be sending me a letter?" Brooksie ripped the top off and jerked the letter out. "I don't believe it."

"What?" Mom and Darlene asked at the same time.

"I got a scholarship."

"Eeee," Darlene squealed and slung her arms around Brooksie.

"I'm so proud of you." Mom wrapped her arms around

them both.

"That's enough." Brooksie shrugged them off and backed up.

"Cuz, that's awesome." Darlene clapped.

"It's an answer to my prayers," Mom exclaimed. "Which one did you get and how much?"

"It's the F.H.B. Memorial Scholarship for children who have lost one or both parents. And it's for full tuition and books if I attend the University of Tennessee. According to this, I don't have to do anything but sign up for classes. The money will be sent straight to UT."

"This is such a relief. I was worried that you would have to work your way through school, and it would take longer for you to get out. I even thought about getting a second job again."

"I'm thankful, too, Mom, but it's strange."

"Who cares? I hope you're not thinking of turning it down." Mom tapped her foot.

"No, it's just that I didn't apply for this scholarship. In fact, I've never heard of it. And there's no way to contact anybody." Brooksie flipped the letter over. "There's not even a return address on it."

"Somebody in the guidance office or a teacher may have put you in for it," Darlene suggested.

"I don't care who suggested it. I'm just so thankful you got it. Now let's join in on the fun." Mom led the way around the house.

"Isn't that Stinky Crawly's car parked down at the creek?" Darlene whispered.

Brooksie narrowed her eyes. "Yeah, I don't think it was there when we drove by."

"He doesn't seem like the fishing type to me."

"Me, either," Brooksie agreed. "So why is he down there?"

"You mark my word. It's going to bring in criminals from all over the world," Mamaw Mary spat.

Darlene and Brooksie came to a halt. Standing around the

holes they dug were Mamaw Mary, Papaw Clyde, and Officer Lanigan.

"Momma, the World's Fair is miles away in downtown Knoxville and we're out in the country on the edge of Knox County. If criminals are coming in for the fair, there's a lot more places they would go instead of out here."

"You'll see. I heard at the hair salon that this fair thing is gonna bring in the wrong type of people." Mamaw Mary jammed her finger into Mom's face.

"You can't believe everything that comes out of the hair salon." Mom crossed her arms.

"Whoever did it threw Fuzzy Wazzy's bones to the side." Mamaw Mary covered her mouth. "He was such a good little dog."

"I'll rebury them." Papaw Clyde caressed her back.

Brooksie puffed her bangs up. If she had reburied Fuzz Wazzy like Darlene wanted to do, then Mamaw Mary may not have called the police. And they wouldn't have to deal with Officer Lanigan again.

"Come on up, girls. I have some questions for you," he quipped.

"Why do you have questions for them?" Mom demanded.

"I questioned them the other day about the hole dug in the graveyard at Happy Valley Church. Brooksie and Darlene have been close to two separate diggings within a short time."

Great. The policeman remembered how to say her name. This wasn't good.

"So in your mind it's guilt by association? Just because they had been at the graveyard doesn't make them guilty of digging in it." Mom shook her index finger at him. "And the same goes for here. Unless you have some real evidence, you shouldn't be throwing out accusations."

"This is too big of a coincidence not to investigate. Vandalism should not be taken lightly," Officer Lanigan snapped.

"I agree about the vandalism, but that doesn't make the girls guilty of it. When you get back to the police station, I dare you to check on their records. You'll see that they don't have any." Mom's nostrils flared.

"My granddaughter wasn't raised to do such a thing and I don't appreciate your accusations either. As far as I am concerned, this matter is over and you can leave now." Papaw Clyde lifted his hat and wiped the sweat off of his forehead.

Brooksie had mixed emotions. On one hand, it was nice to have people stand up for her. On the other hand she felt guilty since she was the one who dug the holes in the backyard and left out Fuzzy Wazzy's bones. How disappointed would they be in her to know that?

"Have a good day." Officer Lanigan folded his notepad and stomped off. Papaw followed along behind him.

"All of this is your fault," Mamaw Mary hissed at Brooksie

"How? You're the one who called the police." Mom reminded her.

Mamaw Mary's voice became shrill. "She's the one who had Mr. Crawly hunt for that stupid Goliath mask."

"I already told you Momma, Brooksie is working on a special project about our family history."

"It's causing too much trouble. Do another project instead." Mamaw Mary's mole turned a fluorescent pink.

"I can't do that." Brooksie wasn't going to back down this time. "I won't do that. I'm not doing anything wrong."

"Our family history is nobody else's business," Mamaw Mary screeched. "Stop it right now."

"Momma, calm down. All of this is nothing more than a coincidence." Mom tried to calm her down.

"She doesn't need to tell anybody else about our family."

Brooksie was tired of Mamaw Mary's attitude. "It's more than that. I picked this project because the circumstances of my daddy's death have bothered me for years. I don't believe the police's theory that he interrupted a burglar. I think his death has something to do with the family history and I want to find out why."

"How dare you," Mamaw Mary screamed. Her face turned scarlet as she pulled at her hair. Brooksie had seen her do that before, but she couldn't remember when or where it was. "How dare you think anybody in the family could have anything to do with his death. You need to quit coming up with such farfetched ideas when you have no idea what you're talking about."

"Momma, why in the world are you so upset? You'd think Brooksie was accusing you of something." Mom put her hand on her mother's shoulder.

Mamaw Mary cried harder and pulled at her hair with both hands. Papaw Clyde ran to her and embraced her. "Nobody's accusing anybody of anything."

Brooksie was the one who has the guilt of her father's death in the back of her mind. Why was Mamaw Mary so upset?

Chapter 24

Sunday afternoon the whole family visited with Papaw Asmus at the Union County Nursing Home. There was one good thing about him moving there. Now Brooksie didn't have to worry about bees or snakes when she used the bathroom.

"Ow." She massaged the back of her aching neck.

The wooden chairs at the nursing home were uncomfortable and stiff. There was a nice recliner next to Papaw Asmus' bed, but Mamaw Mary always got it. Brooksie pivoted around in the chair. Whoa.

Standing at the nurse's station was a cute dark haired intern. Brooksie had noticed him a few times working on the floor, but this was the first time she had the chance to take a good look at him. He had a full head of thick dark wavy hair. Even though he wasn't tall, he had a muscular build. And he had a slight Asian look to his eyes. Talk about cute. If he were on a poster, she'd hang it up when they finished repairing her room. He glanced up and their eyes met. His were a dark chocolate brown she had never seen before. They reminded her of a Hershey's bar.

"Brooksie."

"Huh?" She jerked around. Everybody was staring at her.

"I was telling Papaw Asmus about your scholarship." Mom raised her chin.

"Your mother is very excited about it. I hope you are going to take advantage of it." Papaw Asmus was actually talking to her. He had never done that before. Mamaw Mary usually cut him off too soon to really talk to anybody else.

"Yeah, I'm looking forward to going to college."

He nodded. "Good. I expect great things out of you. Now what do you plan on majoring in?"

"Do they have classes in day dreaming?" Mamaw Mary scowled at her. Brooksie almost expected her to stick her tongue out.

"Now Momma," Mom said.

Brooksie knew Mamaw Mary would say something like that. As the conversation changed, she turned her attention back to the desk. The cute intern was gone. "I'm going to stretch my legs. Be back in a few." She sprinted out of the room before anybody could ask her any questions.

She peered into the different rooms as she moseyed by. That was too obvious, plus she didn't like some of the things she saw. She slowed her pace down and gently slung her arms. Soon she reached the picture window at the end of the hallway. Abruptly she twirled around. Her body came into contact with someone else. The impact threw her into the wall. There were loud tingles and cracks of glass breaking.

Sprawled out on the floor in front of her was the cute intern with food and broken dishes lying around him. There were pinto beans strewn across his chest and little piles of gravy covered mashed potatoes dotted all over him.

"I'm so sorry. Let me help you." Brooksie bent down the same time he tried to get up. The force of their heads hitting together knocked them both to the ground.

"Are you all right?" he asked.

"I think so." Brooksie held her throbbing head while stars danced in front of her eyes.

He crawled over the mess to her. "I don't want to touch you with this stuff on my hands." He yanked a tissue out of his pocket and feverishly wiped mashed peas and beans off.

Was he was going to touch her? Brooksie didn't move.

She couldn't even if she wanted to.

"Let me check you out." Putting her face into his strong soft hands, he gazed deep into her eyes.

Those mesmerizing brown eyes. It was like they were the only two people in the universe.

"Your pupils are normal. Do you feel sick at all?"

She opened her mouth, but nothing came out.

"Are you having trouble breathing?"

"No, I'm okay," she whispered.

"Then you don't need CPR." He chuckled.

Maybe she should pretend to pass out.

"My name is William, but everybody calls me Will. What's your name?"

"Brooksie." Mamaw Mary's screeching broke the spell. She clinched up and pulled away Will's hands. That wasn't the way she wanted him to hear her name. If only she could beam away to somewhere else.

"We can't take you anywhere and you not do something embarrassing." Mamaw's Mary's shrill voice echoed as she stomped down the hallway. "We need to leave soon, but now we have to wait for you to help clean this mess up." She threw her arms out.

People stuck their heads out their doors and were staring at them.

"I'll hurry Mamaw." There was no way Brooksie could look directly at Will now. She kept her face down while grabbing pieces of broken dishes. "I'm so sorry about running into you. Ow." Blood oozed from her thumb.

He pulled a Band-Aid out of another pocket. Gingerly he wrapped it around her thumb. "I'll pick this mess up." He stood and held his hand out. Brooksie clasped it and he pulled her up with gentle ease. "Accidents happen," he whispered and gave her hand a small squeeze.

"They happen to her all the time," Mamaw Mary hissed.

"It's not all her fault." Will dropped her hand. "I was hurrying and not paying attention either."

Mamaw Mary narrowed her eyes into thin slits and scowled at him. Her mole was pulsating. Will didn't flinch, instead he smiled at her.

Brooksie's breath caught in her throat. Will was her knight in shining armor. Selfishly he confronted the pink Cyclops threatening to destroy her.

"We insist on helping," Mom's voice cut into Brooksie's thoughts. She and Papaw Clyde had walked up.

"I can do it by myself and get it cleaned up faster. And this was also my fault. Please go and enjoy your afternoon." Will smiled at them.

As they drove back, Mamaw Mary fussed. "I swannie. That made my nose want a sip of coffee. Do you know how many people saw the commotion you caused?"

Brooksie bit her lip. They wouldn't have known if Mamaw Mary hadn't been yelling.

"It's over now Momma. We can't undo what happened." Mom looked at Brooksie and rolled her eyes.

"It shouldn't have happened at all," Mamaw Mary continued to fuss.

"Like Mimi said, it's over now," Papaw Clyde cooed. "It's a beautiful day, let's just enjoy the ride."

"Umph." Mamaw Mary crossed her arms.

Brooksie looked out of the window, but instead of seeing the scenery, she saw the cute intern in full knight's armor and riding on a white horse.

Chapter 25

"You'll never guess what happened at the nursing home." Brooksie closed Darlene's bedroom door.

"Knowing you, Cuz, I'd say you were playing on a wheel chair and ran into somebody."

"Not just anybody. I ran into the cutest guy on the planet." Brooksie rubbed her hands together.

"So you were playing in a wheel chair?"

"No, don't be silly." Brooksie proceeded to tell her everything that happened in one breath.

Darlene scratched her head. "I think I caught everything, but what's this about a Cyclops and a knight?"

"That's me being me." Brooksie shrugged.

"Oh, I get it. Aunt Mary is the Cyclops and this cute intern is the knight coming to your rescue. I like that." Darlene nodded.

"He was so sweet about everything. And I hit him hard, twice." Brooksie held up two fingers.

"No, you swept him off his feet. Or how about knocked him for a loop? Either way, it sounds to me like he's interested in you. I don't know if I could have been that nice to somebody who knocked me down and then butted heads with me. And he bandaged your thumb as well."

Brooksie's chest tightened and heat radiated from her face. She fanned herself with her hand.

"Are the Sunday trips to the nursing home looking better

now? I may have to go with you one time."

"And get your stamp of approval?"

"That's what best friends do. I need to check this guy out for myself." Darlene smacked her chest.

"I think you'll approve. But right now, I want to read about all the spy stories in Papaw Asmus' letters."

"Or we'll read about Mr. Asmus being chased by polar bears." Darlene pulled the letters out of her purse. "Where do you want to get?"

"Are you kidding?" Brooksie plopped down on the floor and leaned against Darlene's bed.

"I ought to have known." Darlene grabbed the journal and sat down next to her. She spread the envelopes out in front of them. "Since we're not worried about the last letter anymore, let's start with the ones that have the earliest postmark and go from there."

"The date on this one is 1933." Brooksie held it out between them as they read it.

"There's nothing here worth writing in the journal." Brooksie tossed it to Darlene.

"I don't understand." Darlene placed it back in the envelope. "You've mentioned Mamaw Mary and Papaw Asmus having a strained relationship, but in this letter Mr. Asmus talked about how much he missed and loved her. What happened?"

"Who knows?" Brooksie held out the next one. "This is odd." She ran her finger over a line. "'*You know I didn't mean for that to happen at the diner.*' Did he go out to eat with Aunt Brooksie and throw up on her?"

"Maybe he got mad and made a scene like Eddie did at the Pizza Barn." Darlene snarled her nose. "I'll write it in the journal. It's the only thing we have so far."

"I hope they get more exciting." Brooksie held out the next one. "There's not even a bear chase. Why would you keep such boring letters?"

"Patience, dear Cousin." Darlene ran her finger down the page. "Listen to this, '*It saddens me that Mary learned the de-*

tails about Laura's death that way. I had planned on explaining it to her face to face one day so she wouldn't get the wrong idea of how it happened.' I take it Laura was Aunt Mary's mother?"

"Yeah, and this is the first time I've ever heard anything about her death."

"To me, it reads like it was an accident and your Papaw Asmus was involved somehow. Laura could have gotten sick and your Papaw Asmus didn't get her to the doctor in time."

"They lived in Union County 50 years ago and not on *Little House on the Prairie*." Brooksie shook her head.

"Okay. Maybe she was killed in a car wreck and he was driving. Or it could have even been a crazy farm accident similar to Uncle Clyde crashing his truck into your room."

The doorbell rang.

"Is that Aaron?" Brooksie asked.

"No, it's probably somebody here to see Momma or Daddy."

"Okay, you've got a point about it being an accident," Brooksie conceded.

"And look at this line, '*This has made my nightmares worse.*' Whatever it was, your papaw had a lot of guilt."

"Hmm?" Brooksie tapped her chin, "Laura's death could be the reason he left to go to Alaska. He couldn't stand the constant reminders of what happened."

"Eddie's at the front door to see Brooksie so he can apologize. And he has a dozen red roses," Alfie called through the door.

"Not now," she whined.

Darlene shoved the letters under the bed. "Come in, Daddy."

Alfie stuck his gray head through the cracked door. "I'll tell him to leave unless you want to talk to him."

"I don't want to have anything to do with him ever again," Brooksie answered.

Alfie smiled. "Then you need to tell him face to face. I'll be standing next to you and praying while you do."

Brooksie's heart pounded with each step she took down the hallway.

Alfie grasped the door knob. "It'll be all right. Are you ready?"

"I think so." Even though Alfie was with her, she still felt awkward.

As soon as Alfie opened the door, Eddie tried to take step in, but Alfie put his hand out and stopped him. "You'll talk to Brooksie from the porch." He stepped behind the door with his hand still on the handle.

Eddie's eyes widened. He was wearing the same cowboy hat and plaid shirt he had on when he changed their tire. In his hands were a dozen long stemmed roses. His cologne overpowered their smell. "Bruc...Brooksie, I'm sorry for my behavior at the Pizza Barn and I'm ready for a second chance. To prove it," he thrust them into her face, "I brought you some roses without thorns. And they ain't cheap either."

Brooksie pushed them back to him. "We're supposed to forgive others if we expect it ourselves. So I forgive you."

"So when are we going to The Crowing Roster?" He thrust the roses back at her.

She pushed them back to him again. "We're not. Just because I forgive you doesn't mean I will ever go out with you again."

"But you said..."

"We're done. After the way you acted at the Pizza Barn, I don't trust you. By the way, you can take another girl to The Crowing Rooster and give the roses to her."

"Don't come back." Alfie shut the door and locked it.

Brooksie hated the way she was feeling. She didn't like being put in that position. "Thanks for not leaving my side Alfie."

"You know you're like my daughter."

"Yeah, I know." Brooksie gave Alfie a quick hug. She immediately jolted down the hallway and almost ran into Darlene.

"Whoa." Darlene barely managed to step out of the way in time. "Did you hug my dad?"

"Kinda." Brooksie shrugged. "He did help me get rid of Eddie for good."

Chapter 26

"Listen to this, '*I am now a partner in a gold mine with the Heims and the Fields. I will be able to give a nice dowry to Mary. I want her to have a better start to life than I did.*'"

"Gold Mine," Darlene shouted.

Brooksie put her finger up to mouth. "Shhh."

"Sorry," Darlene whispered. "Your dream of a buried treasure wasn't so farfetched after all."

"Why did they tell us Papaw invested in a natural resource instead of saying gold?"

"Who knows? Let's see if there's an answer in here." Darlene held out the next letter.

"He had a girlfriend," Brooksie yelled. She put her hand over her mouth and rested her elbow on her knee.

Darlene read, "*In the last 3 months, I have fallen in love with Hannah, the Heim's daughter. She is wonderful and I haven't felt this way since Laura. I have just asked Hannah's father for her hand in marriage.*"

"This is getting weird." Brooksie ran her hand through her hair.

Darlene continued reading the letter. "*Maybe now I can have a happy and settled life. The nightmares have finally stopped. I would love for Mary to be up here for the wedding, but I do not have the extra money right now. We had to make* some expensive repairs to our mining equipment and it cost us our profits this month.

"I used to get irritated when you talked about God working, but I see it now. I was unsure that Mr. Heim would give his permission since I am a Gentile and not Jewish."

"Jewish," they both shouted.

"Rats!" Brooksie covered her mouth.

"Your Papaw had some exposure to Hebrew in Alaska after all." Darlene lowered the letter. "Hannah had to have helped him write the clues or at least the first one."

"That's just part of the answer. We still don't know what was in the doll that made it so dangerous that it had to be hidden twice." Brooksie picked up the last letter. *"Everything is off with Hannah. I am heartbroken and I don't know where Hannah and her family have moved to. I shouldn't have let it gone so far and done something sooner, but I was so afraid. Charles knew everything, but he didn't step in. He had been such a help to them and they trusted him. Just goes to show that you can't trust anybody from the government."*

"Never mind what I just suggested. If the Heims moved away, then Hannah couldn't have helped your Papaw Asmus write the clues."

"Hmm?" Brooksie tapped her chin. "What did he let go so far? And how bad was it that the Heims moved away? And what did this Charles guy know and not tell them."

"I like the names. Charles was my grandfather's name, Daddy's daddy," Darlene sang.

Brooksie titled her head and raised her eyebrows.

"Sorry, Cuz. Anyway, I think I may have an answer and you won't like it."

"Go ahead." Brooksie put her elbows on her knees and rested her chin on her fists.

"Your Papaw Asmus may have had access to gold as it was mined. In that case, it would be easy for him to slip out small pieces of it here and there."

"You think he smuggled gold back home in the doll? Why

would he do that?"

"Not in the doll, but in the letters. Bear with me here, Cuz." Darlene scooted out from the bed. "When we first discovered the doll had been opened up, I suggested that whatever was in the doll may have led to something else."

"Yeah." Goose bumps crawled up the back of Brooksie's neck.

"Your Papaw may have been worried that he wasn't sending enough money back home to Aunt Brooksie and Mary. As time went on, there may have been some gold left that Aunt Brooksie didn't use and he sent instructions back inside the doll telling her what to do with it. Somehow the Heims found what he had been doing and became upset. Who would want their daughter marrying a thief?"

"It makes sense." Brooksie hopped up on her knees. "Charles may have been some kind of inspector or auditor and he caught on to what Papaw Asmus was doing. He confronted Papaw about it and Papaw gave him a sob story about Aunt Brooksie and Mary." Brooksie tapped her chin. "But that doesn't explain why the Heims moved away when they could've just had him arrested."

"I may have an idea." Darlene retrieved a book off of her desk and sat back down. "This in one of the books you wanted out of Daddy's library, *Alaska in World War II*. I remember reading something about Jewish people in it."

Darlene ran her finger down the glossary. "Here it is. There's a chapter on Jewish refugees in Alaska." She flipped through the pages. "Kristallnacht is also known as the Night of Broken Glass. In 1938, the Nazis terrorized Jewish people in Germany and Austria. They let some of the Jews leave, but they had to give the Nazis their wealth first. Because of this, there was a push from within the US to relocate some Jews in Alaska. Skagway was the only Alaskan city to accept them. In 1940 the King-Havenner Bill was introduced. It was supposed to help in the development of Alaska, but it didn't have any support, especially from the Alaskans."

Darlene placed her finger in the book and closed it. "What if Charles was a government man assigned to help the Heims and other Jews settle in Alaska. Hannah and her family may have been Jewish refugees. "

"Wow." Brooksie wrapped her arms around her knees. "Who would have thought I would have a relative in something as cool as this?"

"Remember, Cuz, we're just guessing. We have no real facts about what happened in Alaska between your Papaw Asmus and the Heims."

"Then we'll go to the source to get them."

Darlene furrowed her eyebrows. "You want us to go to Alaska?"

"Yeah, right. We're going to visit Papaw Asmus ourselves. He may be more willing to answer questions without Mamaw Mary around."

"If your Papaw Asmus finds out you have the doll, he may ask for it back," Darlene warned.

Chapter 27

Darlene pulled into the Pizza Barn parking lot Monday after school. "Thanks, Cuz, for agreeing to take a break. We've been at this since Uncle Clyde ran his truck through your wall."

"I got carried away as usual. Papaw Asmus seems to be happy there, so he won't be going anywhere soon."

"Tomorrow we'll go after school to see him."

They joined their friends inside. Brooksie had forgotten how nice it was to just have fun and laugh. The door swung open. "Oooh," the girls at their table crooned. Brooksie forced her chocolate milk down. What was he doing there?

He sauntered straight to their table. "I hope you ladies are doing well today. Brooksie, it's good to see you again." Will smiled revealing the dimple in his left cheek.

Her chest tightened. If she talked now, she'd squeak.

"Well, you all have a good lunch." He sat a nearby table.

"What's wrong with you? Why didn't you say something?" Amy asked.

"Did you see that dimple?" Susan tapped her left cheek.

"He's cute. Where'd you meet him?" Nikki sighed.

"Shh." Darlene quietened the table. "Cuz, you gotta go over and talk to him."

"I think he's cute. I'll talk to him if you won't." Susan peered toward Will.

"What are you waiting for?" Amy asked. "He keeps looking over here."

"Do you like him or don't you?" Darlene peered into Brooksie's eyes

Brooksie wiped her sweaty palms on her jeans and walked toward his table. Soft giggles followed her.

Will's eyes met hers and he smiled again. She stopped. She didn't mean to stop. What now? He would ask her why she stopped. What would she say? Should she just turn around and go back to the other table?

"Please join me, Brooksie." He rose and pulled out the chair across from him.

Ricky Sharp did that for her back at the eighth grade prom. When she bent to sit down, he shoved the chair and her into the table so hard that she had a bruise across her stomach for a week. Like she needed any help getting bruises.

Closing her eyes, she slowly bent down. The chair barely tapped the back of her knees. Brooksie sat all the way down and he gently scooted her up to the table's edge.

"Thank you for coming over." He took his seat across from her. "I don't like to eat alone."

"Me, either. And thank you." She tucked her hair behind her ear.

"Thank you for what? We've not eaten yet." He raised his right eyebrow.

"The thank you is for saying my name right. Most people mess it up." Brucie and Brosky echoed in her mind. "That's one of the reason's I don't like my name."

"I think it's like you, beautiful and different."

Her heart fluttered. No boy had ever called her beautiful. Not that she was ugly, but she had never considered herself to being anywhere near beautiful. She wasn't a girlie girl.

"Mr. Asmus is very happy that you carry his sister's name."

"I didn't know that. Papaw's never said anything to me about it. But then again, every time we visit I don't get a chance to say much. Mamaw Mary does most of the talking."

Will smiled and nodded.

Will smiled and nodded.

"You all ready to order or do you need a minute?" Lynda winked at Brooksie.

"It's up to the lady."

Brooksie raised the menu up to cover her face. Why did Lynda have to do that? "I would like a pepperoni with hamburger meat on thin crust."

"That sounds delicious. Make it a large please."

"And what to drink?"

"I'll have a sweet tea, please," Will ordered.

"My chocolate milk is at the other table." Brooksie put her hands on the table and started to stand up.

Will laid his hands on hers. "I'll get it." He walked to the other table and retrieved her glass. "Excuse me ladies." Giggles followed him as well.

"I don't want a lady to be thirsty." He sat her glass down without spilling a drop.

"Thank you, but you didn't have to go to all that trouble."

"That was no trouble at." He tilted his head sideways and narrowed his eyes. "So, do you like your name better now that you know how Mr. Asmus feels?"

"Not really."

"Why? Is there something else?"

Brooksie shrugged and focused on her glass.

"You can tell me. I want to hear it. Please," he pled.

"All right." She sucked in a deep breath. "When my mother was carrying me, she had picked out my first name, but she couldn't decide on a middle name to go with it. One day she was listening to the radio and heard a song by the Four Seasons, *Dawn Go Away, I'm no good for you.* Viola, Brooksie Dawn. I'm named after a dead aunt and a rock song."

"That makes you special. How many people can say that about their name?"

"Not many that's for sure." She took a bigger sip of chocolate milk than she meant to. Keeping her head down, she wiped her mouth. No way was she going to have a chocolate mustache.

"I hope you didn't get in trouble with your family about what happened Sunday."

"I have a lot of accidents, so I guess they're used to it." Great, she just told him about what a klutz she was.

"Only boring people don't have accidents."

Brooksie needed to change the subject before she discussed anything else embarrassing about herself. "What about you? The only thing I know about you is your first name and where you work."

"I'm a sophomore at the University of Tennessee where I'm a pre-med major. I want to specialize in geriatrics." His voice took on a serious tone. "I love older people. Our society doesn't treat them right. In Asian cultures, the elders are treated with honor and respect for their wisdom. Here it's all about youth. Knowledge and wisdom about life isn't appreciated."

"I used to love to sit and listen to my Grandma Emma talk about how it was when she was growing up." Sadness swept over Brooksie. She hadn't let herself think of those memories in a long time.

"Brooksie?"

"Sorry." Heat radiated from her face. "Did you say something?"

"I asked if you enjoyed Mr. Asmus stories about Alaska as well." Will furrowed his thick eyebrows.

"I've heard him try to talk about Alaska, but Mamaw Mary would always change the subject."

"Would you like to hear them now?" He gazed into her eyes. She felt like he was searching, but for what, she didn't know.

"Yes, I would." More than Will knew.

"You need to come up by yourself and spend some time with him. I know he would enjoy it. And if you like adventure, you'll enjoy his stories."

God just opened up a door for her. Darlene would be proud she noticed it. "Darlene and I were just talking about visiting him."

"Really?" His eyes lit up. "When are you two coming up?"

"We were thinking about one day this week. Maybe to-morrow. But don't tell him. I want it to be a surprise."

"I won't say a thing. Is Darlene at the other table?" Will gestured toward it.

There were more giggles.

"She's the one who was sitting on my right. Not only is she my cousin on Papaw Clyde's side, she's also my best friend."

"Here you go." Lynda sat the pizza and plates on the table. "Enjoy."

"Thank you." After she walked off, Will leaned over to Brooksie. "I hope you don't mind, but I like to pray before I eat."

"Please do." Brooksie lowered her head. Wow. He was something else.

Will placed a piece of pizza on her plate first. When he ate, he didn't make loud smacking or slurping noises. Did he make any loud noises when he kissed? She reached down to take hold of her glass, but stopped when she realized her hands were shaking.

Chapter 28

"I can't believe you told him all that stuff. A little personal for the first date don't you think?" Darlene asked as they drove back to her house.

"It wasn't a date. Besides, it was so easy to talk to him." Brooksie sighed.

"Did he ask for your phone number?"

"No and I didn't even think of it until you mentioned it." It felt as if her heart sank to her knees. Why didn't Will do that? He had plenty of opportunities. Could Darlene have been right about telling him too much about herself? Did she scare him off?

Darlene pulled into the garage. "I'm sorry, Cuz. I shouldn't have brought it up. He may've been nervous and forgot to ask you for it. Don't worry about it. We could all tell you two were hitting it off."

"I hope you're right." Brooksie closed her door. She followed Darlene inside and up the basement steps.

"Hello, girls." Aunt Bobbie had flour dotted across her nose and cheeks.

"Hi, Momma."

"Hey, Aunt Bobbie."

"How would you all like a homemade strawberry cobbler for dessert tonight?"

"That would be awesome." Brooksie rubbed her stomach. "I'm gonna put a bunch of vanilla ice cream on mine."

"Then you two can help me make it. Brooksie, do you care to get down the blue cookbook from on top of the refrigerator?"

"No problem." She stretched up and pulled it down. "Cool. Check out the title." Brooksie flipped the cookbook around.

Darlene's eyes bulged. "'*Cooking and Baking are Women's Work.*'"

"What's wrong with you two?" Aunt Bobbie yanked it out of Brooksie's hand. "You'd think you all had never seen a cookbook before."

"Wasn't that Grandma Emma's?" Brooksie asked.

"Yes, it was. Mary knew I liked the recipes in it so she gave it to me after Mom passed away." Aunt Bobbie licked her finger and turned the pages.

"Momma, do you mind if we look at it again after supper?"

Aunt Bobbie crinkled her eyebrows. "Is there anything special about it?"

Brooksie and Darlene exchanged glances.

"I want to look through it." Brooksie shrugged. "You know, for old times' sake."

"I don't mind at all, just be careful with it."

க்கூ

Brooksie scanned through the recipes later that evening. "Here's Za Jiang Mein. Grandma Emma would never fix anything Beijing style."

"Why not?" Darlene asked.

"Are you kidding? Do you think Papaw Clyde and Mamaw Mary would every eat anything like that? I'm surprised they eat spaghetti."

"True, but Aunt Mary knows how to fry okra just right." Darlene licked her lips.

"Zucchini Bread. Grandma Emma always fixed it for Mom's birthday." Brooksie rubbed the page between her palms.

"What are you doing, Cuz?"

"The next page is stuck to the back of the Zucchini Bread one and I think there's something between them."

"Stop doing that or you'll tear the pages. Then Momma will skin you alive. I have just the thing." Darlene retrieved her tweezers and slowly maneuvered them through the tiny slot between the pages. "I got it." She pulled out a small folded piece of paper.

"Cool." Brooksie reached for it, but Darlene pulled it back.

"I'll open it and then you can read it." She carefully pried the crinkled page apart and handed it to her.

"'*Over an old heart is a special key. Use it to open a box up and set it free. But before you do the last chore. Look under the guardian forever more.*'" Brooksie's breath caught in her throat. "This is the last clue. We're almost to the answer."

"This one is complicated. It's like there's two in one. We have to open a box and set what's in it free. But before we do that, we have to look under some guardian. These could mean anything." Darlene rubbed her temples.

"If it's like the other clues, then it has something to do with Mamaw and Papaw's house."

"'*Over an old heart.*' Is there or was there anything heart shaped in their house? A picture or wall décor?"

Brooksie shook her head. "Not now. After Grandma Emma died, Mamaw Mary replaced her pretty decorations with hog things and a few green tractors for Papaw. I bet they're stored upstairs somewhere. We'll go back out to Mamaw and Papaw's Saturday morning. And," she flopped across the bed on her stomach, "are we still going to see Papaw Asmus tomorrow after school?"

"Sure. I want to meet him in person and see what he's like."

"Since Will encouraged me to see Papaw Asmus, our going up there won't look suspicious. It's all perfect." Brooksie rubbed her hands together. "Everything is falling into place and soon we'll have answers to all of our questions. I can't wait."

"Be careful, Cuz," Darlene warned. "You may not like all

of the answers."

Chapter 29

“Was your Papaw Asmus moving in here Aunt Mary’s idea?”

“No, it was his. That’s surprising since he has always been independent.” Brooksie glanced into the rooms.

“Not seen Will yet?”

Brooksie jerked her head around. “Is it that obvious?”

“Oh, yeah.” Darlene laughed.

“Here’s Papaw’s room.” Brooksie strolled in and came to a sudden stop.

“Hey.” Darlene rammed into the back of her, causing them to both stumble further into the room.

Sitting on Papaw’s bed was Will and an older lady. Brooksie’s heart fluttered. Will must think she’s the biggest klutz on the planet.

“You know how to make an entrance.” Papaw Asmus laughed and slapped the arm rest on his recliner.

Brooksie nodded. Words escaped her like lightning bugs on a summer night; teasing you with their light, but always out of reach.

“It’s good to see you all here.” Will stood and helped the older lady up.

She straightened her suit and extended her hand. “Hello, I am Mrs. Fields, the nursing home administrator.”

Thick gray curly hair framed her delicate face. Her eyes

were dark brown.

"Nice to meet you. I'm Darlene." She shook her hand.

"And you must be Brooksie." Mrs. Fields gripped her hand and held on. She narrowed her eyes and studied Brooksie's face. Finally, she let go of her hand. "We always love to see company. I hope you all have a nice visit." She patted Papaw Asmus on the back and left.

"Darlene, we haven't officially met, but I saw you at the Pizza Barn." He stuck his hand out to her. "My name is Will."

"Nice to officially meet you," she replied.

"I need to get back to the floor. It's good to see you all again."

Brooksie watched him walk away.

"Will is a nice young man and a pre-med student." Papaw Asmus explained.

It almost sounded like Papaw was trying to get her interested in Will. That boat had definitely sailed. "I know. We met last Sunday and I ran into him yesterday at the Pizza Barn."

"Did you knock him off his feet again?" Papaw Asmus cackled and smacked his knee.

Heat rose from her neck up into her face and she looked down to her shoes.

"No use getting embarrassed about what happened last Sunday. Let me tell you, your Papaw Clyde has done worse." Papaw Asmus gestured toward his now empty bed. "Do you all mind sitting there? I'm pretty comfortable in my recliner."

Brooksie and Darlene sat on the bed.

"Darlene, you look familiar. I may know your parents. What's your last name?" Papaw Asmus squinted.

"Clark."

His eyes popped open. "You're Bobbie and Alfred's daughter."

"Yes sir," she answered. "And I try to keep Brooksie in line."

"Glad to hear it. Since Mary's not here, we can get to know each other a little better." He bent forward. "When you all were up here Sunday, we didn't get a chance to discuss what you're going to major in."

Brooksie had never seen him seem interested in anything before. Usually he looked as bored as she had felt. "I love astronomy, but there's not a lot of call for astronomers here in East Tennessee. Now that I think about it, I could be a science teacher."

Papaw Asmus leaned toward her. "I could always tell how smart you were."

"How?" Brooksie tilted her head. "I never got a chance to say much around you."

"For one, you're always restless. And I can tell by your facial reactions to some of the stuff said around here." Papaw Asmus snuggled back in his recliner. "I may be old, but I'm on to more than you realize. I know you're here for more than just a visit."

"To be honest, I do have some questions about the family that I can't get answers for back home."

"I'll see what I can do. Go ahead." He motioned with his left hand.

"I have no idea how Mamaw Mary's mother, Laura, died."

"I wasn't expecting that." He rubbed the top of his freckled forehead and stared at the floor.

Brooksie wondered if he was going to answer her.

"Laura was killed when somebody broke into the house. I was away on business."

That explained why he felt guilty about her death. "I still don't understand why we can't talk about it back at home."

Moisture pooled at the corner of his eyes. "Probably because Mary was there when it happened."

"What?" Brooksie almost jumped off the bed. "Do you think she remembers any of it?"

"I'm not sure how much she remembers. She was only a toddler."

Brooksie knew she had to choose her next words carefully. "But didn't you leave for Alaska right after that?"

Papaw Asmus folded his hands together and twiddled his thumbs. "I needed to get away for a while. I read an advertisement from an oil company recruiting brave, hard working men to work in Alaska. The pay was good and Brooksie agreed to keep Mary for me." He paused and took a deep breath. "I felt that Mary would be in better hands with Brooksie than with me. I worked long hard hours so I could fully support them. At first it was hard, but I did it."

Darlene raised her hand.

Papaw Asmus furrowed his eyebrows. "You have a question?"

"Mr. Asmus, did you do anything else while you were in Alaska?"

Brooksie remembered her asking the same question before. Maybe she'll get a better answer this time.

"Why yes, I did. For a while, I helped deliver mail." He sighed and looked out of the window. "That was a grand adventure. I remember this one time I was in a small boat with another mailman when an ice storm came up out of nowhere on the Baltic Sea. We had no idea it was heading straight for us. Weather satellites weren't even thought of in those days. The wind and waves were so bad that I thought we were going to capsize. Fortunately, we found an iceberg with a large crack in it. So we sailed into it and waited for the storm to pass."

"Wow." Darlene's mouth dropped open.

"Wish I could have been there. All I get to look at are tractors and cows." Brooksie snarled her nose.

"We didn't realize how dangerous it was. We didn't know what was going to kill us first: the storm or the cold." Papaw Asmus chuckled.

Darlene raised her hand again.

"This isn't school. You don't have to raise your hand when you want to ask me a question."

"Sorry, old habit. Did you continue to deliver mail after that?"

"Of course, I did. I cherished the letters I got from home

and I wanted to make sure the workers stayed in contact with their families, too."

Brooksie couldn't pass this up. "Papaw, did you help to deliver anything unusual or even dangerous?"

He crossed his arms. "What did you have in mind?"

"You weren't far from Russia and you were up there during the start of the cold war. I didn't know if you ever came across any...you know...spies?"

"Spies?" He shook his head. "Hate to disappoint you, but Russian spies were not the problem."

The image of a spy holding out microfilm to Papaw faded away. Brooksie didn't want to see it go.

"You look disappointed." Papaw Asmus narrowed his eyes. "Did you think I was a spy?"

Darlene cleared her throat.

"Well, no...it's just that....," Brooksie shrugged. "I think that would be exciting. Nothing exciting ever happens back on the farm. No, I take that back. A couple of years ago, one of Papaw Clyde's bulls found a hole in the fence and got out on the road. One of the neighbors tried to drive around it and ended up going down the embankment into Cow Walk Creek."

"I remember that." Papaw Asmus laughed and slapped his knee again. Then he laid his arms on his legs and bent forward, looking straight into Brooksie's eyes. "You don't like living on the farm much do you?"

It was as if he was looking into her soul. "I don't fit in there. As soon as I'm out of college, I'm moving. I want to be where there's real excitement and there's always interesting things to do."

"Nice to know somebody took after me and has my restless spirit." He puffed out his chest. "You know, I still like to have an adventure every now and then."

Brooksie's chest tightened. Her desire for adventure came from Papaw Asmus. Her imagination came from her daddy. She couldn't help but wonder what her daddy would have thought about their conversation. Would he have encouraged her to get away?

Darlene started to raise her hand, but put it back down. "Mr. Asmus, is it true you invested in the oil company? That's a huge natural resource in Alaska."

He raised a gray eyebrow. "I take it nobody talked about me being a partner in a gold mine?"

Brooksie knew she couldn't fake a surprise reaction. "No. We were told natural resource, so we assumed it was oil."

"I asked Mary and Clyde not to talk about it. After I got back from Alaska, people asked me for money all the time. But the most aggravating thing was this woman who kept digging around my property looking for buried gold she thought I brought back. I chased her away, I don't know how many times. Sometimes she yelled that I owed her. I told her she was crazy and to never come back."

Brooksie imagined a woman with a hairy mole's nose wearing a miner's hat with the light on. Dangling from her belt were a pick ax and whip. When she bent down to dig, her hands morphed into huge claws.

"Did you have a lot of friends back in Alaska?" Darlene asked.

"My best friends there were Nanook and his wife Anana. They owned a trading post in Skagway for years. They recently retired and handed it over to one of their sons."

Brooksie remembered Aunt Bobbie saying "Nookie." She bit her lower lip to keep from laughing.

"Those are Inuit names, which means they were Native Alaskans," Darlene stated.

"Yes, they were." Papaw Asmus nodded. "I think of them every day."

"Do you want to go back to Alaska?" Brooksie asked.

"Not anymore. Everything I need is here."

Brooksie stiffened her back. This next question may upset him. "Papaw, did you have a..."

"Pardon the interruption, but it's time for Mr. Asmus to take his walk." A nurse came in and went straight to Papaw's chair.

"Let's get this show on the road." Papaw Asmus stood and took the nurse's arm.

"Thanks for talking with us Papaw."

"You and Mimi can come up here anytime for a visit. You don't need to be with Mary and Clyde. Darlene, you're welcome to come, too. I'm glad Brooksie has such a good friend as you." Papaw limped out the door while holding on to the nurse.

"Thank you," Darlene called after him.

"I didn't realize Papaw limped that much."

"Cuz, did you notice anything else?"

"Yeah, Papaw Asmus isn't who I thought he was at all."

"I'm talking about the interaction between him and Mrs. Fields. I think they like each other. Did you see the way she patted his back earlier?"

"I thought she was just being nice."

"It's so sweet and romantic. You're never too old to fall in love." Darlene sighed.

"I wanted to catch you before you left." Will rushed into the room.

Brooksie's heart thumped so loud she was sure he heard it.

"Thank you for visiting Mr. Asmus. I know he enjoyed the company. Will you be coming back to see him again?"

"Yeah," Brooksie squeaked.

"Good. I have classes in the mornings, so I am here most afternoons between three and seven. And I usually work every Sunday afternoon. I look forward to seeing you again." He smiled and ran back out.

"What a sweet grin." Now Brooksie was the one to sigh.

"He wants to take you out on a real date," Darlene sang.

"Then why hasn't he asked for my phone number? Maybe he doesn't want to call me and he's just being nice."

"You're jumping to conclusions again, Cuz. I think he wants to do it in person or he wouldn't have told you when he was working."

Brooksie saw Will in his Knight's armor and getting down

on one knee in front of her.

"Where are you now?" Darlene snapped her fingers.

Brooksie jumped and lost her balance. "Oops." She fell off the bed and into the nightstand, knocking two pictures off. "Thank goodness they didn't break." She picked them up. "This one has a woman holding a toddler. It's faded, but I think her hair is red. Wait a minute. It's Mamaw Mary and her mother. I remember her saying she could have been born with red hair."

"Aw, he still has a picture of her. That's so sweet."

"Look at this one." Brooksie handed it to her.

Darlene took it. "Cool. Check out the sign above the door."

Brooksie scanned over the old black and white picture of four people standing in front a store. It was also faded, but she could make out the one in the middle was Papaw Asmus. Her eyes wondered up to the sign. "Nanook's Trading Post."

"The people on Mr. Asmus' left look like natives. I think that's Nanook and Anana and they're the ones who made Mimi's doll."

"I bet the girl on his right was Hannah." A strange feeling crept up Brooksie's spine.

"Too bad we can't see all of her face, but look at all that dark hair. Oh. I just had a thought. Wouldn't it be sweet if the doll had old love letters inside it?"

"You are a hopeless romantic." Brooksie sat the pictures back down.

"Hey, what was the question you were going to ask when the nurse came in?"

"If Papaw had a girlfriend back in Alaska. I hoped he would talk about Hannah. That's it." Brooksie tapped the side of her head with her open hand. "What if Papaw left letters or diaries back in his cabin?"

"What do you have in mind now, Cuz?"

Chapter 30

"Aw." Darlene jumped out of her car. "This place is like something out of a fairy-tale book. Even the outhouse is cute with the crescent moon carved in it." She ran across the gravel road and onto the wooden bridge. "Look at the little brook. I could sit in one of the rockers on the porch and listen to it gurgle for hours."

Brooksie joined her. "That's easy for you to say. When we visited Papaw, I usually had to sit and listen to them talk for hours."

"Why didn't you go outside? With your imagination, you could have had lots of adventures out here." Darlene spread her arms out and twirled around.

"I did go outside when it was warm. And I loved to do this." Brooksie picked a purple flower and placed it upside down in the stream. "I used to pretend I was riding on the flower and using it as a raft. T-Rexes were roaring at me from the cliffs...er stream banks."

"I never would have thought of that."

"Let's see if I can remember where the key is hidden." Brooksie strolled around the porch. In the corner sat a cracked flower pot with weeds growing in it. She burrowed her hand in the dirt and pulled out the key. "Voila."

"Cuz, I'm not so sure about this. I'm not comfortable breaking into somebody else's house, even if it is your papaw's."

"If I have access to the key, then it's not breaking in. Besides we're not going to steal anything. We're doing research."

Brooksie opened the door and they stepped into the living room. Goose bumps ran up her back. Everything was as Papaw left it. None of the furniture was covered. There were two coffee cups sitting on an end table next to a lamp. One chair had a paper lying open as if somebody had intentions of coming back to finish reading it.

"You can tell a man lived here. Nothing feminine here at all," Darlene observed.

"Why don't you look in the drawers in here and in the kitchen? I'll go into his bedroom."

"Okay, but it still feels weird." Darlene went around pulling out drawers and books.

Brooksie walked into his bedroom. Papaw always kept his door shut and didn't let anybody in. She pulled out drawers to find odd socks with holes in them and ratty underwear. No wonder Papaw left them. There was nothing else personal in there. She stepped back into the living room. "Did you find anything?"

"Nothing but a pile of tabloids in the corner."

"I remember those. I could never understand why a man as smart as Papaw would read them."

"Maybe it was for entertainment?"

Brooksie scooted a chair out of the way and plunked down on the floor next the tabloids.

"Cuz, tell me we're not going to read them?" Darlene whined.

"Why not? We may find something." Brooksie opened one.

Darlene sat down next to her. "Like what, the Loch Ness monster?"

"Here." Brooksie dropped a small stack in front of her. Dust and paper particles flew up in the air. A sneeze exploded out of her. "Sorry."

After a while, Darlene tossed her tabloid to the side and rubbed her eyes. "Cuz, so far all I've read are stories about aliens in the Bermuda Triangle, Lincoln's ghost haunting President Reagan, and Nazi treasure hunters in America."

"I've seen articles about UFOs hovering over Graceland, a diver found the lost continent of Atlantis in the Mississippi River, and Nazis hiding in America."

Brooksie and Darlene exchanged glances. "Nazis in America."

"The dates are up to January of this year. That's when Papaw moved to the nursing home. I guess he quit buying them then." Brooksie flipped through her tabloid pile. "And the dates are not consecutive. If Papaw bought them every week, he only kept the ones about Nazis being seen in the United States."

Darlene wiped her nose with the back of her hand. "Was he afraid they would make a comeback in America?"

"Or he could have been looking for a particular Nazi. Who knows what happened to the Heims back in Germany. A Nazi could have done something to them and Papaw wants revenge."

"Cuz, do you remember what Mr. Asmus said when you asked about Russian spies?"

Brooksie tapped her fingers on her leg. "Yeah, he said they weren't the problem."

"I wonder if some Nazis made it to Alaska."

Brooksie snickered. "Can you imagine Hitler being chased by a polar bear?"

"How about if he was chased by one of the T-Rexes you used to imagine?"

"Oooh." Brooksie rubbed her hands together. "I like that even better. I'm rubbing off on you."

"That's a scary thought." Darlene stood up. "I need to go to the bathroom. I haven't seen one, where is it?"

"You saw it from the bridge and liked the moon carved in it."

Darlene twisted her mouth.

"Can't wait till we get back to your house, huh?"

"Afraid not."

"I don't know if there's been any toilet paper put in it since Papaw left. I saw some napkins still on the table. Better grab you some." Brooksie flashed a sweet smile.

Darlene grimaced. "I'll be back."

Brooksie picked up a tabloid from another pile. *Alien Hitch-hikes Ride on Space Shuttle. NASA Demands Payment for the Ride.* "This is gonna be good." She settled back and started reading.

"Brooksie!" Darlene burst through the kitchen door and ran into the living room. Her eyes bulged and her face was pale.

"What's wrong? Did you see any bees or snakes?"

"Worse," Darlene exclaimed. "I saw…"

Brooksie glanced to the tabloid in her lap. "You saw an alien in the woods?"

"Stop joking." She stomped her foot. "I saw a car pull up and stop just down the road. A guy in a red ski mask got out and is walking this way."

Chapter 31

"We need to get out of here." Darlene yanked Brooksie to her feet

"Wait." She plied her arm out of Darlene's grip. "We don't know which door he'll use and we don't want to come face to face with him."

"Then how do we get out of here?" Darlene's eyes darted around the cabin.

"He's parked that way right?" Brooksie pointed down the road.

"Yeah."

"Then we'll go out the window that's on the opposite side of the house from where he's parked. We'll hide in the bushes until we hear him come in. Then we'll make a mad dash for your car."

Brooksie unlocked the window and opened it. "I'll go first." She leapt out and helped Darlene climb out. After lowering the window back down, they squatted down behind a bush. Darlene closed her eyes and her lips moved. She knew Darlene was praying.

A low creak emanated from inside. "He's opened the kitchen door." Brooksie whispered. "Let's go toward the porch, but stay down below the window ledge,"

They walked hunched over until they reached the edge of the front porch. Brooksie turned her head. The footsteps grew louder. He was heading toward them. *God, please don't let him look out the windows or walk out on the porch.* The footsteps stopped. After a few seconds, they resumed and began to fade.

"C'mon." She grabbed Darlene's arm and lunged out into the front yard. Blood gushed in her ears. Darlene's car seemed so far away. Would they get to it in time? She glanced down the road and saw an older model green Buick. "Humph." She bounced off the side of her car.

"Quit messing around and get in," Darlene screeched.

Brooksie yanked the door open and jumped in.

"Hey!" The masked guy ran through the front door and jumped off the porch. He stumbled and slid down the embankment to the stream.

"Oh, my." Darlene shoved the car in gear and tromped on the gas pedal. The engine roared and gravel flew everywhere.

Brooksie peered back through the dust cloud behind the car. "He's climbing back up. We need to gain some distance before he gets to his car."

"I'm afraid to drive any faster. I've never driven on a gravel road before and we've already slid twice." Darlene slowed down to make a couple of sharps turns.

"Don't slow down too much. If he's a local boy, he's used to driving on these graveled roads. If you don't speed up, he'll catch up to us." Brooksie drummed her fingers on the console.

"He'll catch us for sure if I lose control and we get stuck in a ditch." Darlene's knuckles had turned white.

In her side mirror, Brooksie saw dust flying up. "He's closing in on us. Take a right turn at the red barn up ahead."

The back of Darlene's car spun around as she made the hard right.

"Weeee," Brooksie yelled. It was more in excitement than fear. Darlene skillfully straightened up the car and sped down the narrow paved road.

"You did a good job keeping control of the car. I'm impressed."

"That's because we're back on pavement." The engines roared as the car picked up speed. "I hope no wild animal gets in front us."

"If it's a deer or cow, we're done for." Brooksie looked back just as the Buick made the hard right turn. "His car can't take the curve. The back end's slinging sideways and it's slammed into a mailbox. He doesn't drive as well as you."

"Thanks, Cuz. That makes me feel so much better. Where am I speeding off to?"

"This road runs into Maynardville Hwy. in a few miles."

Brooksie pivoted around in her seat the best she could with her seatbelt still on. "There's a big black car closing in on the Buick. I think it's a Cadillac. I don't know anybody around here who would be able to afford a car that nice."

"Who cares as long as it's going to help us?"

"The Cadillac is beside the Buick and...look." Brooksie pointed to the back window.

"What? I'm afraid to take my eyes off of the road."

"It veered toward the Buick. It's doing it again. The front left wheel of the Buick is off the road. Stop," Brooksie screamed and latched onto the back of her seat.

Darlene slammed on the breaks and the car screeched to a halt. "What's happening?"

"The Buick plowed through a fence and into a corn field. It was awesome. Wood and corn stalks flew everywhere."

Darlene kept her death grip on the steering wheel. "We need to get away while we still can."

"The Cadillac's pulled over and stopped, too." Brooksie pried Darlene's hands off of it. "Relax. It's gonna be okay."

Darlene rose up in her seat. "You don't know that. What if they start shooting at each other or us? We need to get out here."

"Not yet. I want a better look at the masked guy if he gets out of his car and I have to know who's in the Cadillac. Why don't you crouch down?"

"I can't believe I'm agreeing to this." Darlene hunkered down in her seat with her hands over her head.

"I need the binoculars." Brooksie jerked the glove compartment door open. "Boy, Officer Lanigan left this in a big mess. Ah, here they are." She climbed into the back seat and raised them up to her eyes.

"See anything yet Cuz?"

"The door of the Buick is opening and the masked guy is getting out. His left side is covered in mud. And there's an emblem or something on the front of the ski mask." She adjusted the lens. "The emblem is a black pig. Uh oh."

"What's wrong?" Darlene asked.

"An old truck is barreling across the field toward him. In the back is a bunch of boys in suspenders with guns. This must be the Lester place."

"You know them?"

"Nope, but I've heard Mamaw Mary and Papaw Asmus talk about them. They're okay as long as you don't mess with their property. Most people think there's a still somewhere in the woods behind their house. The masked guy is getting back in his...no, he's getting something out. Stay down." Brooksie lowered her head.

A gun fired.

"Eee!" Darlene screamed. "He's firing at us."

Brooksie rose back up. "No, I think he fired above the Lesters' heads. He ought to have known better."

"I can't believe this is happening to us."

"Cool, huh?" Brooksie lowered the binoculars. "We'll be telling this story to our kids one day."

"If we live long enough to have them."

Another gun shot rang out.

"Eee!" Darlene screamed again. "Who's shooting now?"

Brooksie crammed her eyes back into the binoculars. "The Lesters just shot out the Buick's windshield."

"Are they trying to kill him?"

"If they meant to do that, they wouldn't have missed. He's getting back in his car. He's heading back for the road and he's turned this way. Stay down."

Again Brooksie crouched down in the back seat. The

Buick's engines roared as it sped past them.

"Is it safe to get up now?" Darlene asked.

"I'll check." Brooksie peeked up over the back seat. "The Cadillac has turned around and is headed back the way we came. The Lesters are out of their truck and checking out the damage to the fence."

Darlene slowly raised her head. "Did you get the license plates on either car?"

"No." Brooksie climbed back into the front seat. "I didn't really get a chance to see either one. Well, I could've the Buick's, but I didn't know what he might do when he drove by."

"Thankfully this is over and I went to the bathroom, or should I say outhouse, before we left." Darlene started her car up.

"Did Alfie or Aaron teach you to drive like that?"

"Daddy did. He thinks everyone should know how to handle a car in any situation." Darlene wiped the sweat off of her forehead with the back of her hand.

"Do you think Alfie would teach me how to handle a car?"

"After all of that, all you can think of is Daddy teaching you how to drive?"

"Your driving saved us as much as the driver in the Cadillac. And let's not forget the Lester boys." Brooksie clicked her seat belt. "We going back to your house?"

"We're heading to Aaron's. No argument. We're including Aaron or I am out."

Chapter 32

"How's my two favorite girls?" Aaron flung the front door open.

Darlene shoved the journal into his hands. "We were chased down a gravel road by a guy in a red ski mask with a black pig on his forehead."

Brooksie was also talking. "It was so cool. After we read about Nazis in America, we got chased by this guy in a ski mask driving a granny car."

Aaron shoved the journal under his arm and put his hands up. "One at a time." The girls kept talking. "Stop talking." He raised his voice above theirs.

"Well," Darlene huffed and jammed her hands on her hips.

"I'm sorry, but I can't make out what you two are saying if you're talking at once." Aaron glanced back into his house. "I don't think Mom or Grandpa heard you. Let's go down to my study and then you all can tell everything, one person at a time."

In reality, his study was a cleaned out corner in the basement. There were two bookcases, a desk, personal computer, and some chairs. Aaron sat on the edge of his desk and laid the journal down. "I know I could've not heard this right. You two were chased by an American Nazi with a black pig on his head and he was driving a granny car?"

Brooksie started talking, "It all started the day I found Mom's doll in a secret room."

Darlene joined in. "This is getting dangerous and I'm tired of outhouses."

Aaron put his hands up again. "I'm not even going to say what that sounded like."

"Don't you care that we were chased?" Darlene scolded.

Aaron's eyes grew wide. "You two were really being chased by a Nazi?"

"No." Darlene stomped her foot. "It was a guy in a red ski mask with a black pig on it."

"And he was driving a green granny car," Brooksie added.

"Yes, I'm concerned that you two were chased, but you obviously got away from this masked pig guy. What happened that made him chase you? Did he try to rob you?" Aaron scrunched his face up.

Brooksie and Darlene exchanged glances.

"Well?"

"Part of the answer is in here." Darlene grabbed the journal and shoved it into his hands again. "That's why I gave it to you to begin with."

Aaron opened the journal in the back.

"Only read what's in the front." Brooksie flipped the journal pages to the first one. "It all started six years ago when I was playing in my grandparent's attic and found a secret room off to the side." Brooksie proceeded to tell him everything that had happened.

Aaron scratched his head. "So you two think finding that doll has triggered everything?"

"Isn't it obvious?" Brooksie puffed her bangs up. "We're getting close to something that somebody wants to get to first. And I think whatever it is may be what the clues are leading us to."

"Did you stop to consider that this masked pig guy may've been going to break in the cabin anyway?"

"He's got a point. Your papaw talked about some woman digging in his yard looking for gold. Maybe this guy was looking for it too," Darlene suggested.

"And," Aaron held up his index finger, "he saw that you two were already there and thought you may have found some gold and he wanted it."

"So you think we were at the wrong place at the wrong time?" Darlene asked.

"Just like when my daddy walked in on the burglar who happened to be in my room. I didn't buy that story then and I don't buy it this time." Brooksie crossed her arms and stiffened her back.

"I know you need answers about things, but you still need to consider the fact that some of this could just be coincidences. Can you do that?" Aaron asked.

"I don't know. In a way I don't want Daddy's death to be from bad timing, but on the other hand," she balled her hands into fists to keep them from shaking. "I don't want it to be my fault either."

Darlene rested her hand on her back. "It's okay, Cuz."

"There's no way it was your fault. If it was me, I would've done the same thing you did." Aaron spoke in soothing voice. It reminded her of how Alfie talked sometimes. "I would've wanted to give the doll back to my mom also."

"I still have to know what's going on with that doll. I've started this and I'm going to finish it."

"Okay, I'll help you and Darlene with this doll mystery of yours, but you all have to keep me updated on everything and take me with you when you do something like this again."

"Thank you." Darlene jumped and draped her arms around Aaron's neck, knocking them both back onto his desk.

"Excuse me." Aaron's mother walked into the basement. "Hope I'm not interrupting anything."

"I was just…" A red faced Darlene popped back up.

"It was an accident like I have all the time." Brooksie shrugged it off.

"Oh, okay." His mother nodded. "Darlene, your mother called. Apparently she has company. Mimi is there and she said something about seeing somebody named Emma."

Darlene's face went from red to pale. "Thank you Mrs. Summers."

Brooksie waited for her to walk away. "I don't know what's worse, the fact that I forgot about my mom or the fact that Aunt Bobbie saw our dead grandmother."

Darlene let out a puff of air. "She's going to worry about this for days."

❧

Brooksie propped her feet up on the side of the bathtub and wrote on a piece of paper. She'd rewrite it when she got her journal back from Aaron.

April 27, 1982. What a day. I actually had a real adventure and it was exciting. I didn't have to make it up and write about it. While Darlene was scared, I enjoyed the thrill of it.

And I got to see Will today. I would love for him to ask me out on a real date, but then again, I may scare him off once I talk about spaceships. He did seem okay when we talked at the Pizza Barn. I hope he wasn't just being nice. And I hope Darlene's right about him wanting to take me out. Maybe he'll ask me out when we visit Papaw Asmus Sunday.

Brooksie wiped her moist palms off on her pajamas.

Chapter 33

"There's been nothing yet." Aunt Bobbie wrung her hands after getting ready for church Wednesday night.

"Have you been praying about it?" Alfie lowered the newspaper.

"Of course I have."

Brooksie and Darlene were sitting on the couch and across from Alfie.

"Then everything will be all right." He winked at them and raised his paper back up.

"Maybe it's already happened and you don't know about it." Brooksie took a sip of chocolate milk.

They were startled by the ringing of the doorbell.

"This is it," Aunt Bobbie cried. "Why else would anybody come here on a church night?"

"I'm sure it's nothing." Alfie rose. "I'll answer the door."

"Maybe it's Eddie again?" Darlene suggested.

"I hope not. If it is, Alfie'll get rid of him." Brooksie had no doubt about that.

Alfie opened the door. "Mimi, what a pleasant surprise. I hope everything in all right."

"Mom?" Brooksie jumped up off the couch.

"Hello, everybody." Mom waved as she entered the room. "I know you all will be leaving for church soon, but I couldn't wait until you got back home."

"Please, have a seat." Alfie gestured to the couch. "I'll get you some tea."

"Mom?" An eerie feeling washed over Brooksie. "What's wrong? You shouldn't be in from work yet."

"There's nothing wrong. Just a little excitement." Mom kissed Brooksie on the top of her head and then she kissed Darlene next. She sat down on the couch between them.

"First, let me say that Papaw Asmus is all right, but some-body broke into his room last night and attacked him."

"I knew something was going to happen. I saw Momma yesterday," Aunt Bobbie exclaimed.

"What? Oh…Yeah." Mom looked over at Brooksie and Darlene.

"Is there anything we can do?" Alfie handed her the tea.

"Thank you. I appreciate the offer, but the police were there this morning. There's nothing else to do but keep Mom-ma calm."

Brooksie wondered if Mamaw Mary pulled at her hair again.

"I would like to hear what happened if you don't mind." Alfie sat back down.

"About 10 o'clock last night, the attacker crept in through the window, crawled on top of Papaw and put a knife to his throat."

"Oh my word." Aunt Bobbie covered her mouth.

"Was his window open?" Alfie asked.

"Yeah, he likes fresh air when he sleeps. The attacker un-derestimated how strong and daring Papaw is." Mom scooted up closer to the edge of the sofa. "Papaw smacked the knife out of the guy's hand and wrapped his arms around his throat in a head lock. The attacker managed to grab Papaw's reading lamp on the night stand and hit him upside the head with it. Ac-tually, he sideswiped Papaw. Then he wrapped the lamp cord around Papaw's throat and started screaming at him. Of course the staff heard the commotion and came running in the room. The attacker jumped off of Papaw. On the way out, he picked up his knife and pushed a nurse down. He leapt through the window and disappeared into the woods."

"Mr. Asmus is blessed that he wasn't hurt," Aunt Bobbie said.

"Papaw was just bruised and mad. He's always been tough. That's why he did so well in Alaska."

Brooksie noticed Alfie gave a small grin and nodded.

"What was the attacker screaming?" Aunt Bobbie asked. "Was he asking for money?"

"This is where it gets strange. He yelled that he was tired of digging up old skeletons and he demanded Papaw to tell him where the rest of it was buried."

"Is he a grave robber?" Aunt Bobbie fanned herself.

"I doubt that since Mr. Asmus isn't dead." Alfie chuckled.

"Papaw doesn't like for us to talk about it, but the natural resource he invested in was gold." Mom took a sip of tea. "Some of his neighbors believed he brought gold nuggets back with him and buried them somewhere around his cabin. So the police believe the attacker was looking for Papaw's supposedly buried gold. Who knows where all he's dug."

"You know, now that you mention it, I do remember hearing something about that rumor years ago." Aunt Bobbie scrunched her face up. "I believe Flossie from church has talked about some old man burying gold up in Union county. I didn't realize she was talking about Mr. Asmus."

"Has anybody dug around his place lately?" Alfie creased his eyebrows.

"No, but the police went to Papaw's Cabin to see if anybody had broken in it. They found the front door wide open and there were tabloids lying on the floor as if somebody had been reading them."

Heat rushed into Brooksie's checks. She and Darlene had totally forgotten about the tabloids. They were too busy trying to get away from the masked pig guy.

"You mean somebody broke into his home only to read some tabloids? Nothing was missing?" Aunt Bobbie scrunched her face again.

"There were no signs of breaking or entering. They think somebody climbed in through the window and for some reason wanted to read them." Mom took another sip of tea.

"Do they have any clues about who the attacker was?" Alfie asked.

"No. All they know was that he was wearing a red ski mask with a black hog on the forehead." Mom popped her forehead with her index finger. "And Papaw said he smelled like mud."

Brooksie had just taken a sip of chocolate milk. She spit it across the coffee table. "I'm so sorry." She grabbed tissues and dabbed it up. Maybe she shouldn't drink when people were talking.

"Darlene. You look sick."

"I'm fine, Mom. If you'll excuse me, I need to go the bathroom." Darlene rose and trotted down the hallway.

Brooksie didn't dare look up as she cleaned her mess.

"This whole thing is weird." Mom took another sip. "Actually, everything's been weird since Daddy ran his truck into Brooksie's room."

"I'm concerned about your papaw's safety. This attacker is getting desperate to find gold that isn't there and that can be very dangerous." Alfie rubbed his mouth.

"The police will keep an armed guard at the nursing home for a while. Once the attacker realizes there's no gold, I think he'll leave Papaw and his place alone," Mom answered.

"You call me if you need anything," Alfie told her.

"I will." Mom looked at her watch. "I need to go so you all can get to church early enough to eat. Brooksie, are you coming back home again this weekend? You don't have to go to the nursing home with us if you don't want to," Mom offered. "I know you get bored up there. I do myself sometimes."

Brooksie saw Will's smiling face. "I might go up. We'll see." She didn't want her mom to know she was interested in Will yet. There were too many other things to deal with right now.

After Mom left, Brooksie went straight to the bathroom

door and knocked on it. "Are you okay?"

"Yeah, come on in."

Darlene was sitting on the toilet the way Brooksie does when she writes in the journal.

"I had to get out of that room before I said anything. The more I think about it, I wished I had." Darlene slipped her feet off the side of the tub and laid her arms across her legs. "We need to tell the police what happened to us yesterday."

"No, it's too soon. Besides I don't need a cop to make the connection between the Civil War skeleton dug up at the church and the attacker talking about digging."

"I didn't think about that. But," Darlene held up her index finger, "they occurred in two different counties."

"And they both happened after we left somewhere. First it was the church graveyard and now the nursing home."

"We'll tell Aaron about it at church supper and see what he says."

Brooksie didn't care what Aaron said as long as he didn't try to stop them.

Chapter 34

"Yum." Brooksie tilted her nose up. "There's nothing like the smell of fried chicken." She liked eating Wednesday night supper in the fellowship hall. Her small church didn't have one.

The line inched up to the piles of food on the serving tables.

"I heard about that. Nursing homes aren't safe anymore either." An elderly lady ahead of them jabbed her fork into a big piece of chicken.

"Reckon he's okay. I hope that robber didn't get a thing." The lady behind her dumped a spoonful of fried okra onto her plate.

Brooksie elbowed Darlene. "I think the elderly ladies in front of us are talking about Papaw's room being broken into."

"They talk all the time about stuff that happens in Union County," Darlene said.

"Really?" Brooksie watched the elderly ladies go through the line and sit down. She and Darlene sat with Alfie and Aunt Bobbie at the end of the next table.

She took a bite of her chicken leg and peered back at the elderly ladies eating and chatting. She took another bite and peered back again. Now the ladies were all hunched across the table in deep conversation and she bet the topic was Papaw Asmus. She needed to hear what they were saying.

"I need another drink." Brooksie jumped up and dashed

off. As she neared the table, she slowed down, trying to hear what they were saying.

"Trouble always seems to follow him."

"It's his own fault."

"Do you think those old rumors are true?"

They may know some details about Papaw's past that could answer some of her questions. Dare she ask? Yep, she would. She'd watched Mamaw Mary and her hair salon buddies carry on for years.

"Excuse me, ladies. Do you all mind if I sit down for a second?" Brooksie tried to sound sweet and pleasant.

"Please do," the lady with a large broach patted the empty seat next to her. Even though the other three nodded in agreement, Brooksie saw the confusion on their faces.

"I'm so sorry to bother you, but I couldn't help but overhear your conversation in line earlier. What's the world coming to for somebody to break into a nursing home?"

"Oh my, yes."

"In my day, you didn't have to worry about such as that."

The Broach lady said, "I say it's because of the rumors about him."

"Oh my, yes. I've heard those for years, but I don't listen to rumors." The lady on the broach lady's right side pushed at her tall blue beehive hair.

The lady with black horn rimmed glasses scolded the beehive lady. "Yes, you do. You believed it when we heard the preacher had bought a motorcycle and a leather jacket. You followed him around for a week."

"I most certainly did not." The beehive lady defended herself.

"Yes, you did. We all saw it," the broach lady reminded her.

"Excuse me, but what might some of those rumors be?" Brooksie asked.

The beehive lady put her hand next to her mouth. "I heard somebody's neighbor's cousin saw the preacher standing in the middle of a motorcycle shop."

"No, not that rumor." Brooksie shook her head. "When I sat down, you all were talking about something else."

A lady with her eyebrows plucked and painted on leaned forward. "William Asmus brought back a treasure chest of gold with him. He was the one whose room got broken into last night."

"Really? Where or how did he get a chest of gold?" Brooksie tried to sound nonchalant.

"Alaska." They all answered except for the beehive lady who said, "Mexico."

"Mexico?" The other ladies asked at once.

"He didn't go to Mexico?" The beehive lady looked around the table.

"Everybody knows he brought back gold from Alaska." The broach lady glared at the beehive lady.

The lady with black glasses said, "I don't think all that gold's in Union County for that matter."

"And why not?" The broach lady demanded.

"Because nobody has found any of it yet. I think he's got it hid somewhere else. He's a pretty clever fellow from what I hear," the lady in glasses answered.

"Oh my, yes. I've heard he's quite the rascal." The beehive lady's cheeks turned pink and she fanned herself.

Brooksie wasn't sure why the beehive lady blushed. It was probably best if she didn't know. "Has anybody ever seen the gold? How do you know it's not just some old rumor?"

The broach lady answered, "Because he worked in a gold mine up there. We heard that he sneaked some back here."

Brooksie inhaled. Darlene had suggested that.

"Oh. I thought he held up a train in Mexico." The beehive lady bored her finger through her hair and scratched her head.

"Brooksie." She pivoted around in her chair. Alfie was waving at her.

"Are you a friend of Alfred's?" The lady with glasses asked.

"He's married to my Aunt Bobbie," Brooksie answered.

A collective "Ohh." went around the table.

"We love Alfred and Bobbie."

"Wonderful people."

"Did they ever go to Mexico?"

"Thanks for letting me sit with you all. I've enjoyed our chat." Brooksie waved bye to them and walked back to Alfie. While she didn't learn anything new, she did get reinforcement about the rumor of Papaw Asmus burying gold.

"Do you mind to get Bobbie a piece of chocolate cake?" Alfie asked. "She forgot it when we went through the line."

"Yeah, sure." Brooksie went back and grabbed the biggest piece she could find. When she spun around, she saw Aaron had arrived and was sitting next to Darlene.

"Thank you so much." Alfie took the cake and placed it in front of Aunt Bobbie. "Where's your drink?"

"Huh?" Brooksie asked.

"You went up front to get another drink. Did you get distracted by the ladies and forget about it?" Alfie gestured to them.

"I think what's left of your chicken is getting cold." Aunt Bobbie put a napkin up to her mouth to hide the big piece of chocolate cake in it.

Brooksie felt the heat in her cheeks. "I'll be right back." She went back up to the serving line again. The only drink left was lemonade. Having no other choice, she grabbed a cup and took it back.

"Was there something wrong with your chocolate milk?" Aunt Bobbie asked.

"Nope." Brooksie sat down and placed the glass of lemonade toward the middle of the table and away from her.

"Then why in the world would you get a glass of lemonade. I didn't think you liked it." Aunt Bobbie furrowed her eye brows.

"I wanted to try something different." Brooksie took a bite of chicken.

"Well, aren't you going to drink it?" Aunt Bobbie tapped the glass of lemonade with her fingernail.

Darlene rested her elbow on the table and laid her chin on her palm. Everybody else's eyes were on her too. Brooksie picked up the glass of lemonade and brought it up to her mouth. The smell was sickeningly sweet. She closed her eyes and took a gulp. "That was different." She sucked her lips over her tingling teeth.

Alfie raised both of his eyebrows. "Bobbie and I are heading on over to the sanctuary. I expect to see you all in a few minutes."

After they left, Darlene scolded her. "That's what you get for fibbing about your drink."

"Very funny, but it was worth it. I learned some things." Brooksie leaned over and whispered, "I think the one with the beehive kinda likes Papaw Asmus."

"Flossie?" Darlene turned in her seat to look over at the ladies.

"Ssh." Brooksie tapped her on the arm. "Don't look at them."

"Flossie has always been feisty and a little off," Aaron added. "Why else would you wear your hair like that?"

"No joke. She thinks Papaw got his gold in Mexico."

"What?" Darlene asked. "Why Mexico?"

"She thinks he held up a train down there. Anyway, there is definitely a rumor going around that Papaw brought back gold and buried it up in Union County somewhere."

"That makes perfect sense. It's also a good explanation for why you two were chased. Case closed." Aaron crossed his arms.

"You haven't told him about last night yet have you?" Brooksie asked Darlene.

"Tell me what?"

"How could I?" Darlene huffed. "Mom and Dad were sitting here and you don't want them to know what we've been doing."

"What happened last night?" Aaron tapped his hand on the table.

Brooksie scooted her chair over next to his. "The same guy who chased us, broke into Papaw Asmus' room last night and attacked him. Papaw's okay, in fact; he fought the guy off."

Aaron's eyes bulged. "How do you know it's the same guy?"

"He was still wearing the same ski mask with the pig," Darlene answered.

"And he smelled like mud. I saw him fall down the creek bank at Papaw's cabin when he ran after us."

"This is worse than I thought," Aaron rubbed his forehead. "Not only is this attacker dangerous, but apparently he's stupid as well."

Chapter 35

"You didn't look in the back?" Brooksie asked Aaron after school Thursday.

"No, you asked me not to." Aaron handed the journal back to her. "I like the night shot of the space shuttle. Didn't they have any with dinosaurs?"

"They did, but I liked this one better." Brooksie patted the cover.

"Well, I have to say, you two have done a lot of work on this doll mystery of yours. Is there anything else I need to look at?"

"There's stuff in her diary from the first time she found the doll," Darlene chimed in.

Brooksie winced. "I read some of it to Darlene the night Papaw Clyde ran his truck into my room. I stopped at the day of Daddy's murder."

"I think it's time you got it back out. There might be something in it to help jar your memory." Aaron tapped her head with his finger. "And that could lead to answers."

"I don't know if I'm ready to do that." Brooksie's chest constricted and she looked down at her shoes.

Darlene squeezed her hand. "It's okay, Cuz. You can wait until you're ready."

"Don't wait too long," Aaron warned. "This attacker seems to think you two can lead him to buried gold. Again, it makes sense. You are Mr. Asmus' great-granddaughter."

"It may be more than that. Hmm?" Brooksie tapped her chin. "Word may have gotten out about us having Crawly find the old Goliath mask. He called Mamaw Mary and had her riled up. Who knows who else either one of them told about it. The masked pig guy may have heard it and figured out we have the doll and the clues."

"He may not know the full extent of everything like you think his does," Aaron suggested.

"What're you getting at?" Brooksie titled her head.

"In the journal, there's a suggestion that your Papaw sent back instructions inside the doll. What if," Aaron clasped his hands on top of his desk, "people don't know about the doll per se, but think he sent back a treasure map to his buried gold."

"And they think we have it." Darlene twisted her mouth.

"I just realized something. If Aaron's right, then that means Papaw Asmus knows where the gold is buried. And he's the only one alive who does. Why didn't he warn us about how dangerous the doll is? And furthermore," Brooksie scooted up to the edge of her seat, "why didn't he dig the gold up and help us out after Daddy died? For a while, Mom had to work two jobs."

"In all fairness, we're speculating. And if it's true, he may have had a good reason for what he did and the way he did it," Aaron answered.

Brooksie stood and paced around the room "What if somebody else found out about the doll and Papaw had to hide it. He or whoever left the clues so the gold could be found in case something happened to him or Aunt Brooksie."

"And he hid the doll and kept it as a secret way of protecting everybody," Aaron added.

"It worked until I came along." Weight crushed down on her heart and she plunked back in the chair. "I should have left that stupid doll in the secret room where I found her. If I had, then my daddy would still be alive." Brooksie's eyes burned.

"You don't know that for sure," Aaron said in a soft voice. "The one responsible for your daddy's death is the one who broke into your house."

"But the burglar was trying to find the doll because he thought it would lead him to gold." Brooksie wiped a tear before it could fall.

"It's still not your fault." Aaron handed her some tissues. "Who all did you tell about the doll?"

A memory tried to surface, but she didn't feel like reaching for it. It was too much at once. "Daddy's the only one I can think of right now."

"Would your diary have that information?" Aaron asked.

"I remember you mentioning somebody coming to the door and talking to your dad after you brought the doll home."

"When Daddy came back in the house, he took Mom's doll away from me and hid it."

"And you don't know who it was at the door?" Aaron leaned back in his chair.

Brooksie shook her head.

"If this person had your daddy hide the doll, then they didn't want anybody else to know about it either. To me, it sounds like somebody in your family."

"We've thought about that too, but nobody fits." Brooksie shrugged.

Aaron rubbed his forehead. "We're missing some vital information that somebody else has or knows about. This masked guy could be somebody who's close to your family and knows its history."

"We said the same thing about the person who helped write the clues." Cold chills ran down Brooksie's spine, causing her to shiver.

"What's wrong, Cuz?"

"We don't know how old the masked guy is. Could he be the burglar who broke in and killed my daddy?"

"I didn't think of that." Darlene covered her mouth with both hands.

"All of this is still speculation, but we need to be on the safe side. Where's the doll now?" Aaron asked.

"I've got it hidden in a box on the top of my closet," Darlene answered.

"I'll go over to Darlene's house with you two and get it."

"Wait a minute. That doll is still my mom's. What do you want with it?"

"I think somebody outside of the family needs to hold the doll for safekeeping," Aaron answered.

"Daddy was also going to put the doll up for safekeeping and look at what happened to him."

"It'll be fine. I'll hide it in Grandpa's old vault that's in the wall behind my Farrah Fawcett poster."

Darlene grimaced. Brooksie knew how much she hated that picture. That was why she put one up of Christopher Reeves as Superman in her room.

"Okay," Brooksie agreed. "But can I get it back whenever I want?"

"Yes ma'am," Aaron answered.

"I'd feel better if we call the police," Darlene said.

"No way am I calling them. They would just mess everything up. And with our luck, they'll send Officer Lanigan."

"Here's a suggestion. You all only go from school to home by yourselves. Since the school is just down the road, it shouldn't be a problem. Anywhere else you go, I'm going, too, or you find a way to get Alfred to go. Understood?" Aaron asked.

"Okay," Brooksie agreed.

"I know where we can get more information." Darlene snapped her fingers. "We'll go to The Lawson McGhee Library downtown. Daddy does research there all the time."

"I'm off Saturday. I'll come by and pick you two up that morning."

"But that's when we were going to go to Mamaw and Papaw's house to look for the last clue."

"We can go next Saturday, Cuz."

Brooksie sighed. It was going to be a long week.

Chapter 36

Brooksie bobbed her head from side to side watching the microfilm at the library Saturday.

"What's the matter? Having a hard time sitting still?" Aaron snickered.

"Being still for thirty minutes is too long for me." Brooksie pushed away from the micro-fiche machine and rolled her chair over next to Aaron's. "You've not found anything either, huh?"

"Nope." Aaron blinked his eyes. "I'm up to November 1932. But I did find this old interesting newspaper article."

"Hello, everybody. I didn't expect to see you all at the library on a sunny Saturday morning." Alfred appeared behind them.

"Hi, Daddy." Darlene clicked her screen off.

"Hey, Alfie, we're just doing research for my project. What're you looking up?"

Alfie glanced down to the papers in his hand. "I'm doing some historical research. See you at the house later."

"Bye, Daddy." Darlene gave him quick hug.

"See ya later, Alfie." Brooksie waved.

"Goodbye, Mr. Clark." Aaron shook his hand.

"Why did you shut your screen off?" Brooksie asked.

"As soon as Daddy walked up, I found something. Look at this." Darlene flipped her screen back on.

Brooksie rolled her chair over, thumping into Darlene's.

"Sorry about that."

"It's okay. I should've expected it. In one of Mr. Asmus' letters, he mentioned something happening at the diner that was an accident. You were wrong about him throwing up on somebody." Darlene tapped the screen. "Read this."

The Blue Bowl diner blew up late yesterday evening. Surrounding businesses were damaged by flying debris. Mr. William Asmus, the owner of the diner, is suspected in its destruction. When investigators looked into the cause of the explosion, they found a still in the basement for producing moonshine.

Authorities now believe the diner was a front for Mr. Asmus to produce moonshine as well as his headquarters for its distribution. The explosion killed a Mr. Frank McCoy. It is reported that Mr. McCoy worked for Mr. Asmus as a runner. It has yet to be determined if the blast was an accident or on purpose. Authorities are looking for Mr. Asmus. They have reason to believe he may try to leave the country and head toward Mexico.

"So this is where Flossie got the idea of Mexico from." Aaron nodded.

Brooksie massaged the constricting muscles in the back of her neck. "Is there more on this?"

"Probably." Darlene flipped through the screens.

"I'm getting out of this uncomfortable chair." Brooksie shoved the chair back into place and dropped down on the floor next to Darlene. She loved sitting in the floor. Leaning back, she closed her eyes.

Will was running across a field toward her with his arms open wide. Brooksie was doing the same. When she was almost to him, Eddie swung in between them on a vine. He was dressed like a pirate with a patch over his right eye. In his free hand was a large rooster that was crowing and flapping its wings. Eddie threw it at her.

"Found something," Aaron called out.

Brooksie jerked so hard she banged her head into the wall. "Where's the rooster?"

"Cuz, what are you talking about? What rooster?" Darlene crinkled her eyebrows.

"Nothing." She jumped up and stood behind Aaron. "What did you find?"

"It was in the paper two days after the explosion." Aaron pointed at the screen.

Homicide in Hogskin. Mrs. William Asmus was found lying lifeless on the floor with her two old daughter, Mary, crying next to her. Mrs. Asmus had been strangled. There is a rumor that a warning note was pinned to Mary's dress by the murders. The authorities have been unable to find the rumored note. According to some Asmus family members, the note threatened Mr. Asmus saying he had intentionally killed Frank McCoy in the explosion of his diner, The Blue Bowl. Authorities believe Mrs. Asmus' murder was an act of retaliation for Mr. McCoy's death. Mrs. Asmus' daughter is staying with a relative. People in the Hogskin community are taking up money to help them.

Brooksie's knees buckled. She grasped the back of Aaron's chair and steadied herself. "He said he was away on business when Laura was killed. Was he hauling moonshine?"

"I'd say he was in hiding from the authorities," Aaron answered. "He didn't take Laura or Mary with him, so he underestimated how mad the McCoys were and what they were capable of."

Bile surged up in Brooksie's throat. "I feel sick."

"That's enough for one day." Darlene turned her micro-fiche machine off. "We're leaving now."

Except for the radio, they drove back in silence. Brooksie sat in the back seat feeling numb inside. When she was little, she loved turning her Magic Eight Ball upside down to see what answer would pop up. Now she felt like the triangle floating in the window. All turned around not knowing what was going to come up next

"Are you okay, Cuz? I know that was a lot to take in." Darlene twisted around in her seat.

"I'm not sure what to think about things anymore."

Brooksie ran her hand through her hair.

"I don't know about you, but I feel sorry for Aunt Mary. It would be horrible to find out your father's actions brought about your mother's death."

"Alfie made a comment to me that day after we dug out the Goliath mask. He said I would be surprised at what it would be like to walk in somebody else's shoes." Brooksie fiddled with the hem on her shirt. "That would explain the strange relationship she and Papaw Asmus have."

"It goes deeper than that. Aunt Mary may also feel abandoned by her father."

"But Papaw Asmus sent enough money back to them that helped them live comfortably. He even gave Mamaw a nice dowry when she married Papaw Clyde," Brooksie argued.

"I wasn't talking about financially. He was never there for Aunt Mary when she was growing up. He made Alaska his life and he chose it over her. And she's still carrying anger toward him."

"It's not just Papaw Asmus. She isn't any nicer to me. What did I do to her?"

"You're like him," Darlene answered. "He noticed it and told you that. You both want adventure and excitement. That's why you're not content to stay on the farm all the time like everybody else there. Aunt Mary recognized that quality in you and she reacted to it. She may not even realize she's doing it."

Brooksie leaned up as far as her seat belt would let her. "Even so, I'm not a criminal. What if Papaw Asmus really did have a hand in that Frank guy's death? Doesn't that make him a murderer? Is he any different than the guy who killed my daddy?"

"Papaw Asmus' situation was different. He wasn't a burglar." Aaron rubbed his chin. "During prohibition, times were tough. Bootlegging was the only way some people could feed their families."

"Are you defending him?" Brooksie challenged.

"No. What he did was wrong. I'm just saying desperation

may have been what got him into bootlegging and things got out of hand."

"And that was where he learned to smuggle," Darlene added.

Brooksie sighed. "I think I could have handled this better if Papaw had been a spy. At least he would have been heroic."

"Spy?" Aaron looked at her through the review mirror.

"It's nothing." Brooksie looked away.

"That day we visited him, he seemed happy and laughed a lot. I didn't get the impression that he was a bad guy at all. If he was at one time, then he changed his life and that makes him heroic," Darlene said.

Brooksie puffed her bangs off her forehead and leaned back in her seat. "I want to know what kind of man Papaw Asmus really is."

෬ඁ෴ඁ

Aaron and Darlene dropped Brooksie off at her grandparent's house. Mom immediately knew something was wrong, but Brooksie just said she was tired.

She didn't want to go to church the next morning. Alfie would tell her she needed God now more than ever, so she went on with a heavy heart. The sermon was about the reunion of Jacob and Esau. Jacob had wronged Esau by stealing his blessing and he thought Esau wanted to kill him. Instead, Esau loved and forgave Jacob. Was there hope for her family?

She dreaded going to the nursing home while she looked forward to it at the same time. Even though she wanted to see Will, she didn't know how she was going to be able to look Papaw Asmus in the eye now. And he would expect that after her visit the other day.

Once there, Mamaw Mary dominated as usual. Papaw Asmus tried to ask Brooksie some questions, but Mamaw Mary kept interrupting and giving Brooksie the evil eye. That's what Mom calls it when Mamaw Mary scowled with her eyes squinted into thin slits. It reminded Brooksie of robots from old science fiction movies. Mamaw Mary should be shooting death rays from her eyes any minute now.

What she needed was her knight in shining armor. That's when she realized she hadn't seen Will yet. While Mamaw Mary droned on, Brooksie kept an eye on the hallway. No Will. Was he sick? She couldn't ask about him without giving anything away. Her heart sank.

The following week went by so slow. When Mom came by after work Monday, she said they had gotten everything cleared to start repair work on the house. The workers would be there tomorrow. Soon they'd be in their own house again and things could go back to normal like it had been. No matter how things turned out with the doll and the clues, Brooksie knew her life would never be the same again.

Aunt Bobbie came in from the store on Tuesday and told them Eddie had been fired. The manager didn't say why, but the other workers seemed very relieved about it. Brooksie understood why.

Wednesday evening she went by the table with the elderly ladies and said hello to them. Flossie was talking about some old man she liked until his goat tried to eat her new straw hat.

The sermon that night was about Jacob struggling with God. Jacob refused to let go until God blessed him. God touched Jacob's hip and caused him to limp. Brooksie couldn't understand how that could be a blessing.

And that was when God changed Jacob's name to Israel. Jacob was a different man after that. It made Brooksie think about Papaw Asmus. Was he like Jacob? Is that why God had her hear about Jacob at two different church services? Did Papaw have some struggle that changed his life for the better? Did it involve Hannah? Is that why she left? Maybe one day Papaw Asmus would explains things to her.

Chapter 37

So what did you find that's so important?" Brooksie asked Aaron when they came to his house on Friday.

Aaron flipped the light on in his study. "Did you bring your diary?"

"Just like you asked." She held it up. "What gives?"

"Do you feel up to reading about the day you found your daddy?"

Brooksie's chest tightened. She knew she couldn't put it off any longer.

"Do you want me to read it, Cuz?" Darlene offered.

Brooksie almost said yes, but that would be the easy way out. "I'll do it."

They sat around Aaron's desk. She opened her diary up to the last entry. *Please give me your strength God.*

"Dear Diary, today I realized how different sirens sound when they're coming to you. I wanted to go home early, but the extra key to my house was not on the carport column. Grandma Emma came out to the carport and passed ball with me for a few minutes until Mamaw Mary pulled in. She was mad as usual."

Brooksie closed her eyes. Images filled her mind as if she were watching TV. "I remember it now. Mamaw Mary slammed the car door shut. Her mole was bright pink and her face was flushed. Grandma Emma asked if the store was out of baking soda. Mamaw acted like Grandma was crazy, but

Grandma said Mamaw had gone to the store to get it. Mamaw said they didn't have any and stomped into house.

"Grandma Emma asked me to get her some tea. I went inside and lying on the kitchen counter was my house key. I crammed it in my jean pocket and took Grandma some sweet tea. A storm was almost to us, so I ran home as hard as I could.

"Daddy's car was sitting in the driveway behind the house. I thought he didn't come and get me because we hadn't spoken much since he took Mom's doll away from me the Saturday before. The house was dark and the TV wasn't on. I knocked on the front door and yelled for him, but he didn't answer. Then the storm hit. I put the key in the door and that's when I heard a banging noise. I ran toward the back of the house to see what it was. The back door was swinging in the wind. I stepped inside and shut it."

Brooksie stopped and took in deep breaths. "Daddy was lying in the hallway outside my room. His blood had mixed with the paint from the can still in his hand and he was surrounded by blue and red swirls." She trembled all over.

Darlene laid her arm around Brooksie's shoulders and held her close. "I'm sorry, Cuz. Too bad we didn't get anything from it."

Brooksie stiffened her back and shrugged Darlene's arm off.

"Maybe we have. Did your house key fit both the front and back door?" Aaron asked.

"Yeah, so?" Brooksie shrugged.

"You said that your daddy interrupted the burglar. Who told you that?" Aaron continued.

"I don't know." Brooksie shrugged again. "I've heard that since it happened. What's with all the questions?"

"During my lunch today, I went back to the library and found an article on your daddy's murder," Aaron answered. "I remember you saying the burglar started in your room. Most robbers go after valuables first; getting the most they can in the shortest amount of time. The burglar didn't do that in this case.

So that tells me either he was stupid or looking for something he thought would be in your room."

"I said the same thing years ago, but the police totally dismissed me." Brooksie leaned up. "What exactly did the article say?"

"According to the police, there were no signs of breaking and entering. They think the burglar forced his way in after your daddy opened the back door. If that was the case, then he obviously didn't interrupt anything. And after you said the house key opened both doors, I realized another possibility."

The blood gushed in Brooksie's ears. "I've missed it for years. Mamaw Mary had the house key with her while she was gone. That's why it was on the kitchen counter and not on the post. She didn't go the store. She'd been in my house."

"Are you all saying Aunt Mary killed Brooksie's daddy?" Darlene squeaked. "We all know she may have anger problems, but she's no murderer."

"No, that's not what I mean." Aaron held his hands up. "I think Mary had been in the house and accidently left the door unlocked. This burglar may have been watching and gone in after she left. If that's the case, then Brooksie's daddy may have interrupted him."

"But why would Aunt Mary be sneaking into her house?" Darlene asked.

"The doll," Brooksie answered flatly. "I don't know how, but she figured out I had found it."

"You're sure you didn't show it to anybody else after you left the attic?" Aaron asked.

"I hid the doll under my *Bionic Woman* shirt when Mamaw Mary chased me out that day. Maybe she saw it and decided to get it for herself without anybody else knowing about it."

"Do you think she knows about the map to the gold?" Aaron asked.

"I don't think that was her motivation. Aunt Brooksie thought about hiding the doll from Mamaw Mary. I think Mamaw Mary was angry that it hadn't been destroyed in the fire years ago and wanted to rid get of it once and for all."

"I remember reading about that. They saw the doll burning in your Papaw Clyde's trash fire. That was convenient for somebody's benefit." Aaron got up and walked around while rubbing his forehead. "There's one thing that I don't understand. Why didn't the authorities come after your Papaw for Frank's murder when he came back to Tennessee?"

"That had been twenty years earlier," Brooksie replied.

"There's no statute of limitations on murder."

"Aaron's right," Darlene agreed. "But we didn't see anything where Mr. Asmus was ever officially charged with murder."

"We stopped after we read about Laura's murder," Brooksie reminded her.

"Does your mom know about your Papaw's history?" Aaron rubbed his chin.

Brooksie shook her head. "I don't think so."

"Are you going to tell her?" He asked.

"Not yet," Brooksie answered. "I want more answers first. For instance, who helped him write the clues?"

"Are you sure he had help with them? He knew family history," Aaron said.

"When Papaw came back, he moved back to Union county. I don't think he was around them enough to know about the Goliath mask or Grandma Emma's cookbook," Brooksie answered.

"There's something else I've been thinking about as well. I have an idea who Mr. Asmus' attacker could be and you're not going to like it," Aaron warned.

"Who?" The muscles in the back of Brooksie's neck tightened.

Aaron took in a deep breath. "I think it was Will."

"Are you kidding?" Brooksie raised her voice. "It doesn't make sense."

"Yes, it does. He could've followed you two when you left the nursing home. When he saw you were snooping around inside Mr. Asmus' cabin, he put on the mask to stop you all from finding the gold before he could find it." Aaron answered.

"Aaron has a good point. Nobody else knew we were there but Mrs. Fields, Will and Mr. Asmus." Darlene nodded.

"Aaron didn't see the interaction between Papaw Asmus and Will at the nursing home. It's obvious they're close. Papaw sounded so proud of Will being in pre-med. Why would Will go after his friend's great-granddaughter and then attack him? Will's not the type to do that." Brooksie ran her hand through her hair.

"You've just met him," Aaron argued.

"Will was so kind to me the day I ran into him and he didn't have to be that way. And he was such a gentleman at the Pizza Barn. He even asked us to come back to visit Papaw Asmus. That's not the type of person who chases and attacks people."

"Will's good guy image may be an act to get everybody's trust so he can get what he wants," Aaron suggested. "Maybe he was just trying to gain your Papaw's trust to find where the gold was."

"He may be desperate for the gold so he can pay for med school." Darlene added.

"But wouldn't Papaw recognize his voice or something else about him?" Brooksie asked.

Aaron leaned forward with his hands on his desk. "Here's a thought. Maybe it was a set-up. Your Papaw Asmus may have realized you two were onto finding his buried gold. He and Will have gotten so close that maybe he wants Will to have the gold."

Brooksie finished Aaron's thought "...instead of me."

❧

Brooksie opened up her journal and began to write.

April 29, 1982. I love riding roller-coasters. I like the feeling of my stomach going in my throat as the car flies down the rails. Right now that's how I feel, but it's not fun, it's pain-

ful. I felt like I was discovering my Papaw Asmus for the first time, but I soon discovered his past sins. Darlene thinks he's changed his life. And what about Aaron's suggestions? Does Papaw prefer Will over me? Is Will not what he seems to be? Who are they really and what do they think of me?

Chapter 38

"Have fun girls." Aaron shoved the gearshift into park Saturday morning at Brooksie's grandfather's farm.

"You're not coming in with us?" Darlene shut her door.

"I'm going to the barn and look at the tractors. Would your Papaw Clyde mind?"

"If he was here, he'd take you for a ride." Brooksie chuckled.

"I may take him up on that sometime." Aaron backed out of the driveway.

"That stinker," Darlene fussed.

"Tractors are more his thing." Brooksie plucked the house key off the post.

"I know you're thinking about Aaron's suggestions about Will."

"Yeah, it keeps bouncing around in my head." Brooksie opened the door and crammed the key in her jean pocket. "I really like Will. He's different from all the other boys. As for Papaw Asmus, I don't know what to think anymore."

"We don't know anything for sure yet, Cuz."

"Mamaw Mary left a note on the counter. '*Gertie's still got car trouble. I'll be taking her home again today and will be late getting back.*' That's good. It'll give us more time to look around."

"Can we start somewhere besides the attic?" Darlene

snarled her nose.

"I don't know where else to look. That's where Mamaw Mary sticks a lot of old stuff,"

"Wait a minute." Darlene snapped her fingers. "Your mom talked about enjoying all the old family stuff in her room."

"What are we waiting for?" Brooksie ran up the stairs with Darlene trailing behind.

Brooksie flipped the light on and walked over to her mother's bed. "Too bad we don't have the doll with us. I'd lay it on the bed the way Mom used to."

"Right now we need to look for that clue."

They searched all around the room.

"I don't see anything, Cuz." Darlene sat down on the side of the bed facing the closet.

Brooksie sat down next to her. "Me either."

"Hey, there's something in the back of the closet that's got a blanket over it."

"Let's see what it is." Brooksie hopped off the bed and scooted Mom's clothes over. In one fluid movement she yanked off the blanket. "Wow."

"I forgot how beautiful Grandma's old vanity was." Darlene ran her hand over it.

Brooksie touched it too. "When I was little, I'd stand in front of the mirror and play house. First I would put on aprons, pretending they were dresses. Then I'd put on Grandma's jewelry."

"I remember you trying to get me to do that with you when we were little. I didn't want to go through Grandma's stuff."

"She didn't mind. Sometimes she would join me and pretend to be a visiting neighbor. I wonder if any of her jewelry is still in here." Brooksie slid the drawer open.

"Oooh. Grandma Emma had good tastes." Darlene picked up a necklace with a sparkling swan sitting within a silver circle. "This is so cool." She slipped the swan necklace on over her head.

"I used to wear that one a lot." Brooksie ran her hand

through the jewelry. "It feels good to touch them again. I haven't done that in years." Memories slowly emerged from the back of her mind, but one still refused to come out.

Darlene gingerly picked up an old broach in the shape of a lily pad. "Didn't Grandma Emma pass away soon after your daddy?"

"About six months later." Brooksie picked up a wrist watch.

"Momma said Grandma Emma wasn't the same after his death."

"I don't remember noticing her being any different, but then again, I was still dealing with what had happened."

"Was? Cuz, you still are." Darlene lifted a broach up to her chest. "How cute, it's a lady bug."

"Here's one with daisies all painted on it." Brooksie held it up to her chest too. "I love daisies."

The girls exchanged glances.

"Cuz, the old heart wasn't décor."

"It was Grandma Emma's heart, so the key from the clue is in one of these broaches."

They picked up the different broaches and shook them.

"Not this one."

"Nothing here."

Fido howled.

"Do we need to see what's upsetting Fido?" Darlene shook a rose shaped broach.

"Not now. If he doesn't stop soon, we'll check it out."

"Nothing in this one either. We're soon going to be out of broaches."

"This has to be it. Grandma Emma loved music." Brooksie picked up a broach with musical notes on it and shook it. "Did you hear that?"

"Yeah, shake it some more."

Brooksie turned the broach around. "There's a small slit in the top of it. Stick your hand out."

She shook the broach until a small key fell out onto Darlene's open palm.

"Wow. This is awesome." Darlene twisted the key around. "It's pretty small. I wander what it goes to."

"We'll have to find the guardian first. Why don't you keep the key?"

"I'll put in my purse." Darlene paused. "I'd like to have Grandma's vanity. Do you think Aunt Mary or Uncle Clyde would let me have it?'

"What are you going to say when they ask you how you know about it?"

"Oh yeah. After this is over, I'm going to ask for it, if you don't want it."

"I would like to have some of the jewelry." Brooksie tossed the blanket back over the vanity. "But right now we need to get Aaron."

Brooksie galloped down the steps, missing the last two. Darlene put the key in her billfold.

"C'mon. We have a guardian to find." Brooksie bounced through the door to the carport and came to a sudden stop.

Darlene ran into the back of her. "Cuz, stop doing that."

"Will."

"Will what?"

In the carport, Will was squatted down and petting Fido. "Hello." He stood and shoved his hands deep in his pockets. "I didn't expect anybody to be here. Clyde had mentioned that I might like to fish in Cow Walk Creek sometime."

The back of Brooksie's neck tightened. Something wasn't right about him. Even his voice sounded different.

Darlene crossed her arms. "So you decided you'd do that this morning?"

Will grinned. "I thought it would be a good time for fishing. Guess I was wrong. I'll go and leave you all to what you were doing."

"Where's your car?" There was no missing the challenge in Darlene's voice.

"I parked at the creek where I was going to fish. I'll be

going now."

There was no way Brooksie was going let him walk away. She had to know why he was really there. "What's your hurry? Have a seat." She opened a lawn chair and smacked it. "Unless there's some reason you don't want to stay and talk to us."

"Of course not." He sat down on the edge of the chair and tapped his right foot against the concrete floor.

Brooksie and Darlene sat down across from him. They all stared at each other for a few minutes.

"That's a pretty necklace Darlene. Is it an antique?" Will asked. "I like old stuff like that."

She clasped it in her hand. "Thank you. I forgot I had it on."

An old Volkswagen drove by and backfired.

"Crabby Crawly," Brooksie said out loud. She wondered why he was around so much lately.

"I can see why he's called that. He pulled into the road behind the creek until he saw my truck there. He shook his fist at me and yelled in some foreign language. I'm not sure what it was." Will furrowed his eyebrows.

"Yeah, we've heard it before," Darlene agreed.

Brooksie shoved her foot into Darlene's.

Will tapped his right leg and glanced around. "I love Clyde and Mary's old white farm house. It's like something out of a book. Was it a great place to play in when you were a child?"

"At times." Brooksie tilted her head.

"When I played at my grandmother's home, I loved the attic. There were all kinds of old things up in it."

Her neck tightened. "Mamaw Mary chased me out when she caught me playing in there."

"I see." He gave a smile so weak, she couldn't see his dimple. "I'll come back another day to fish." He stood. "Tell your family I said hello, and you all have a good day."

"You, too." Brooksie stood.

He waved and walked away.

Darlene whispered, "He was fishing all right, but he was

trying to see what you would say about the attic. He has to know about the doll."

Watching Will walk away was like watching her hopes for a good boyfriend fade away. It seemed like he was interested in her and liked her being different. Was all that just a front to get close to the doll? Was Papaw Asmus doing the same?

"Cuz, are you all right?"

"Yeah, just thinking. Maybe Aaron was right about Papaw wanting him to have the gold and he told Will where the doll was hidden."

"Should we go in and lock the doors?" Darlene asked.

"Why? He's halfway to the bridge. Besides, Fido liked him and Fido doesn't like just anybody."

"So he's okay then? Let's see if he leaves or if he's waiting for us to leave."

They ran around to the back of the house and peeked around the corner. There they watched Will get in his truck and drive off.

"There you two are. Your Papaw Clyde's tractors are awesome." Aaron joined them. "Why are you two peeking around the house?"

"Will was in the carport when we came out," Darlene answered.

"What did he want? Did he threaten you two?" Aaron's eyes bulged.

"He claimed Uncle Clyde invited him to go fishing, but I don't buy it. And he asked Brooksie about playing in the attic."

"I hate to say it, but your Papaw Asmus may have sent him down here to get the doll or see if it was gone. Hey, where did that necklace come from?" Aaron pointed to it.

"It was Grandma Emma's and I forgot to take it off." Darlene took hold of the chain.

"Keep it. Just don't let anybody else see it yet." Brooksie sighed. "You know, except for you two and Mom, I'm not sure who to trust anymore."

Chapter 39

Brooksie rolled her window down as they neared church on Sunday morning. "They're ringing the church bell."

"I swannie. They need to stop that racket." Mamaw Mary clapped her hands over her ears. "Makes my nose want a sip of coffee."

Papaw Clyde pulled the gold station wagon into his usual spot. "It's an old tradition."

"I love to hear the old bell ring." Mom sighed and closed her eyes.

"Me, too." Brooksie enjoyed the memories of being up in the tower with her daddy or Papaw Clyde when it was their turn to ring the bell. "That's it."

"What's it? What's wrong?" Mom crinkled her face.

"Ah…Papaw, pull in the right parking space." Brooksie jumped out and sprinted toward the church.

❧❧

"Hello?" Brooksie slammed the front door and skipped up the stairs after lunch. Alfie was asleep in his chair. The Sunday paper was lying open in his lap and his head was titled to the side. Aunt Bobbie was stretched out on the couch and making soft hooting noises like an owl.

Low voices emanated from the deck behind the kitchen. She tiptoed out the back door. Darlene and Aaron were snuggled up on the covered swing.

"I didn't think you'd go to the nursing home today." Darlene smiled. "I'm sorry, Cuz."

"It doesn't matter. It's still a beautiful day."

Darlene furrowed her eyebrows. "What's happened?"

"I figured out the last clue this morning." Brooksie plunked down in a lawn chair, almost sending it backward. "When we pulled into the church parking lot, the bell was ringing."

"You think it's in the bell?" Aaron asked.

"Not exactly." Brooksie scooted her chair closer to them. "My church has a very old tradition of a child and a family member ringing the bell on Sunday mornings. I couldn't wait for my turn. It was kinda like waiting for Christmas Eve or my birthday. Either Daddy or Papaw Clyde would go up with me. And standing in the corner was big white ceramic angel. I always thought of it as a guardian angel."

"That's a sweet story," Darlene sang.

"And you think the key goes to something hidden inside the angel?" Aaron rubbed his forehead.

Darlene clapped her hands together. "It could be a little treasure chest of gold. That would be so awesome."

Brooksie held up a key. "We're going to find out tomorrow night."

"That's not the key we found. It's still in my purse."

"This is Papaw Clyde's key to the church. He only uses it when he sets up communion. I sneaked it out while I was helping to clean the kitchen after lunch. I'll put it back next weekend. Knowing Papaw, he won't notice its missing."

౷

"Be careful, Cuz. These steps are steep." Darlene whispered Monday evening as Brooksie opened the door to the church belfry.

"I can't believe you never fell down or up them. Wouldn't that make it a miracle?" Aaron snickered.

"I did pray before we left," Darlene hummed.

"Good thing. Back then, Daddy or Papaw stayed in front

of me or behind me," Brooksie said.

"You know, our flashlights don't put out enough light to see the steps very well." Darlene raised her light up. "And we still have a few more to go."

"What was what?" Brooksie leaned over the hand rail.

"Watch it." Aaron clasped her upper arm. "Did you see something?"

Heat rushed up Brooksie's cheeks. "I thought I saw something dart across the floor below."

"Anybody there?" Aaron yelled down.

"Guess I'm just being paranoid. It's kinda creepy in here with all the lights out except for ours."

"I feel strange being in a church and not being here to worship," Darlene added.

"We shouldn't be here too long." Aaron lifted the trap door in the ceiling. He climbed into the tower and helped Darlene and Brooksie up.

"It's sitting in the same place." Brooksie ran her hand over the angel's wings. "I haven't seen it since before Daddy died. Our Sunday to ring the bell was the one after he took Mom's doll away from me. I let Lynda and her dad do it instead." She gripped the angel as if it would give her strength. "I wouldn't do it after that with anybody else."

"I'm sorry, Cuz. Do you need us to come back later?" Darlene asked.

"No. What I need are answers." Brooksie squatted down and wrapped her arms around the angel.

"Wait." Aaron closed the trap door. "Don't' do that yourself." He grasped the bottom. "Put your arms under the wings and around the chest. We'll slowly and gently lay her down."

"Hear that?" Darlene cupped her hand behind her ear.

"Footsteps," Aaron whispered. "We're not alone."

Chills ran up Brooksie's back all the way to her head causing her to shake all over.

"Whoever it is, he's climbing up the steps." Darlene stepped away from the door.

"It's more than one person." Aaron added.

The trap door flung open and hit the floor. The noise echoed in the empty sanctuary below.

Chapter 40

A head full of honey blonde hair popped up through the hole.

"Eddie?" Brooksie balled her fists and moved toward him. "You've got no business being here, so why don't you leave."

"We're not going anywhere." He reached in his jacket and pulled out a gun.

"Oh my." Darlene covered her mouth.

"It's clear Mamaw." With his free hand, Eddie reached down and helped a gray headed lady up.

"Gertie," Brooksie yelled.

"My name's Gertrude." She squawked. "I hate being called Gertie. I only let Mary do it to keep her happy."

"And to think Papaw named the last calf born after you."

"What?" Aaron asked.

"Gert...Gertrude is one of Mamaw Mary's hair salon buddies."

"Ha ha." Eddie bobbed his head from side to side. "Now you have to look at her old sour wrinkly face again."

"What did you just say about me?" Gertie smacked him upside the head.

"That's what Brucie called you when we were at that stupid Pizza Barn." Eddie rubbed his head.

"It's Brooksie, you idiot. And I'll deal with her after we get what we came after." Gertie jabbed Brooksie in the chest with her bony finger. "I was never one of Mary's salon buddies. I only went there to hook up with her so I could get to the Alaskan gold her no good father buried. He owes it to me and Eddie."

Brooksie pinched her nose shut. "Maybe he'll give you a toothbrush?"

"Cuz." Darlene gave a furtive whisper.

"William Asmus killed my daddy when he blew up that diner of his. I saw it happen. One of his men called Daddy and told him to meet him there to discuss business. Daddy had just walked through the door when it exploded. I was sitting in the car with my momma when it blew. Me and Momma had nothing to live on and had to move to Flat Lick, Kentucky to live with my mamaw." Gertie wiped her nose with her sleeve.

"Your daddy was Frank McCoy?" Brooksie asked before she realized the connection.

"Did William brag about it?" Gertie shouted.

"I read about it in an old newspaper article. I've never been told anything much about Papaw Asmus' life."

"Thanks to him, mine was miserable. When I was seventeen, I got a job in Corbin and saved enough money to move what little I had back to Tennessee. I was going to do what was necessary to avenge my daddy's death. He had the right to ask your papaw for more money. He earned it."

"And now we're gonna collect," Eddie sneered.

"Collect what?" Brooksie held her hands out with her palms up. "I have nothing to give you. My daddy was killed, too."

"Don't play dumb with me, girl," Gertie hissed. "I know you have that Alaskan doll and the treasure map that was hidden in it. Mary thought it burned up until she saw you show it to Emma years ago."

The memory exploded out of Brooksie's mind. Mamaw Mary had just chased her out of the attic after she found the doll. She bounded out to the carport were Grandma Emma was sitting on a glider.

"Grandma." Brooksie leapt onto it, causing it to sway.

Grandma Emma laughed. "What's all the excitement about?"

Brooksie cupped her hands around her mouth. "I gotta a secret, but you can't tell anybody."

Grandma Emma made an x over heart with her right hand. "Cross my heart and hope to die."

Brooksie pulled the doll out from under her Bionic Woman shirt. "I found Mom's Alaskan doll. Isn't she beautiful?" She caressed the doll's dark braids.

"My word." Grandma Emma's mouth dropped open. "Why don't you let me hold the doll for a while?" She reached out for it.

"No." Brooksie jerked it back and held the doll up to her chest. "I'm the one who found it, and I'm the one who's gonna give it to Momma when she gets in from work."

Brooksie bent down and cupped her hands over her knees. Darlene laid her hand on her back. "What's wrong?"

"You heard Gertie. Mamaw Mary knew I found the doll. I remembered showing it to Grandma Emma. Mamaw Mary had to have been listening to us at through the screen door and we didn't see her. Grandma would've been the one who came to the door and talked to Daddy. Did she also put the other doll in the fire?"

"But why?" Darlene asked.

"Who cares about Emma? As for Mary, she hated that doll. But I knew I finally had a way to the gold." Gertie pointed to herself and smirked.

"You're the one who dug around in Mr. Asmus' yard," Darlene accused.

"For years and for naught. I don't know how many times he shot over my head or chased after me with pitch forks. I was almost to the point of giving up on finding the gold when Mary told me about the doll Brooksie found. I knew that doll was the connection. William didn't do stuff like that.

"After Clyde ran his truck into your room, Mary was afraid

the doll would show back up. She wanted to find it before you did so she could get rid of it, but it wasn't anywhere. And then a strange thing happened. Within a few days, somebody dug in Mary's back yard and left an empty burlap sack next to the hole. I knew you all had the map from the doll and it lead to the gold that was in that sack. And you two are still looking and snooping around, so that tells me there's more gold buried in different places."

"You all confirmed it that day at the store when she," Eddie gestured toward Darlene, "said you all had been digging for buried treasure."

"She was only joking." Brooksie puffed her bangs up. "We dug up worms and Fuzzy Wazzy's bones. There was no gold."

"And you didn't even rebury them. Tsk. Tsk." Gertie shook her finger. "Eddie, you know what to do."

"You," Eddie aimed his gun at Aaron. "I'm keeping my gun on you to make sure you do what I want."

"Not him." Gertie turned his gun toward Darlene. "Isn't this one his girlfriend?"

"What do you want me to do?" Aaron asked.

"You're gonna smash that angel against the wall." Eddie gave a toothy grin. "The only people getting the gold in it is me and Mamaw."

"I'm sorry Brooksie." Aaron picked up the angel.

Brooksie closed her eyes. She saw the angel leap out of Aaron's hands and spread it wings. Its robe morphed into armor and it pulled out a sword.

The cracking sound was sickening. It felt like her heart had cracked open as well. Something hit the side of her foot. She opened her eyes and saw the angel's face peering up at her with a peaceful expression.

"Move." Eddie shoved Aaron out of the way. He knelt down and searched through the pieces. "Ouch." He stuck his finger in his mouth.

"Found any nuggets?" Gertie crouched down next to him

"Not yet, Mamaw."

"The gold has to be here," Gertie whined.

Aaron cleared his throat and pointed to the angel's head at Brooksie's feet. Then he gestured to the trap door. She nudged the angel head toward him with her foot. He snatched it up and whacked Eddie in his upper back.

Chapter 41

"Hmmph." Eddie lunged forward. His hand holding the gun slammed into the floor.

The bullet careened off the bell and imbedded itself into the wall above Aaron's head.

"Eee!" Darlene ducked down with her hands over her head.

"Eddie," Gertie yelled. "What've they done to you?"

Brooksie pushed her down on top of him. "Giving him what he deserves."

"Let's go." Aaron lifted the trap door and motioned for them.

Darlene went down first and Brooksie came next. Aaron hopped down and latched the door shut. "That should hold until we can get away."

They burst through the church's front doors.

"Don't look back, run." Aaron bellowed.

Brooksie prayed, *Deliver us and keep us safe.*

"Lock your doors." Aaron started the car and spun rocks toward Eddie's truck. "We're going back to my house and call the police."

An image flashed across Brooksie's mind. "No. We're going to Papaw's barn. The answer to the last clue is there."

"We can go there after we call for help." Aaron shook his head.

"We'll drop Darlene off at my house and she can call the

police from there. The two of us will drive up to the barn and park the car behind it. That way Gertie and Eddie won't see it. We'll stay in place until the police arrive."

Aaron turned down Cow Walk Road. "I probably shouldn't do this."

"I want to be with you all instead of calling for the police," Darlene protested. "You may need me."

"We need you to call them as soon as possible." Aaron peered at her through the rear view mirror.

Darlene huffed and crossed her arms.

"Turn your lights off when you pull into the back driveway. I don't want my family going up to the barn and getting involved in anything." Brooksie told her.

"Okay, but I will have to drive very slow since I can hardly see where I'm going." Aaron explained.

He stopped behind Brooksie's house. She dug her house key out of her pocket and handed it back to Darlene. "Now I need the one you have."

Darlene opened her billfold and plunked it in Brooksie's hand. "Here."

"Please stay inside until we come back down." Aaron clasped her hand and kissed it.

Darlene nodded and climbed out of her car.

"I didn't like doing that." Aaron drove toward the barn.

"Me either, but it's not like we have a communicator from *Star Trek* where we can call the police from the car."

"Was it Eddie or Gertie you saw in the lobby as we were climbing up?"

"Neither." Brooksie hesitated. "I could have sworn it was Grandma Emma."

Aaron turned the car off. "You know who you sound like?"

"Yeah, Aunt Bobbie. I hope the warning was about what happened in the bell tower." Brooksie jumped out of the car. "I need to shut the barn doors before the lights are turned on."

"I'll do it." Aaron closed them and secured the lock bar. "I didn't come in here Saturday morning. Actually, I've never been in a real barn that had animals."

"And one that stinks. Look up and see what real barns have," Brooksie pointed.

"Whoa." Aaron stepped back.

"It's okay, it's only Sedrick. He likes to lie on the rafters. Smart farmers always keep a black snake in their barns. They eat rodents and chase away poisonous snakes. Oh look, he has a bulge. He's still digesting a snack."

Aaron's eyes grew wide. "He's lying on the rafters."

"So the answer to the clue is buried in the dirt floor underneath him."

"If these clues were written years ago, maybe the snake from that time laid on another rafter?" Aaron rubbed his chin.

"Every snake Papaw's ever had has stayed on this end. The woods aren't far behind us and that's where the little animals come in from." Brooksie grasped two shovels and handed Aaron one. "Darlene and I used these in Mamaw and Papaw's back yard. You know how to dig?"

"I can dig better and faster than you can." Aaron crammed the shovel in the ground. "Ready?"

"Ready"

After a few minutes of digging, Brooksie stopped and wiped the sweat from her eyes.

"Too much work?" Aaron teased.

"Not for me." She crammed her shovel into the ground with renewed force. "Did you hear that?"

"Yeah, your shovel hit something metal." Aaron crouched down and reached into the hole. "Whatever it is, it's lodged in there." With his bare hands, he loosened the dirt around it. "I've got my hands on it."

"Well?" Brooksie gripped the shovel handle so tight her hand tingled.

"This is so awesome." Aaron pulled out a small metal lockbox.

A car's engine caught their attention. "Your Papaw must've seen the lights."

"No, that doesn't sound like his truck." Brooksie's neck tightened. "Rats! Toss the box."

Aaron immediately threw it into a stall, almost hitting a calf.

"Let's crawl through that open stall window." She slung open the stall door.

They were almost to the window when Eddie popped his head through it. "You're not going anywhere until I tell you." There was a trail of blood from his neck down his shirt. He looked like something out of a slasher movie. "Back up out of the stall." He aimed his gun at them.

Brooksie and Aaron did as he asked. She held her breath as Eddie struggled to crawl through the window. *God, don't let him accidently fire his gun.*

Eddie's feet hit the floor. "Go open the door and let Mamaw in."

Aaron and Brooksie walked to the door with Eddie behind them.

"How did you know we were here?" Brooksie asked.

"Shut up and just open the door."

Aaron lifted up the lock bar and Gertie barged in with her hands on her plump hips "What are you waiting for? Close the doors and lock them."

Aaron did as she asked and stepped back.

"I see shovels in the back. You dug up some more gold didn't you?"

"They dug up the Momma Load." Eddie's eyes widened.

"It's the Mother Lode, and I think you might actually be right this time. I can't wait to get my hands on all that gold." Gertie gave a sweet smile that made Brooksie want to throw up. "You two take us to it now."

"But, there's no gold."

"We'll see about that," Gertie sneered. "Eddie, give her some motivation."

He aimed his gun at Brooksie.

Gertie sighed. "Point it at Aaron."

"Right." Eddie turned it toward him.

"Okay, okay." Brooksie held her hands up. "What we found is in the stall with Gertie."

"But Mamaw's right here," Eddie sputtered.

"Mary had Clyde name one of her stupid cows after me," Gertie moaned. "Now let's go."

Aaron opened the door. Gertie rushed in, almost knocking him into the wall. "I see something in the hay."

Gertie the calf walked over, stepped on the lock box and mooed.

"Shoo. Go away." She stomped at the calf. "Surely this isn't it." Gertie picked up the metal box and crammed it into Brooksie's face. "Why isn't it bigger?"

She shrugged. "How would I know? It was buried years before I was born."

"Give me the key to it." Gertie held her hand out.

Brooksie closed her eyes. *God, how can you let Gertie win when we've done all the hard work? And you lead us to the clues' answers.*

"I know you're praying." Gertie snarled her pudgy nose. "It won't do you any good. Eddie's got the gun and he'll use it if you don't hand me the key or find a way for me to open it."

Brooksie dug the broach key out of her pocket and plopped it in Gertie's clammy hand.

Gertie gripped it. "Finally, all these years of waiting and putting up with Mary have paid off." She sat the box on a bale of hay, unlocked it, and yanked out a small white box. "Nanook's candy for all ages?"

"Candy? Where's the gold?" With his free hand, Eddie jerked the lid off. Inside it were small round pieces wrapped in colored foil paper.

Eddie's face turned blood red. "Here's your old candy." He snatched the box out of Gertie's hands and slung it toward Brooksie and Aaron, sending the foiled pieces flying at them. Having quick reflexes, Brooksie was able to dodge them, but Aaron wasn't as quick.

"Ouch." Aaron cupped his cheek. "I didn't know candy could get that hard."

Brooksie moved his hand. "It scratched your cheek and it's gonna leave a nasty bruise."

"Who is this Nanook and does he have our gold?" Gertie growled.

"It sounds like an Inuit name, so he's probably not from around here." Aaron cupped his cheek again.

"What do you mean by idiot name?" Eddie asked.

"Inuit are Natives Americans from Alaska." Brooksie struggled to keep the sarcasm out of her voice.

"This is a trick and you're in on it." Gertie jabbed her finger in Brooksie's chest again.

"Are you deaf? I wasn't around when the box was buried, so how can I be in on anything?"

"I'll tell you what, Missy," Gertie hissed. "You don't mess with me. Your daddy found that out the hard way."

Brooksie's chest tightened and blood gushed in her ears. "What do you mean?"

"I'm sure you still remember the day he died?" Gertrude gave her sickening smile again. "Like I said, Mary knew you had found that doll and she was all tore up over it. I don't know how many sips of coffee her nose took that day. I promised her I would destroy the doll once and for all if we could get our hands on it.

"That Saturday morning, Mary had sneaked the key to your house out and we went in through the back door straight to your room. We searched it from top to bottom and didn't find that stupid doll anywhere. Mary had to go back home and she told me to clean up my mess and leave. I agreed, but after she left, I slashed open anything I could. That's when your daddy walked in.

"He yelled at me to get out and he threatened to call the police. I panicked and rushed at him to knock him out of the way. I forgot I still had the knife in my hand. It plunged into his chest. I didn't want them tracing the knife back to me, so I jerked it out."

"That was the wrong thing to do," Aaron said. "If you hadn't done that, he may have lived."

"I realized that after I pulled the knife out. That's when he started to bleed real bad. It mixed with the blue paint from the can he had in his hand. Then I heard Brooksie pounding at the front door. I ran out the back and into the woods."

The world spun around Brooksie and her knees buckled. Aaron caught her and slowly sat her down against the barn wall. Hot tears ran down her face as her pain exploded out of her. "It is my fault. She was looking for the doll."

"No, it's not your fault. It's Gertie's and Mamaw Mary's." Aaron held her close.

"Eddie, get over here," Gertie barked.

"I hate to bring this up now," Aaron whispered into her ear. "I don't think the police will get here in time and we need to get out of here before it's too late. Gertrude just took Eddie to the middle of the barn and they're talking in hushed tones. They're planning something."

The truck's engine roared as it came to life.

Gertie walked toward the doors. "Bring your gun Eddie. Nobody's gonna stop me."

The booming mufflers grew louder.

"Get down." Aaron shoved Brooksie over and behind the bale of hay.

"Aahh!" Gertie's screamed.

Chapter 42

Brooksie coughed and fanned the dust from her face. "Are you okay?" Aaron still had his hand on her back.

"Yeah, you? What happened?"

"A truck ran through the barns doors."

"Brooksie. Aaron." Darlene knelt in front of them. "Thank goodness you two are okay. We were so scarred."

Brooksie leaned up on her elbow. "We who?"

"Did anybody get hit by flying wood?" Will sat on his knees and cupped Brooksie's chin in his hand. "I don't see anything in your face." He looked her arms over. "Nothing here, either."

He turned toward Aaron who put his hands up. "I'm good man. Just got a scratch. I don't need to be examined."

Brooksie wobbled as she tried to stand up. Will took her arm and steadied her.

"Cuz, you've been crying." Darlene wiped her tears away with the back of her hand.

"We need to get back in the truck and get to safety now." Will warned.

"Nobody's going anywhere." Eddie stumbled up to the truck with his gun in his hand. Slivers and bigger pieces of wood jutted out of his hair and face. Blood trickled down from the bigger pieces. "I hate splinters. And I hate you all. You've been nothing but trouble."

"My leg," Gertie moaned.

"Who said that?" Eddie turned his head from side to side.

"It's Gertie, the calf in the stall," Brooksie snipped. Darlene nudged her.

"Shut up, you weirdo." His cheeks turned pink.

"Eddie, get over here and help me," Gertie moaned. "I'm on the other side of the truck."

"Mamaw? You okay?" Eddie called out.

"No, I'm not okay. I need to go to the hospital."

Eddie inched toward Gertie. He stopped and grabbed onto the truck bed. Aaron tapped Will's shoulder.

"Mamaw, there's a piece of wood in your leg." He dropped the gun and gagged.

Aaron and Will raced to him. Aaron reached him first and lunged at him, knocking them to the ground. He rolled Eddie over to his stomach. Will put his knee into Eddie's shoulder and grabbed his flailing wrists.

"Get off me," Eddie screamed.

"We need rope," Will yelled.

"Got it." Brooksie pulled a long strand out of Papaw's twine box. "I'll do the knots, you two hold him still."

"Stop it. Let me go," he squealed.

Aaron dug his knee deeper in Eddie's back. "Don't think so."

After Brooksie tied his wrists, she tied Eddie's ankles with the other end. "Done." She hopped up.

"We have a new record for the roping of a bad guy." Aaron held her left hand up high in the air.

"I'm gonna get all of you when I get lose." Eddie spurt obscenities as he struggled against the ropes.

Will picked up Eddie's gun and disarmed it. "We'll give this to the cops when they get here."

"It's ironic. This truck," Brooksie patted the hood, "is the same one Papaw ran through my room."

"It wasn't by chance." Darlene shook her head. "I was almost to the barn when Will came up the driveway. We peeked through a stall window and saw Eddie holding his gun on you all. I told Will if that truck could go through your wall, it could go through the barn doors."

"Smart thinking." Aaron took her hand and squeezed it.

"Please help me," Gertie called out.

"We forgot about Gertie." Brooksie and Darlene rushed to her.

"Oh my." Darlene covered her mouth.

"I need help." Gertie held her leg with the piece of wood sticking out of it.

"Did my daddy ask you for help after you stabbed him that Saturday morning?" Brooksie asked.

"What?" Darlene paled.

Gertie glared at them. Like Eddie, she had pieces of wood sticking out her face and hair. She looked like an evil version of the Scarecrow.

"I take that as a yes. Don't worry. I'm not going to do to you what you did to my daddy. I'm going to get you help." Brooksie spun around." Will, we need you here."

He bent down and examined Gertie. "I don't think it's as bad as it looks. The piece of wood in her leg has probably nicked an artery. It needs to stay in until she gets to the ER."

"Why can't you take it out now?" Darlene asked.

"Because it's acting like a plug. If we take it out, she may bleed profusely."

"Just like when you stabbed my daddy in the heart and pulled your knife out." Brooksie crossed her arms.

"She was the one who was in your room that day," Darlene exclaimed.

"I was right all along. It wasn't a regular burglary and she was looking for Mom's doll. You and Aaron were right about people thinking there was a treasure map in it," Brooksie told Darlene.

"You still have the doll right?" Will asked.

"Yeah, we do," Brooksie answered. "So, you were at Mamaw and Papaw's Saturday to get the doll instead of going fishing."

"Yes, Mr. Asmus suspected you had found Mimi's doll, but he wasn't sure. If you had, he was afraid you and Darlene would be in danger and he asked me to watch out for you two. I followed you to the church earlier. I left to report in to Mr. Asmus. When I got back, I saw Eddie and Gertie running out and getting into a truck. I didn't know what had happened. I just knew I needed to follow them."

"Hmm?" Brooksie tapped her chin. "And you were the one driving the Cadillac when the Buick chased us. How did you know we were in trouble?"

"I didn't. Mr. Asmus sent me to his cabin to retrieve something for him. I saw you two running out and then I saw a masked guy coming after you."

"I knew you were a kni...nice and cool guy." Brooksie almost called Will a knight in shining armor to his face.

Gertie moaned, "I need an ambulance."

"Darlene has already called the police and they're on their way," Brooksie reassured her.

"Actually I called Daddy and he's gonna call them. Sorry, Cuz, but I told him everything. Hey, did you and Aaron find what the clues led to? Was it anything like we thought?"

"There's nothing but a stupid box with old hard candy in it," Eddie whined.

"What? That can't be right." Darlene twisted her mouth. "What's so dangerous about that?"

"I don't think its candy." Aaron pointed to his cheek. "See this place on my face?"

Darlene caressed it. "I thought a piece of flying wood cut you."

"Eddie pitched another fit and threw the contents of this box at us." Aaron handed it to Darlene. "It was in a small lockbox we dug up. That's what the key opened."

"It's small enough to fit inside the doll. So there was no real treasure map in it."

Aaron snatched up a couple of pieces of foiled wrapped

candy. "Let's see what's really in here."

Brooksie held her breath as he unwrapped one. If it had been her, she would've ripped that foil to shreds.

Aaron placed it in his palm. "It's a diamond."

"Cool," Brooksie gasped. "I bet all those pieces are diamonds."

"I wonder how many karats it is." Darlene narrowed her eyes.

"I'll be taking those now," a voice said behind them.

Chills ran down her spine. "Crabby Crawly."

"I hate being called that." He hissed through clinched teeth. In his hands was a rifle.

"Hey, that's my hunting rifle." Eddie cried. "You stole it out of the back of my truck."

"You idiot. I was in the back of your truck when you left the church. I heard the gunshot and the bullet bouncing off of the church bell. When I got to the church, I saw that girl's car drive off in a hurry." He pointed the gun at Darlene. "I saw your truck there, so I climbed into the bed of it and laid down."

"I want my metal detector back too," Eddie spat.

"In case you haven't noticed, you are in no position to demand anything from me," Crawly sneered.

"Your metal detector? I get it now." Brooksie pointed her finger at Eddie. "You and Gertie have been the ones following us. After we left the graveyard, you went back that night with a metal detector to look for buried gold. I bet that was a shock to dig up a skeleton instead. Then you got mad. You let your temper get the best of you again and you went after Papaw Asmus."

"I was madder than an old wet hen. All that dead guy had on him was some old coins. It was hardly worth all the digging I had to do." Eddie twisted around in his ropes.

"And you gouged the hole in Darlene's tire so you could come to our rescue and get an 'in' with us. How did you keep track of where we were?"

"I put a homing device on Darlene's car when you all

stopped by the store. You two owe me for those crazy Lester boys blowing the windshield out of Mamaw's car."

"I don't owe you anything. You shouldn't have been chasing us." Brooksie bobbed her head.

"Enough of this stupidity," Crawly roared. "I have been stuck in this horrid place since the fifties. I want the diamonds now."

"What diamonds?" Brooksie shrugged

"Don't play that game with me girl. I listened from outside and I know you found them." He aimed the rifle at Darlene. "I want you and your girlfriend to pick up all the pieces, put them back in the box, and give them to me. Now."

Neither Brooksie nor Darlene spoke as they gathered the pieces. After they finished, Brooksie carried the box to Crawly.

He smirked. "William and Nanook were the clever ones. But not as clever as…"

"We are since we figured out where to find them," Brooksie blurted out. She really needed to quit doing that.

Crawly shoved her into the truck. Her teeth jarred, but she wasn't going to give him the satisfaction by saying anything. Will inched toward them.

"Nobody moves until I tell you to," Crawly commanded.

"But where's the gold?" Eddie asked.

"Boy, you are thick. There is no gold," Crawly snarled.

"Who do the diamonds belong to?" Brooksie asked.

"They rightfully belong to the Third Reich." Crawly furrowed his thin eyebrows. "My real name is Franz Kantor and I have been searching for these diamonds for years."

Brooksie's heart leaped into her throat. That explained the tabloids Papaw Asmus had kept.

"After the fall of Berlin, I escaped to Alaska. I knew German Jews were taking refuge there and they had smuggled out some of their wealth that belonged to Germany." Crabby Crawly began to cough and wheeze. Then he spit toward Brooksie.

"Oohh," Darlene grunted.

"I was the assistant to the officer over the Heims. I always

215

thought they had more wealth, and I was determined to get it. From my research, I knew William had been close to them. After they suddenly left Skagway, I followed him back here. I thought they had entrusted their valuables with him, and I was right."

"Just for curiosity's sake, who was the officer you assisted?" Brooksie asked.

"Gunther Bauer." Crawly puffed his chest out. "I was proud to work for him."

"What are you going to do with the diamonds, scalp them and run off to Tahiti?" Will asked.

"I'm going to Argentina and meet up with my fellow comrades, including Gunther," he announced.

"Why don't you take the diamonds and just go?" Aaron gestured toward the door.

"We've got the woman who killed my daddy. So you can go and do whatever." Brooksie shoed her hand at him like Papaw Clyde had done her.

"I know the police are already on their way. I don't want any clues left behind of who I really am or where I'm going." Crawly laid the white box down at his feet and put both of his hands on the rifle. "Girl, you go first. You have always got on my nerves."

Brooksie sucked in a deep breath. *Where are you God? Please don't let it end like this. Don't let the bad guy win.*

Baring his teeth, Fido charged down the passageway toward Crawly. Fido never went all the way to the barn by himself, so Papaw Clyde and her mom weren't far behind.

"You little mutt." Crawly spun around and aimed at Fido.

In her mind, Brooksie saw Mom and Papaw Clyde running into the barn. Crawly laughed while he gunned them down. Then he stepped on their dead bodies and gave the Hitler salute.

"No way." She held her hands out in front of her and lunged.

Chapter 43

"Huh?" Crawly jerked his ahead around the same instant Brooksie slammed into his ribs, hitting him with the full force of her body. He smacked into the barn wall. The rifle went off, sending a stray bullet through the roof.

Something black dropped onto Crawly. "Get it off me!" He slung the rifle and jerked his body around. If it wasn't for Sedrick hanging around his neck, Brooksie would think Crawly was having convulsions.

"Get it off." His foot slammed into an empty feed bucket and he fell to the ground with it still on his foot. Sedrick slinked off.

"Argh," Crawly roared and crawled toward the rifle.

"I don't think so." Brooksie clomped her foot down on top of his hand.

"You little freak." With his free hand, Crawly smacked the back of Brooksie's legs at the bend of her knees. The next thing she knew, she was on her hands and knees with her face inches away from the wall. Sedrick slithered through underneath her.

Aaron jerked the rifle up and pointed it at Crawly. "Don't move again."

"Are you okay?" Will gently pulled her up. Brooksie's insides quivered. Was it from her sudden fall or Will's strong hands?

"Brooksie." Mom ran in through the gaping hole in the

217

doors. "Are you all right?" She engulfed her in a tight hug. Will and Darlene stepped back.

"I'm fine, Mom." Brooksie wriggled herself free. "How did you know we were here? Did you see the light from the barn?"

"Alfred called. He said some dangerous people were threatening you all in the barn" Mom stroked Brooksie's hair. "I was so afraid."

"Is everybody all right?" Papaw Clyde ran in with a baseball bat in his hand. "Who fired a shot and what happened to my barn doors?"

"It's going to eat me," Eddie screamed as Sedrick crawled across his back.

"He's just trying to get away." Brooksie waved her hand.

"Alfred said it may be strange up here." Papaw Clyde took his hat off and wiped his forehead. "Why is he tied up like a calf at a rodeo?" He pointed to Eddie. "Why is Aaron holding a gun on Mr. Crawly? And who's lying over by the truck?" He stepped around it. "Gertie, what happened to you?"

"That girl and boy tried to kill me and Eddie with your truck," Gertie screeched.

"Papaw, that's not what happened. The guy tied up is Eddie, her grandson, and they were holding me and Aaron at gunpoint."

"At gunpoint." Papaw's eyes bulged.

"Will and I looked through the window and saw what was going on. We knew we had to do something quick. I'm sorry we messed your doors up Uncle Clyde." Darlene lowered her head.

He hugged Darlene. "You did the right thing. Barn doors can be replaced."

Mom's faced turned red. "Why would they do that?"

"It's a long story, Mom." Brooksie puffed her bangs up.

"I want to know what's going on here and why you held a gun to my daughter." Mom towered over Gertie. Her nostrils flared and the end of her nose turned pink.

"Me and Eddie are due," Gertie screeched.

"Due what, jail?"

Brooksie took in a deep breath. "She's talking about the gold she thinks Papaw Asmus sent back from Alaska."

"But that's just an old rumor. And that doesn't explain why she would be after you?"

"She knew I found your Alaskan doll and she thought it had a treasure map to the gold in it."

"That's impossible. My doll burned in Daddy's trash fire years ago." Mom cupped her cheek.

"No Mom, it didn't. Somebody wanted you all to think that."

"It was William. He didn't want anybody to get his gold. But I'm not just anybody." Gertrude sneered. "I watched my daddy get blown up."

"You're Frank's girl?" Papaw Clyde wiped his forehead again.

"Papaw, you know about Frank?" Brooksie asked.

"We all knew except for you, your mother, and Bobbie," he answered. "That was back in the thirties and we saw no need to talk about it. How did you find out?"

"When I found Mom's doll, there were old letters from Papaw Asmus to Aunt Brooksie in the box with it. Aaron and Darlene helped me do some research on them. We read old articles about Laura's murder, Papaw Asmus' bootlegging moonshine, and his diner blowing up killing Frank."

"What?" Mom's mouth dropped open.

"Papaw, why don't we take Mom and go outside for a minute." Brooksie didn't want her mother around Gertie when she explained everything.

As they walked by Crawly yelled, "Clyde, make them let me go or I'll sue you and have you arrested."

Papaw Clyde squatted down next to him. "I never did understand why Mary trusted you so much. I'm going to step outside and find out what you're up to."

Crawly raised his head up and started to speak.

"Keep it to yourself." Aaron warned.

"I'll stay here with Gertie until help gets here." Will bent back down next to her leg.

They walked out through the hole in the door. Brooksie told everything that happened since she found the doll and what she had found out. Papaw Clyde filled in with what he knew.

The color in Mom's face drained as fast as Darlene's usually does. Brooksie expected her to get angry and upset, but she didn't. Instead, she leaned against the barn wall and inhaled a deep breath. "Mom, are you all right?"

"I think your mother's in shock." Papaw Clyde touched her arm. "Mimi?"

"What I am is thankful." She embraced Brooksie and cried. "I'm thankful you and your friends are safe. And I'm thankful to know your daddy's death wasn't so senseless."

She didn't push her mother way. Crying didn't feel so awkward this time.

"I hope I'm not interrupting anything." Darlene joined them.

"I'm glad you're okay, too." Mom hugged Darlene.

"I'm thankful God had his hand on all of you." Papaw patted Brooksie and Darlene on their heads. "I guess what gets me the most is Mr. Crawly. I knew there was a meanness about him, but I never imagined him being a Nazi."

"Speaking of meanness, there's something I need to do." Mom lifted her chin.

"Mom?" Brooksie knew this could be bad.

"It's all right." Mom went back in the barn and up to Gertie.

"What do you want?" She hissed.

"I forgive you for all the pain and hardships you've caused us."

"You forgive me." Gertie tried to rise up, but Will kept her down. "What about the pain and hardships William caused us?"

"Did Momma know that you killed my husband and Brooksie's father?"

"She figured it out after Brooksie found him. I told her he charged at me and didn't see the knife in my hand. I also told her we'd both go to prison for the rest of our lives if she blabbed. And being in prison would be like being abandoned by her daddy all over again. But Mary did buck me on one thing. I wanted to go after Brooksie for some answers, but she wouldn't let me. At that point, I was afraid to push her too much or she'd snap."

"So that's why Mamaw Mary got so upset that Saturday when Officer Lanigan was investigating the holes in their back yard," Brooksie said.

"Yeah," Darlene agreed. "She felt guilty."

"And she was afraid I would find out the truth about his death and her involvement." Brooksie twirled around. "Why is Fido howling?"

Chapter 44

"Sirens. Thank goodness the police are almost here." Darlene looked up to the roof.

Brooksie went back six years to standing in the carport after finding her daddy dying. Grandma Emma sang *Beulah Land* while she rocked Brooksie as she sobbed. Mamaw Mary wailed and pulled at her hair.

"Cuz." Darlene snapped her fingers.

"Huh?" Brooksie blinked.

"Are you okay?"

"Yeah, I'm okay now. Let's go outside." Brooksie picked up Fido and they walked back outside. The cool evening breeze soothed her warm face.

Black cars with flashing lights barreled up the driveway and parked in front of the barn. The passenger door opened on the lead car and a tall man stepped out.

"Alfie," Brooksie exclaimed.

"Daddy?" Darlene's eyes widened.

"Uncle Alfred." Mimi laid her hands on her hips.

"Hello, ladies." Alfie was dressed in black and had on a bullet proof vest. "I'll be back to talk to you all as soon as I can. I need to help secure the scene." He charged inside the barn with other officers who were dressed the same.

"Wow," Brooksie gasped. "You never mentioned Alfie was some kind of undercover cop."

"He's not. He's a retired college professor." Darlene

rubbed her temples.

"Here I imagined Papaw Asmus being involved with spies and your dad was some kind of secret agent. That's so awesome." Brooksie imagined Alfie crawling on his stomach under an electric barbed wire fence. Over his head artillery exploded in brilliant lights.

"I know there are things about Daddy's past he doesn't discuss much, but I never thought about that."

"Brooksie, you've always craved excitement and now you've got it," Mom said.

"What I really wanted were answers. The more answers I found, the more questions I had. I had no idea how big it was or how far back it went." Brooksie sat a squirming Fido down.

"Yeah, it's amazing," Darlene agreed. "I've had enough excitement and adventure to last a lifetime."

"Not me." Brooksie took in the whole scene.

"Make way." Officers pushed Eddie and Crawly out of the barn by them. Crawly hands were handcuffed behind his back with a chain connecting to cuffs around his ankles. As they walked by, he spat toward Brooksie. "Mary was right about you being a little freak."

"Ignore him." Alfie marched back with Will, Aaron, and Papaw Clyde behind him. "He's angry he didn't have the capability to find the diamonds himself."

"You knew about them, Daddy?" Darlene asked.

"And the doll and the clues." Alfie nodded. "I knew Mr. Asmus back in Alaska when I was still working for the government."

"You never mentioned that to me or Momma." Darlene twisted her mouth.

"I'm sorry, but it was for everybody's safety. We'll discuss this more down at Mary and Clyde's once we get everything straightened up here. I will need Brooksie and Darlene's statements before we leave. Now," Alfie crossed his arms, "I want to know why any of you didn't tell me what was going on."

Brooksie kicked at some rocks. "I wanted to figure this

out for myself and prove that there's nothing wrong with the way I am."

"We never thought there was anything wrong with you." Mom laid her hand over her chest. "I can't believe you thought that way."

"I know you don't, Mom." Brooksie's eyes met Papaw Clyde's.

"Excuse us a second." Papaw Clyde took Brooksie by her arm and led her off to the side. "I never thought you weren't capable of anything."

"Papaw, it's no big secret I don't fit in out here. I never have. I know it's been hard for you and Mamaw to accept how I am."

"Is that what you thought?" Papaw lowered his head. "I'm so sorry you felt that way. To be honest, I have never understood how you think or how a tractor could be a dragon."

"I have a vivid imagination and there's nothing wrong with that. It doesn't make me weird."

"I've never thought of you that way. As for your Mamaw, I know she has problems, but I love her despite them. And don't you ever doubt how much I love you." Papaw Clyde took her in his arms.

"I know that, Papaw." Brooksie snuggled into his chest. She hadn't been held like that since before her daddy died.

An ambulance sped down the road and turned into the driveway as Fido howled.

"I'm going to go back in and see what they say about Gertie's injuries."

"Okay, Papaw."

Darlene came up next to her. "Wow, you hugged him back."

"Yeah, so?" Brooksie shrugged.

Another car plowed up the driveway.

"Move back everybody. I think Mary's in this car." Alfie stretched his arms out and shoved everybody backwards. He opened the back door. "Glad you could make it, Mary."

She stepped out in her housecoat. And she was still wearing her hair net with the fuzzy ball on top. "I swannie. What kind of trouble have you caused now, Brooksie? Why can't you ever be satisfied like the rest of us?"

"Momma. That's enough. You have no idea what is going here," Mom scolded.

She scowled at Mom. "We'll see about that? Where's Clyde?"

"He's inside checking on Gertie," Brooksie answered matter-of-factly. "She's already told us some interesting things about how Daddy died."

Mamaw Mary's mouth dropped open. "No." She ran inside.

Gertrude called out to her, "They know Mary. They know everything."

Mary wailed and jerked her hair net off. "I only wanted to get rid of the doll. My daddy never did anything like that for me. He abandoned me." She yanked the pins out of her hair and pulled at her curls. Papaw Clyde embraced her in his arms. Collapsing against him, she buried her face in her hands and let out loud sobs.

"I can't believe Momma's carried so much guilt and pain." Mom covered her mouth.

Alfie laid his hand on her shoulder. "It's over now."

"Sir, what do you want me to do with these?" An officer handed the white box to Alfie

Alfie took it. "I'll make sure they go to their rightful owner."

Brooksie stuck her hand out. She was the one who found the doll that lead to the diamonds and she helped to dig them up as well.

"I believe this belongs to you." Alfie placed the box in Will's hand.

Chapter 45

"I can't believe my doll was in here the whole time." Mom twisted the hat box around after Brooksie showed them where it was. "I used to go with Grandma Emma to Myrtle's Milliner shop on Market Square. I guess Papaw Asmus got the box out of her closet."

"She gave it to him," Alfie told her.

"We didn't even think of Grandma Emma being involved at all. I kinda blocked some of my memories from the day I found the doll until the day Daddy died." Brooksie peered at the hatbox.

"It's hard to imagine Grandma Emma doing such a thing. She knew how much I loved that doll." Mom put the box down.

"But she loved you more, Mimi. She knew as long as that doll was around, you and everybody else could be in great danger," Alfie answered.

Mom cupped Brooksie's cheek. "Where's my doll now?"

"Aaron has it hidden at his house. An officer went back with him to get it. " Brooksie twirled the Chinese fan in her hand. "I'm gonna clean this off and hang it in my new room."

"Brooksie, why don't you finish asking me your question?" Alfie crossed his arms.

She furrowed her eyebrows. "What question?"

"The one you really wanted to ask me after Officer Lanigan searched Darlene's car and found your earring and phasor." Alfie's lips turned up into a wide grin.

"Oh yeah, the sword. Do you think it belonged to the soldier Gertie and Eddie dug up and who he was?"

"Yes, it did belong to him and I know exactly who he was." Alfie picked up the sword. "After William hid the doll, he told us about the sword laying in here. Emma had heard stories about the family hiding two Union soldiers here during the Civil War. I knew I couldn't draw any attention to the room, so I didn't look into it any further. I forgot about it until they dug him up. I went to the Lawson McGhee Library to do some research."

"Is that what you were doing when we saw you there?"

"Yes, it was. This house was built at the beginning of the war. Your great-great-great-grandfather George thought they needed a place to hide since he sided with the Union.

"Two Union soldiers who were brothers were fleeing from an ambush and came here for help. They fought under General Burnside in the siege of Knoxville in the autumn of 1863 and were the only survivors from their regiment. George hid them in his attic for a while. One of the brothers died from abdominal wounds. They buried him in the middle of the night. The other brother stayed here and married. He is your great-great-grandfather on your father's side."

"John said something about one of his ancestors fighting for the Union, but that was all he knew," Mom said.

"A lot of people aren't fully aware of their family history. Since Brooksie here is a descendant, the sword is hers. I would say it's worth a lot of money to some collectors. You could sell it and use the money for tuition," Alfie suggested.

"Didn't I tell you or Aunt Bobbie?" Brooksie asked. "I got a full scholarship to UT."

"No, you didn't." Alfie patted her on the back. "Congratulations. Which one is it?"

"The F. H. B. scholarship."

"F. H. B.?" Alfie raised his eyebrows.

"Is there something wrong with it?" Brooksie asked.

"Not at all." Alfie grinned and shook his head.

An officer popped his head in the door. "Sir, Mr. Asmus and Mrs. Fields are down stairs. They brought some hot Krispy Kreme Donuts, and your daughter is making some coffee."

"Thank you Tim. Let's go downstairs, eat, and sort out this mess." Alfie laid the sword back down. "This is dangerous. I'm going to leave it up here for now. We know where it is." He closed the door to the secret room and left the attic after them.

In the kitchen Papaw Asmus and Mrs. Fields were sitting around the table with the other officers. She had her arm draped around him and his head lay on her shoulders. Darlene was right. There was something going on between them.

Three dozen donuts sat in the middle of table. Brooksie chose a chocolate one with sprinkles. "Yum." She wiped her mouth. "Alfie, what about Mamaw Mary? Will she be in trouble? Even though she didn't have anything to do with Daddy's murder, isn't she an accessory or something like that?"

"Technically, she is an accessory after the fact. I'm going to talk to the D.A. about it, but she's on her way to the mental hospital for a psychiatric evaluation. I'm glad Clyde stayed with her. To be honest, she should have gotten treatment long ago. And I will bring up the fact that she kept Gertie away from you." Alfie raised a frosted donut. "William, thank you very much for the donuts. Now it's time for you to tell your side of the story."

"You're welcome. I appreciate you being there for my family." Papaw Asmus folded his hands and twiddled his thumbs. "During prohibition, I bootlegged moonshine. Frank McCoy was my best runner, but I found out he was terrorizing some of my customers. He threatened them if they didn't buy more or he upped the price on them and kept the extra for himself. I told him to stop and he refused. He said he brought in so much money that he deserved to be an equal partner.

"I decided to teach Frank a lesson and I had Buford, one of my guys, do it. I should've known better. He wasn't the sharpest tool in the shed, but he was the biggest and meanest.

Anyway, he decided to use the still to scare Frank. He set it to go off right as Frank entered the diner. He over did it and blew up the diner and damaged some nearby businesses. I was the next block over when it blew. After the explosion, I heard Gertie screaming for her daddy. I had nightmares for years about it." A tear ran down Papaw's face.

"Mr. Asmus," Darlene spoke up, "were you ever charged with Frank's murder?"

"No. In the early forties, Buford admitted to the police what he had done when he was on his death bed with leukemia."

"Sorry we're late. I was so nervous that I forgot the combination to my vault." Aaron and an officer stepped into the kitchen. "I believe this belongs to you." He handed Mom the cookie tin.

"These were his favorites." Her hands trembled so much she couldn't take the lid off.

"Here, Mom." Brooksie did it for her.

"Oh," Mom gasped.

Brooksie reached in and gingerly lifted the doll out and handed it to her.

"Thank you." Her voice was barely above a whisper. She kept her head down while she caressed the doll's braids. Brooksie saw her mother's tear splash onto the cookie tin.

She had to get everybody's attention off Mom. Who wants to be stared at during such a personal time? "Papaw Asmus, why did you send the jewels back in the doll when you knew how dangerous it was?"

"That's straightforward," Mrs. Fields scolded.

"It needs to be." Papaw Asmus squeezed her hand. "They deserve an answer. If you found the doll, then you found my letters as well."

"Yeah," Brooksie answered. "Darlene and I read them. We hoped we might find some answers in them."

"So you know about Hannah?"

"You did something to cause her and her family to run

away." Brooksie drummed her fingers. "I can't help but think it had something to do with your last name."

"Since Asmus is a German name, I was afraid the Heims would think I was related to or in cahoots with the Nazis, so I lied and said my last name was Brewer. It was my mother's maiden name. I went into business with the Fields and Heims using that name."

"Wait a minute." Brooksie smacked the table. "That has the same initials as my scholarship. F.H.B."

Papaw Asmus grinned. "I wanted to do something for you without you finding out everything I did in my past. After your father died, I knew Mary and Clyde would help take care of you and Mimi. I decided to wait and help with your college expenses. My father died before I was born from appendicitis. I had no help and I wanted you to have a better start on life than I had."

"I didn't know that, Papaw. I'm sorry." She should have never thought he wanted the gold to go to Will.

"Me either," Mom added. "Momma never discussed any of that with us."

"Your helping Brooksie is very honorable." Alfie reached for another donut.

"Lying isn't honorable. When I first met Hannah, I was swept off my feet. I hadn't felt like that since Laura. I should have told the Heims about my name, but I was too afraid. The Nazis terrorized them and took their wealth in exchange for their lives. They managed to smuggle some diamonds out with them. I was honored when Mr. Heims asked me to keep the diamonds safe for them."

"We read about that in our research. It's called the Night of the Broken Glass," Darlene sounded like Alfie.

Papaw Asmus nodded. "That's right. One day I had invited them over for supper and left the mail on the table. There was a letter from Brooksie to me and she had used the name Asmus. They were so upset and wouldn't listen to me when I tried to explain everything. That night they left without getting their diamonds."

"So you never saw Hannah again?" Brooksie imagined what it would be like to not only never see Will again, but to have him think she was some kind of awful person would be too much.

"She's sitting at this table."

"It's you." Brooksie immediately turned to Mrs. Fields. "And you have the last name of one of the investors."

"I married their son. After my husband and parents passed away, I looked William up. I moved here and took the position of administrator at the nursing home."

"So that's why you moved in there, Papaw." Brooksie winked at him.

"My grandson came down as well." Mrs. Fields smiled Will kissed Mrs. Fields on her cheek.

"I should've seen the similarities before now? And Will was named after Papaw."

"Yes. I believed William, but my parents didn't." Mrs. Fields squeezed his hand.

"Alfie, that's why you handed the diamonds to Will." Brooksie crossed her arms.

"I knew exactly who he was." Alfie grabbed another donut. "My father Charles was sent to Alaska to help the German Jewish refugees settle in. I went back years later when I got word that a Nazi was looking for the Heim's diamonds."

"The Charles we read about in Mr. Asmus' letter really was my grandfather. That's so cool." Darlene clasped her hands together.

"Yes, he was a good man and I was unfair to him. It was easier to blame him than myself." Papaw Asmus looked down to his hands.

"Wait a minute," Mom spoke up. "Papaw, why did you smuggle the diamonds back in my doll knowing a Nazi was looking for them." Her nostril flared again.

"I acted impulsively." Papaw Asmus rubbed the top of his freckled forehead. "At the time, it seemed like the perfect answer. I didn't think anybody would suspect a little girl's doll. I really thought everybody would be perfectly safe."

"So it was your idea?" Brooksie asked.

"Not exactly. My friend Nanook and his wife Anana owned the local trading post in Skagway. The Heim's diamonds were hidden there in one of his candy boxes. An unusual man lurked around their trading posts for a few days. Then Alfred visited me and told me they suspected a Nazi treasure hunter was looking for the diamonds. I went straight to Nanook. Anana had just finished the doll for Mimi. It was Nanook's idea to put them inside the doll. Like I said, I thought it was the safest answer. I was wrong."

"That unusual man was Kantor, also known as Crawly." Alfie added. "After William came back to Tennessee, Kantor tried to coerce the truth out of Nanook and his wife. My men got there just in time, but Kantor got away. He had enough information to figure out the diamonds were sent back here."

"There's something I don't understand. Why didn't you just take the diamonds out of my doll," Mom held it up, "and give it back to me?"

"That danger was too great to risk. We didn't know if Kantor knew about the doll or not," Alfie answered. "William contacted me for help with the diamonds. After I came here to Knoxville, he told me what he and Nanook had done."

"Alfred and I told Emma the whole story. She was afraid for her family's safety while being mad at me for putting her in that position. And she was right to feel that way. The three of us put our heads together and came up with a plan to not only protect the family, but the diamonds as well. Emma told me about the secret room and where the house key was hidden. One Sunday night while everybody was gone to church, I went in and put the doll in the hat box Emma left. I put some of my letters in there, too. If I had passed on by the time somebody found the doll, I wanted my side of the story to be better understood." Papaw Asmus sighed.

"Now that I think about it," Mom rubbed her mouth. "That

explains Grandma's reaction. I didn't give up on finding my doll until it, or the other one, was seen in Daddy's trash fire. Momma told me it was just a silly doll and to get over it. But Grandma Emma cried with me and rocked me while singing her favorite hymn *Beulah Land*. She must've felt so guilty."

"Mimi, we all felt that way," Alfie said.

"Alfie, didn't you get suspicious when we had Crawly search for the Goliath mask or when you heard about Mamaw and Papaw's yard having a couple of holes dug in it?" Brooksie asked.

"I didn't know about the holes dug in their yard and I didn't realize the Goliath mask was a clue. William helped Emma write the first one. She did the rest herself and was the only one who knew all the answers. It was her idea of added safety. She typed all her clues on the typewriter in the attic. Have you ever seen it?"

"Are you kidding? I used to play on it all the time." Brooksie tapped the table with her fingers.

"Yeah, it was her control panel to the spaceship. She showed it to me the other week." Darlene winked at Brooksie.

Papaw Asmus chuckled. "It does have all those fun buttons to press."

Alfie twisted around in his seat. "I didn't realize what you all were doing until Mr. Asmus called me Saturday afternoon. He was afraid you all may have found the doll and could be in danger. He thought it was strange he got attacked the same day you two visited him, so he sent Will to see if the doll was still hidden.

"I asked Bobbie if she saw anything unusual and she told me about Darlene trying to hide a doll from her and how you had a fit over one of Emma's old cookbooks. When you were dropped off Sunday, I listened from the kitchen window while you all sat on the deck and talked about finding the last clue." Alfie took a big bite of his donut.

"You weren't asleep in your chair when I came in?" Brooksie crossed her arms.

Alfie wiped his mouth. "I was until you woke me up by slamming the front door."

"Sorry about that. But I have another question Alfie. Did you stay in Knoxville to keep an eye out for the doll?"

"I had originally planned on staying only a few months, but I loved it here so much I decided to stay. I took an early retirement from the government and accepted a teaching position at Maryville College. I was visiting Emma one day and saw how Bobbie had grown into a beautiful woman. I fell head over heels in love with her. A year later we were married."

"Does Momma know about the doll, the diamonds, or Alaska?" Darlene asked.

"Not at all. Emma, William, and I decided the less who knew our secret, the better."

"See, Cuz, there's no reason for you to feel guilty about your daddy's death," Darlene sang.

"Why would you feel guilty about that? Why didn't you tell me?" Mom placed her hand over her heart.

"Because I brought the doll back home after I found it. If I had left it in the secret room, Daddy may still be alive."

"Don't you dare ever think that way." Papaw Asmus rose. Hannah started to rise as well, but he laid his hand on her shoulder. He hobbled over to Brooksie's chair. "I had no idea you were carrying that guilt. If it's anybody's fault, it's mine. I should've never lied to the Heims and I should've told Charles about the diamonds the minute the Heims left. Truth be known, I should've prayed about it, but I didn't know Jesus then. Thanks to Hannah and Will taking me to church, I do now."

"But the Heims were Jewish?" Brooksie looked to Mrs. Fields.

"After I married, I became a Christian and my parents did as well." Mrs. Fields gave a peaceful smile. It was similar to the guardian angel's smile.

Papaw Asmus clasped her hand in his. "I know Jesus has forgiven me for all my stupid and selfish actions, but now I ask for you and Mimi to forgive me."

Brooksie gulped and fought back the tears threatening to escape. Was it from the relief of guilt or the joy of knowing her Papaw had accepted Christ? Maybe it was both. "It's okay Papaw." A peace she hadn't felt in years washed over her.

"Mimi?" Papaw Asmus asked.

She wiped a tear. "I forgive you and I appreciate you helping Brooksie with her college. I also want her to have a good start on life."

"If I may," Alfie held up his index finger. "Let's not forget that Gertie was greedy and obsessed over her father's death. It almost drove her crazy. And she was a threat none of us foresaw."

"That's true," Papaw Asmus agreed. "But I want everybody to know how impressed I am with Brooksie and Darlene."

Aaron cleared his throat.

"...and that young man for figuring out all the clues. Emma was a very clever lady as are all of you."

Heat rushed into Brooksie's face at warp speed. "Thank you Papaw, but God led us to the answers."

Papaw Asmus patted her arm. "God made you the way he did for a reason. He knew nobody else who would have the imagination and the daring to do what you did."

Brooksie glanced over to Alfie who winked at her and smiled.

"Most of you can go to bed. The boys and I will be heading downtown. Darlene, I would appreciate it if you went back to home to be with your mother. Brooksie, are you going to stay here with Mimi?"

"We need to take care of one more thing," Papaw Asmus interrupted. "While I didn't bury gold in my yard, I did hide it other places."

"What?" Alfie's eyes bulged. "There's actually gold hidden somewhere?"

"Good thing I didn't bury it in the ground." Papaw Asmus laughed and smacked his knee. "There are nuggets stashed everywhere at my cabin. That's what Will was going after when he came across you two being chased. I even had my sister hide them upstairs here in the attic."

For a few seconds, Brooksie couldn't move or speak. If the gold pieces were stolen as Darlene suggested, then they also needed to go to Will. But how was she going to ask about that? "Papaw, wasn't it expensive sending all that gold back?"

"It would've been if the Heims and Fields hadn't been so generous. They knew I was trying to support Mary and Brooksie, so they let me send back what I mined on my own time. Brooksie had more than enough and I sent her instructions on where to hide it. That's what I planned on using to pay for your tuition,"

"How much is there?" Mom asked.

"I don't rightly remember now, but at today's prices, it may even be enough to also get Brooksie a car."

"But we've been riding together ever since I got my license," Darlene complained. "Who am I going to talk to while I drive, myself?"

"Why don't we take turns and you ride with me. I do have my licenses," Brooksie suggested.

"That's another adventure." Darlene paled.

"Alfie, would you teach me how to drive on gravel roads?"

"I will do what I can to make you a good driver." Alfie rose. "William, you and Hannah go to the cabin with my boys and me. I need you to tell me where the gold is hidden. Tomorrow I'll exchange it and set up a trust fund for Brooksie."

"Alfie, can I ask you one thing?" Brooksie raised her hand.

Alfie narrowed his eyes. "I will make sure you get a dependable car."

"Now that I think about it," Brooksie tapped her chin. "I'd like to wait on the car."

"What?" Alfie raised his eyebrows.

"I can get a car later. For college, I need a personal computer and a printer. And there's couple of other things I want if I can have them."

Alfie crossed his arms. "What are they?"

"A telescope and a picture at the Christian bookstore that has stars and a verse from Isaiah on it."

"I think I can arrange that. Now, the rest of you will help get the gold out of the attic. William, do you mind telling them where to find it?"

"I don't have to. I wrote it down years ago and hid it behind Brooksie's picture."

"Papaw, I don't think there's a picture of her anywhere in the house," Brooksie said.

"Do you know what she looks like?" Papaw Asmus asked.

Brooksie shrugged. "No, but there's not a picture here of anybody I don't know."

"How did you get the door open to the secret room?"

"I tilted a picture." Goose bumps ran down her spine. "That's Brooksie's picture."

"I've always liked that picture of her. There was an old painting hanging there. After I hid the doll, I put her picture up instead. There's a treasure map behind it."

"You know, Cuz, I think after you get out of college, you should start your own detective agency," Darlene said.

"I'd rather teach science and write adventure books on the side."

Alfie stood and patted her on the head. "You already have a story."

Soon they were in the attic. Brooksie's scalp tingled when Will took the back of the other Brooksie's picture off and found the map. For the next two hours, they moved wall planks, floor boards, and pictures. There were little bags of nuggets down in cracks in the wall. They even found some down in the old typewriter. Finally, they had every piece listed on the map.

❧

"Bye and thanks for everything." Brooksie yelled to Darlene and Aaron as they pulled out of the driveway.

"What a day. I'm ready to go to bed." Mom yawned. "I

have to work tomorrow and Brooksie, you have classes."

"Why don't you go on to bed then Mom?"

She looked from Brooksie to Will. "I think I will." She gave Will one of her tight hugs and kissed him on the cheek. "Thank you so much for all you did. And you, young lady, be up in a few." She kissed the top of Brooksie's head.

"Night, Mom."

After the carport door shut, Will started talking. "I would love it if just the two of us could go out sometime."

"Do you have a place in mind?" She hoped it wasn't The Crowing Rooster.

"There's a big event at Big Ridge State Park this weekend."

Her neck tightened. "You mean the Hog Festival? I'm not squealing like a pig to be Hog Queen."

"Hog queen?" Will laughed. "Who in the world told you that?"

"You mean it's not true."

"There's a squealing contest for fun and anybody can enter it. This is a storytelling festival. They're going to be telling old pioneer and Native American stories by a bonfire next to the lake."

"I would love that." Brooksie rubbed her hands together.

"I thought you would. You know, I've never known a girl quite like you."

"Is that good or bad?" Brooksie tucked her hair behind her ear.

"It's good. I like you just the way you are."

Brooksie was glad it was night. As hot as her cheeks felt, they had to be fluorescent pink.

Will put his finger under her chin and gently tilted her face up. "The next time you find anything unusual though, include me."

"I'll always include you."

Will bent down and placed a soft kiss on her lips. Maybe being lovey dovey wasn't so bad.

❧

Brooksie shut the door and turned the light on. She sat down next to the old typewriter and opened her journal.

May 12, 1982. It's cool that I'm sitting in the attic where it all started years ago. I'm not that 12 year old girl who found the doll any more. I'm not the same person I was when Papaw Clyde ran his truck through my room. But I'm still who God designed me to be. And the only way to be happy in life is to live to please Him, instead of trying to satisfy others.

People, even your family, may hurt you. But I have realized they don't always know they're doing it, if they're hurting inside too. And I know I have hurt others as well. I was too wrapped in myself to realize how much Papaw Clyde missed me and loved me. And how Mamaw Mary protected me from Gertie.

Darlene was right about everything being meant to happen. God took something bad and made it good. And He anointed me to be part of the way in which He did it. If you think about it, as Christians, we are all anointed with something.

So I'm going to keep my eyes and ears open for new adventures, for ways God can use me. Let's face it; nobody has the imagination He does. I hope He wants Will, Darlene, and Aaron along for the ride.

Made in the USA
Charleston, SC
29 September 2015